T0147097

WASH, SET, AND DIE...

The minute they parked at the salon's back door, Olivia raced outside. She was pale, her movements jerky. She grabbed Jazzi's hand and pulled her into the building.

"What did Misty do now?" Jazzi had tried to think of something horrible enough to panic her sister. A load of manure in each washbasin? But it had to be something worse, far worse.

Olivia's face screwed up as she tugged her through the storage room, and Jazzi worried she was going to burst into tears or have a meltdown. What could have happened? Olivia was usually unflappable, squaring her shoulders and dealing with whatever came up. She'd never seen her like this.

Olivia opened the door to the shop and pointed.

Jazzi stared. She could feel the blood drain from her face. Misty was slumped in her sister's chair at the washbasin, her head resting on the edge of the sink and a pair of scissors jammed in her chest...

Books by Judi Lynn

Mill Pond Romances
COOKING UP TROUBLE
OPPOSITES DISTRACT
LOVE ON TAP
SPICING THINGS UP
FIRST KISS, ON THE HOUSE
SPECIAL DELIVERY

Jazzi Zanders Mysteries
THE BODY IN THE ATTIC
THE BODY IN THE WETLANDS
THE BODY IN THE GRAVEL
THE BODY IN THE APARTMENT
THE BODY FROM THE PAST
THE BODY IN THE BEAUTY PARLOR

Published by Kensington Publishing Corp.

The Body in the Beauty Parlor

Judi Lynn

LYRICAL UNDERGROUND
Kensington Publishing Corp.
www.kensingtonbooks.com

LYRICAL UNDERGROUND BOOKS are published by

Kensington Publishing Corp.
119 West 40th Street
New York, NY 10018

All Kensington titles, imprints, and distributed lines are available at special quantity discounts for bulk purchases for sales promotion, premiums, fund-raising, educational, or institutional use.

Special book excerpts or customized printings can also be created to fit specific needs. For details, write or phone the office of the Kensington Sales Manager: Kensington Publishing Corp., 119 West 40th Street, New York, NY 10018. Attn. Sales Department. Phone: 1-800-221-2647.

Lyrical Underground and Lyrical Underground logo Reg. US Pat. & TM Off.

First Electronic Edition: March 2021
ISBN-13: 978-1-5161-1022-3 (ebook)
ISBN-10: 1-5161-1022-6 (ebook)

First Print Edition: March 2021
ISBN-13: 978-1-5161-1025-4
ISBN-10: 1-5161-1025-0

Printed in the United States of America

Acknowledgments

I want to thank the usual suspects for their help with my books. My daughter, Holly, who reads and critiques my work…and who happened to be a hairdresser before she went back to school to become an RN. She knows how much a hairdresser values her scissors, which are expensive. Also, I want to thank my good writer friend and fabulous author, Mary Lou Rigdon/Julia Donner, whose red pen has saved me from many a blunder. And Ralph Miser, who's always willing to share ideas and house project knowledge with me.

I wouldn't have a mystery series without my wonderful agent, Lauren Abramo, and my equally wonderful editor, John Scognamiglio. I get so much support from so many people at Kensington/Lyrical Press, I consider myself very lucky. Thank you, all!

Chapter 1

Jazzi grimaced at her reflection in the mirror. It was Thursday night—girls' night out. She was meeting her sister, Olivia, and their friends for supper. Her sister the hairdresser. Her sister who'd drive to Don Chava's Mexican Grill straight from the salon she and Mom owned. Olivia would be dressed in something trendy, her makeup would be perfect, and her dark blond hair would look stylish and wonderful.

She turned off her curling iron in defeat. Ugh. She'd had bad hair days for two weeks in a row. She'd hear about it. Glancing at her new spring top and bright green pants, she hoped Olivia would focus on her clothes and not her hair. Jazzi rarely bought anything this bright, pants this snug. And she never wore them with heels. Olivia should give her brownie points for that, right?

When she walked downstairs and Ansel looked up at her, he did a double take. "Whoa! Look at you!"

She bit her bottom lip, nervous. "Is it too much?"

His sky-blue eyes lit up. "You look great."

Maybe her plan would work. Maybe Olivia would be surprised by her stab at being stylish. She reached for the cardigan she'd tossed by her purse. It was mid-March and she didn't need a coat, not even a jacket. Her mood brightened. Spring was in the air. More than that, the house she, Ansel, and Jerod were working on in Kirkwood Park was close to being finished and had already sold. They'd reached the part of the job she loved, putting on finishing touches to see how their choices worked.

This time around, they'd gone with a farmhouse theme to fit the older neighborhood and the style of the Dutch Colonial. So far, she was happy with the way everything had worked out. Plus, another cherry on the cake was that everyone could make the Sunday meal this year for Easter. She and Ansel were really looking forward to it. Her Norseman was excited about planning an Easter egg hunt inside and outside for the kids, if the weather held. He wanted to have games in the basement, too—pin the cottontail on the bunny and balancing an egg on a spoon for a relay race. He'd played both when he was a kid.

Walker and Didi's little boy, River, had promised he'd split any eggs he found with his new baby sister, Noreen. She was only three months old. Walker and Didi had given her Brooklyn as a middle name, in honor of River's mother, who'd died. Easter was a month away, though, so she pushed those thoughts away and raised her face for Ansel's kiss.

"Have fun," he told her.

"You too." When the girls met so did the guys. They were going to The Tower Bar and Grill for wings tonight. George, Ansel's pug, opened an eye to watch them walk to the door. He knew the routine on Thursdays. He also knew Ansel would bring home a treat for him. If anyone spoiled a pet more than her Norseman, she hadn't met him. He'd even started doting on her cats. When they left for a night out, on their return he threw cat treats across the kitchen floor for them to chase and eat.

It took her fifteen-minutes to reach Chava's, and when she pulled in the lot she had to park in the last row to find room for her pickup. Her sister's car was already in the lot. Walking into the restaurant, Jazzi scanned the booths until she saw Olivia. She was dressed in a cherry-red jumpsuit, sipping a margarita. Her lips were as red as her outfit, and her hair was scraped into a tight bun. She must have been going for drama today. When Jazzi slid into the booth across from her sister, a frown creased Olivia's forehead and she stared.

"What?" But Jazzi already knew what Olivia's comment would be.

"What did you do to your hair?"

Jazzi pushed the heavy, honey-colored strands behind her ears. "I tried to make it look decent."

"I couldn't tell. When was the last time you came in for a cut?"

She tried to remember. "I don't know. Isn't it on your books?"

Olivia shook her head, annoyed. "I'm not your nanny. I'm your hairdresser."

Thankfully, the waitress came for Jazzi's drink order, offering her a short reprieve. Then she stared at the two empty seats. "Will the other two ladies be joining you shortly?"

Jazzi nodded, and when the waitress left Olivia jabbed a finger at her. "Eight o'clock. Tomorrow morning. You look like crap. We have to get you in before the salon opens. We're already getting busy for the holidays."

That settled, Jazzi leaned back to relax. The waitress brought her strawberry margarita, and she scanned the menu. Silly really. She always ordered the spicy beef chimichanga. Just then, Didi and Elspeth walked in together. Didi still wore a loose-fitting top. She was breastfeeding, and she hadn't lost all the baby weight yet. Didn't matter. She was plenty attractive. So was Elspeth, in a quiet, understated way. She wore her long, light-brown hair twisted back in a soft knot, as usual.

Elspeth's eyes widened at Jazzi's white, flowered top and neon-green pants. Her brows shot to her forehead. "Ready for spring?"

Jazzi laughed. "That, but mostly I wanted to give Olivia a run for her money."

"No, she wanted to distract me from her awful hair." Olivia took another sip of her drink.

Didi sighed, watching her. "I love margaritas, but I still can't have any alcohol. Nursing."

Elspeth made a face. She didn't like hearing any of the messy details of motherhood. "You can't have caffeine either, can you?"

"No, and the baby wakes me up two or three times a night. I could sure use some."

Could Jazzi live without caffeine? Babies demanded a lot from a person. She wasn't ready to take that on yet, but she wasn't getting any younger either. She'd be thirty in two years.

"When I have a kid it's strictly bottles for me," Olivia declared. "I still want to work at the salon, and I'm not pumping myself to freeze milk." She wrinkled her nose in distaste. "With bottles, Thane can get up for night feedings, too."

"Walker would be happy to." Didi closed the menu, having made her decision. "But this time of year his cement business goes berserk. He's working ten hours a day sometimes. He needs his sleep."

"And you don't?" Olivia countered.

"I can work from home doing medical transcripts. My hours are flexible. I don't even have to hire a babysitter."

Olivia reached for a package she'd propped on the floor and handed it to Didi. It was a cute dress for a baby, with rabbits prancing around its hem and a matching stretchy headband.

"It's adorable!" Didi beamed, looking at it.

"I couldn't resist." The outfit looked like something Olivia would pick, with lots of frills and ruffles. She either wore ultrafeminine or ultrachic, bouncing between them.

The waitress interrupted to take their food orders. When she left, Jazzi turned to Elspeth, changing the subject. "I heard that your house is finally coming together."

She and Ansel had been helping his brother and Elspeth renovate the old, brick house they'd bought near downtown River Bluffs. Elspeth smiled. "We're almost ready for furniture. It's been hard living there while we worked on it, but all the big stuff is done."

The women raised their glasses to toast her. "Congrats!" they cheered in unison.

Elspeth fidgeted under the attention and focused on Olivia. "How's the new girl you hired at your salon working out?"

Olivia wrinkled her nose. "Oh, fine."

A noncommittal answer if Jazzi ever heard one. "You don't like her?"

"Most months she can't make her booth rental. And she hasn't brought in the business we expected her to. Things haven't worked out like we'd planned."

"But she's still new, isn't she?" Didi asked. "Doesn't it take a while for a hairdresser to build clients?"

Olivia drained her glass. "That's the thing. When we looked at her résumé she got such high recommendations, we thought she'd bring in clients. She was supposed to know cutting-edge coloring and cuts. Not so much. And the shop's actually making less money than before. I don't know how to explain that."

"Is Dad giving you grief about it?" He'd been against Mom and Olivia hiring someone new.

"Mom's so unhappy about it, he hasn't pushed it. It's a touchy subject." Olivia scowled. "Thane avoids it, too, if he can. He knows it upsets me."

Their food came, and Olivia and Jazzi ordered second drinks. The talk turned to members of the family or kids. By the time everyone paid their bills, they'd covered a wide range of subjects. On the drive home, though, Jazzi thought about Olivia and Mom's salon again.

How could they have hired a new girl who brought in more clients and lose money? It didn't make sense.

Chapter 2

Ansel pulled in the driveway behind Jazzi. She waited for him to park so they could walk into the house together. George, Inky, and Marmalade came to greet them and, as expected, Ansel had brought home a few boneless chicken wings for the pug. While he cut them into smaller pieces, Jazzi tossed treats for her cats.

Once the pets had enough snacks and attention, she and Ansel went to the living room and stretched out on their favorite sofas. The room was so large, it held two seating groups, perfect for entertaining. The men usually congregated in one area, the women in another. For now, though, they headed to the red leather sofas and chairs closest to the TV. The cats jumped on the couch with Jazzi. George nuzzled against Ansel.

"Did Olivia notice your hair?" Ansel asked, a gleam in his eyes.

Jazzi nodded. "I have an appointment for a haircut at eight tomorrow morning. It needs it. It's so tangled in the mornings, I can hardly get a brush through it."

"Did she talk about the new girl at the shop? Thane says she's a pain to work with, and the shop's losing money with her there."

"Olivia didn't say she was a pain." But then, her sister didn't want to admit that she and Mom might have made a mistake hiring a third person.

Ansel situated his pillow to be more comfortable and rested an arm behind his head to prop himself up more. He was so tall, six-five, his feet were propped on the opposite sofa arm. "Thane thinks it's only a matter of time before something blows. He said the new girl has a mouth on her, doesn't mind being pushy. Your sister has a short fuse. She doesn't put up with crap."

Jazzi wrinkled her nose. "I hope she doesn't lose it while I'm there. It's too early in the morning. I don't need the conflict, but I should be safe. We're going in before the salon opens, so hopefully I won't even meet the girl."

"How do you want to work things tomorrow?" George nuzzled to his side, and he reached out to stroke his head. "Will you drive straight from the salon to meet us at the Kirkwood Park house?"

"Might as well, but then we'll have to drive home separately."

"I can pack our lunch and take the cooler to work with me. Then you don't have to worry about it."

He'd never made their lunch before, but it would be easy this time. She'd bought a pound of deli roast beef to make sandwiches and had lots of chips. "Thanks. That's sweet."

He grinned. "I'm a sweet guy. That's why you married me."

"And humble. You forgot to add humble."

He laughed. "I'm humbler than Jerod."

That wasn't saying much. Her cousin could be downright cocky. On occasion, he'd been known to be full of himself, but that didn't last long in their family. Anyone with a big head got knocked off their pedestal pretty fast. Truth was, Ansel didn't realize how good-looking he was, and that was fine with her.

He must have had a good time tonight because he gave her a naughty smirk. "Maybe Jerod and I will stop somewhere for a beer on our way home because you're driving separately. But I won't be too long, so don't worry about us."

If he thought that would bother her, he was wrong. "Good, maybe I'll stop someplace, too."

He raised his brows. "A gorgeous blonde at a bar on her own? Isn't that asking for trouble?"

"Doubt it. I'll be in my work clothes. Not much of a turn-on."

"Honey, you haven't seen yourself in those worn jeans. You even look good covered in sawdust."

She rolled her eyes and yawned. Her husband was biased, bless him.

"Tired?" He rolled to his feet, waiting for George to jump off the couch. "I could call it an early night. How about you?"

She could, too. She followed him up the stairs. And it was a good thing they crawled into bed earlier than usual because she could barely force herself up in the morning, but she had to make it to Olivia's shop by eight. Ansel padded downstairs while she got ready, doing all the morning routines she usually did. He had toast and coffee for her when she came down to join him. "I have everything covered," he said. "Just enjoy your sister and make yourself even more beautiful."

Right. But she stood on tiptoe to kiss his cheek. "You're a keeper."

He tugged her closer for a hug. "Good, 'cause you're stuck with me."

Poor her. She downed the last of her coffee and started to the door.

"Better wear your hoodie," he called after her. "It's chilly today."

That was the thing about spring in Indiana. Temperatures bobbed up and down. It was mild yesterday, but the weatherman said it would only get to the high fifties today. She pulled on her hoodie and headed out the door. The salon was on the southwest side of River Bluffs, and there was more traffic than usual. Olivia and Mom lived close to the shop, but it was a trek for her.

Forty minutes later, she parked near the salon's back door. Olivia wasn't there yet, but lights were on inside and two cars were parked near the front door.

When Olivia pulled in five minutes later she frowned, unhappy. When Jazzi joined her, she motioned toward the vehicles in front. "That's Misty's SUV. I don't know how she got inside. Only Mom and I have keys."

Jazzi gave an inward sigh. The morning might be off to a bumpy start. Olivia had come dressed for battle. She couldn't have known she needed to, but she wasn't wearing her usual style. She'd donned Kate Hepburn trousers and a striped, button-down blouse. Jazzi pursed her lips. "Are you trying for early Hollywood glam?"

"Thane and I watched *Bringing Up Baby* last weekend. He likes old movies and I liked Kate Hepburn's style." Just like her sister. She hadn't wasted any time copying it, but then, Olivia loved to shop. So did Mom.

With a sharp twist of her key, Olivia unlocked the back door, then charged into the storage room. Music blared, so loud even back here, that Jazzi covered her ears. Olivia held up a hand, warning her to advance slowly. Cracking the door to the salon wide enough for them to see, they watched Misty finish highlighting a girl's long, dark hair. That process took a while. Jazzi wondered how early the women had gotten there. She frowned, studying Olivia's new employee. The girl looked rough, with harsh makeup and bleached blond hair and dark roots. Her shirt was too tight, exposing an inch of skin above the waistline of her hip-hugging pants. Not the professional vibe Olivia and Mom tried for. Had she looked like this when Mom and Olivia hired her? Maybe. Olivia had said they wanted someone new and cutting edge.

Neither woman noticed the cracked door, they were laughing and talking so much. When the girl was ready to leave she paid Misty, and Misty put the money in her pocket. Then she went to Olivia's station and took products to her friend.

"They're on sale for half price now."

The friend paid her, and that money went into Misty's pocket, too. Jazzi glanced at her sister. Olivia looked like she might explode but waited until the friend left the shop. Then she stomped to the speaker system and turned off the music.

The abrupt silence felt deafening. Misty whirled to see who was there, and her eyes flew wide. "I can explain."

"How did you get into the shop?" Olivia's hands went to her hips.

Misty's expression turned sly. "Your mom made me a key for when I had an early client and she wouldn't be in until later in the day."

"Mom and I never come in the front door. We always use the back. Why would Mom give you a key to the front?"

"She was locking up for the night and had that key in her hand, I guess."

That didn't sound like Mom. She'd take the time to find the key she wanted. Olivia wasn't buying it either. She'd check on it later in the day when Mom got there.

Olivia arched an eyebrow. "We all buy our own products here. I just saw you take some of mine for your friend."

Misty pressed her lips together. "Sorry about that, but Tish didn't call me until late last night to ask me for a favor. She needed her hair done pronto for a job interview. I didn't have time to run to the beauty supply store. I'll buy new for you, I promise."

The girl was saying all the right things, but Jazzi didn't trust her. Her answers were too glib. She didn't have any solid reason to think she was lying, but she didn't like the girl. And she'd learned to trust her instincts.

Olivia's voice was brittle. "I brought my sister in early for a haircut. I'd better get busy or she's going to be late for work."

Jazzi got the message. So did Misty. Olivia didn't want to confront Misty now. She'd talk to Mom first. Olivia motioned for Jazzi to take the chair at her station and then turned to focus her full attention on her, ignoring Misty. But her brows furrowed when the front door opened and another client zipped inside for Misty to do her hair. Twenty minutes later, Jazzi's waves fell into place like they were supposed to. No one could rival her sister's expertise. She paid for the cut, even though Olivia insisted she didn't need to because they were family, but she didn't leave a tip. Olivia drew the line there. Then she wished her sister a good day and got out of there. Olivia might not say anything to Misty now, but the tension between them was palpable.

As Jazzi drove to the house in Kirkwood Park, she decided she wouldn't want to be Misty when it was closing time tonight.

Chapter 3

Traffic was still heavy on the drive to Kirkwood Park. Most people had already gone to their jobs, but others were venturing out to shop or do chores, or maybe they didn't start work until nine, like Jerod, Ansel, and her.

She wasn't as late as she'd feared when she reached the Dutch Colonial. She found Jerod and Ansel in the kitchen, finishing the backsplash tiles they'd ordered—the last detail to complete the room. White subway tiles and white walls accented the light-gray cupboards the three of them had installed. They'd chosen metal handles for the doors and drawers along with butcher-block countertops, giving them a clean but old-fashioned look. A long, dark table worked as the kitchen island, with chairs along one side for seating.

The kitchen opened into the living room with shiplap siding, built-in bookcases, and a fireplace. An Oriental rug centered two armchairs with white slipcovers, two Federal-style wooden chairs with padded backs and seats, and a love seat facing the fireplace. The space was warm and inviting.

Ansel turned to look at her when she entered the room. He gave a low whistle. "Your sister sure knows how to make you look good. Your hair's all sexy and soft."

Jerod turned to see her, too. "Yeah, you look better." He grinned. Her cousin would rather eat raw liver than give her a compliment. "How was Olivia anyway?"

When Jazzi told them about the new girl, Misty, Jerod shook his head. "Sounds like she's stealing from them. That girl had better say her prayers she still has a booth in the salon tomorrow."

While the guys finished the tiles, she went outside to work on the landscape. The day was still nippy but not terrible. It was too soon to plant flowers, but she could clean up the bushes and beds that were there. They made a point of never leaving work for their buyers, and today was going to be their last day here.

They stopped for a quick lunch so they could finish up. As soon as George got a whiff of deli beef, he was at Ansel's ankle, begging for scraps. When they were done with their meal Jazzi packed up everything and carried it to the van. It took two trips so she could get the coffee urn she carted to each job site, too. Then she finished work on the yard, and the men completed the last detail on the grouting. At the end of the day they walked through the house to check everything out.

The new owner was happy with it and meant to move in over the weekend. It had four bedrooms and two bathrooms up, the kitchen, living room, and dining room downstairs with a half bath, and a beautiful backyard. They'd replaced every window in the house and installed a new roof. They'd fixed the ceilings damaged by leaks. No one would ever know what bad shape it was in when they bought it.

On Monday they'd start work on their next project—a Georgian-style house in Wildwood Park, a short distance for Jerod on the south side of town but a decent drive for them. Jazzi had never intended to live on the north side of the city, so far away from everyone else, but she'd fallen in love with the roomy stone cottage, and Ansel loved all the land that came with it. He'd built a pond at the back of the property the first year he'd move in with her.

When they'd walked through the Wildwood place it needed a lot of updating, like most old houses, but the structure was solid—all red brick with five windows up, four windows and a center door down. A white, arched entry protected the door and the wide steps leading up to it. For once the roof was fairly new. Everything was in such good shape, they wouldn't make as much money flipping it, but it wouldn't take them much time either.

Satisfied with the work on this house, they left it and locked up after themselves for the last time. Jerod would give the keys to the owner tomorrow. Then they had the weekend off. Ansel couldn't wait to work outdoors at their place on Saturday. And then, on Sunday, they'd host the weekly family meal.

On the drive home Jazzi said, "I can't wait to hear what Olivia and Mom have to say when we get together." She'd be surprised if Misty still had a job.

Ansel shrugged. "I remember how excited they were when they hired her. And they did their homework. When they called the last shop she worked at the owner gave her a glowing reference."

Jazzi frowned, remembering that. "Do you think that owner just wanted to get rid of her with no theatrics?"

"If that's true, shame on her. She stuck your mom and Olivia with a bad employee."

Worse. Jazzi agreed with Jerod. "Well, we won't hear anything until we see them on Sunday. Tonight we can have a quiet night and relax."

"I'm ready. It's nice enough out, I thought I'd grill some smoked pork chops for supper."

"It's only fifty-eight." Not Jazzi's idea of grilling weather, but Ansel even wore a poncho and cooked in the rain when he was in the mood. There was no roof over their back patio, and he wanted to change that. He was thinking about screening it in so the cats could go out there. Then they'd pour a bigger cement pad next to it, covered by a pergola with a canvas ceiling.

When they pulled into the garage and started to the back door, Jazzi cocked her head, trying to picture his plans. He was right. A porch would protect them from too much sun, the rain, and insects. The project wouldn't be that hard either. And it would keep her Norseman busy for the summer. Another plus.

The cats ran to meet them when they entered the kitchen. Jazzi stopped to feed and pet her furry beasts. Once the pets were happy, she and Ansel grabbed drinks and sat at the kitchen island to relax. It was Friday night. The end of the week. That deserved a glass of wine and a beer.

Chapter 4

Saturday flew by. Jazzi cleaned the house while Ansel worked in the yard. He'd grown up on a dairy farm and needed his outside time. George had followed him as far as the patio but only stretched on the cement for a short while before scratching to get back into the house. It was too chilly for the pug.

Once the house was in good shape, she and Ansel grabbed their grocery list to go to the store. When they first got together George always wanted to come with them, but he'd learned he had to wait in the pickup while they shopped, and because they were getting a full order for the week, it took longer than he liked. Before Ansel moved in with her, when he lived with Emily, he only ran in for a few items. Emily didn't like to cook. She didn't like to clean or be bothered either. That was why Ansel took the pug everywhere with him. She didn't like his dog. Now George felt loved and content, so he was happy to stay at home and wait for them.

On the drive to the store Ansel asked, "What's on the menu for tomorrow?"

"Since Easter's so close and it's such a big meal, Elspeth, Didi, and I thought we'd make something lighter for the next few weeks. I'm going to make salmon with creamed spinach and a pretzel salad with cranberries for the sides. Didi's making yellow rice with peas and diced onions and Elspeth's bringing orange pudding cakes."

"That's light?" Ansel grinned. "You three don't know what light is."

"If we ever got too healthy, Jerod would have a fit."

"So would I. You've spoiled us. My mom's idea of a big Sunday dinner was fried chicken and mashed potatoes with gravy."

"There's nothing wrong with that."

"Every Sunday. Like clockwork. We could tell the day of the week by the meal on the table."

She shrugged. "My mom didn't like to cook either. We ate a lot of carry-in food."

"Like Olivia and Thane." He shook his head. "I'd have been happy with that if I hadn't married you and gotten spoiled. It's nice having Didi and Elspeth help with family meals, though, because so many people come now."

It was wonderful, especially because over twenty people came now. Of course, Walker and Didi's Noreen was just a baby, but she made twenty-one. "It would have been too much if someone didn't step up to help. We'd have had to change to snacks or pizzas."

Ansel turned into the entrance for the store and looked for a place to park. "Radley and Elspeth will be able to host it every other week after Easter. Radley said they'd be ready by then."

"Even better." She and Ansel had helped them knock out a wall to make the kitchen, dining room, and sitting room big enough to hold everyone. They'd helped install the new kitchen and redo both bathrooms, too, but Radley and Elspeth had insisted on refinishing the floors and painting every room themselves.

"You guys do this for a living," Radley told them. "We're just happy you helped us with the big stuff we wouldn't get right."

It had taken Radley and Elspeth longer than they'd expected, but Radley's apartment manager had let them stay in their small apartment without signing a new lease. There were so many people on the waiting list to live there, he didn't have to worry about filling it when they left. But really, he was just a nice guy and didn't hassle them when he could have.

They were making their way through the store, and Jazzi was reading through her grocery list, when someone parked her cart beside theirs. "Fancy meeting you here." Misty's voice was too loud, bordering on belligerent.

Jazzi snapped up her head to stare at her. Her feet were spread in a fighting stance. What was the girl's problem? "I've never seen you here before." And that was a good thing.

Misty's penciled brows rose. "That's because I had a job and worked during the day, but your witch of a sister and your froufrou mom fired me. If you hadn't come in early that day, I'd still have my booth."

Jazzi couldn't believe her ears. "And you're blaming *me*?"

"Olivia never came in before opening time except to pamper you."

This was too much. Jazzi glanced at Misty's cart, full of cartons of beer and bags of chips. "Are you celebrating? Because my sister probably is. I'm guessing she's glad to be rid of you."

Misty's gaze smoldered. "You're as holier than thou as your mom and sister."

"No, but none of us like to be taken advantage of. You must not have had any good answers for them about why their shop lost money after they hired you."

The smolder turned to a blaze, but before Misty could say anything more, Ansel stepped beside Jazzi and said, "It's time you move on or I'm calling the manager."

"To do what?" She stared up at him, defiant.

The look he gave her could wither green grass. "Do you really want to be booted out of two places?"

She glanced around her at the people staring in her direction. With a huff, she said, "Now that I know what kind of clientele shops here, I won't be back anyway."

A relief. Jazzi hoped she meant it as she stomped away. Ansel watched her, too, then let out a low breath. "That girl's some piece of work."

"She must have put on one heck of a show when Mom and Olivia hired her."

With a grimace, Ansel glanced at the next item on their list before heading down the aisle. "It's easy to sound good for half an hour. My uncle made it sound like I'd be welcome when I moved here from the farm, that he needed another worker. That didn't last long."

She remembered him telling her about that. "It wasn't your uncle. It was his sons, and their construction company does all right, but it's sure not thriving."

He narrowed his eyes at her. "Have you checked on it?"

"Maybe." Then she confessed. "They treated you so badly, I watch for their signs around town. They never get anything big."

He smiled. "You can be pretty fierce when you go into protective mode. Thanks for watching out for me."

"If I had my way, they'd go under."

He laughed and hugged her waist. "My uncle deserves better than that. I'm glad they're making a decent living."

"If you say so." But his uncle had been a wimp and let his boys treat Ansel like crap.

"Come on." Ansel rumpled her hair. "We still have a lot of groceries to buy, and it's a Saturday. Let's not let tacky people ruin our day."

He was right. She knew it, so she pushed Misty and his uncle out of her mind, and she let herself relish the fact that Mom and Olivia had sacked Miss Attitude. They'd have something fun to talk about over the meal tomorrow.

Chapter 5

Jerod and Franny were always the first ones to arrive on Sunday. This time Jerod walked in looking frazzled. He handed Pete to Jazzi and went straight to the kitchen island where the cheeseball and crackers were set, and Ansel went to get him a beer. He looked like he needed one.

Pete twisted in Jazzi's arms to see who was holding him and smiled. He reached to put his hands on her face, as if reading her features in Braille. Then he laughed and smacked them against her cheeks.

"Does that mean he likes me?" she asked Franny.

"Every kid likes you." She made herself some crackers, too. "You have a way with them."

She did? News to her. She squinted at Franny, suspicious. She looked grateful Pete was happy with someone else for a minute. She didn't want him back. The sign of a good parent. Even when a mom or dad loved a kid, it was nice to get rid of him once in a while.

Jerod nodded toward Pete, who was beginning to squirm in Jazzi's arms. "Mr. Wonderful thinks he can do anything since he turned a year old. Every time Franny says 'no,' he looks right at her and does it again. He screamed in the car seat all the way here."

Gunther put his hands over his ears. "He screams really loud," he told them.

"He wants down," Jazzi said, doing her best to hold onto a wiggle worm. "Is that okay?"

"Have you babyproofed everything within reach?" Jerod asked.

Ansel nodded. They'd learned the hard way. Pete had made it halfway up the stairs before anyone noticed a few weeks ago. They had a gate at the bottom of the steps leading to their bedrooms now. And Ansel had installed a hook on the outside of the basement door, so that even when Pete turned the handle, he couldn't open it. There were locks on every cupboard door and plugs in every electrical outlet. Why not? They figured they might as well babyproof the entire first floor and basement; Walker and Didi's Noreen would be careening around them someday soon, too.

"He's a whirlwind," Franny told them, going to get a can of Coke. "But if you're ready to chase him, you might as well set him loose."

The minute Jazzi set him down, he took off. He only crawled right now, but he could pull himself up to anything that interested him. The cats took one look at him and disappeared. A sad thing for River. When he got here he liked to pull a string for them.

She'd no more than thought that than Walker and Didi walked into the kitchen with River and Noreen. Gunther and Lizzie took one look at River and ran to drag him into the basement. Ansel had built a kids' corner down there. Walker had to unhook the door to let them go down, then glanced at Pete, crawling at top speed toward the steps, and locked it again.

"Whoa! That boy's getting faster," he said.

"Tell us about it." Jerod went to peek at Noreen. Jazzi's cousin had a soft spot for kids, especially babies. But with three of his own now, he swore Pete was the last. So did Franny.

Didi pulled back the blanket she'd wrapped around the little girl, and Jazzi went to coo over her, too. Noreen had gotten her dad's chestnut-colored hair and her mom's full lips. She was going to be a beauty when she grew up. Pete crawled to her and used Jazzi's jeans to pull himself higher, trying to see the baby. She picked him up and he stared. When nothing happened he got bored and wanted back down. Jazzi grinned, watching him head for the sitting area across the room. Pete had gotten his mom's carrot-colored hair but Jerod's blue eyes and long lashes. He'd also gotten his mom and dad's stubbornness.

When he reached one of the easy chairs near the bay window, he tried to climb onto it. When he couldn't he let out a bloodcurdling scream. Jazzi blinked. "When did he start doing that?"

"On Monday," Franny said. "We try to ignore him so he doesn't get a reaction to his temper tantrums, but it's not easy."

She could see why. Just then, Jazzi's mom and dad walked inside the house, followed by Olivia and Thane. Gran and Samantha came next. She was taking their coats to hang in the closet on the other side of the basement door when Radley and Elspeth arrived, carrying two trays of pudding cakes. Everyone made room for them. Jerod's parents, Eli and Eleanor, arrived last.

After a quick head count, Jazzi nodded that everyone was there. She and Ansel carried the food they'd made to the huge kitchen island to join Didi's rice and the desserts, and Ansel announced, "Grab your plates."

Jazzi looked at the dishes stacked for people to load their food on. There were three different sets of cheap dinnerware—two sets of eight and one set of four. The bottom white plastic plates had come from her apartment. The Corelle were ones Ansel had bought at a garage sale when he lived with Emily. And she'd grabbed the last four plates from a discount rack at the mall. Every single one of them was sad. She grimaced at the hodgepodge look they made on the long farmhouse table. It was time to buy something better. Not that mismatched dishes slowed anyone down from digging in.

People lined up to serve themselves and grab drinks. Once everyone was seated people started talking about their week. George sat by Ansel's ankle and whined for scraps. When Ansel gave him a nibble of salmon he begged for more. Her Norseman's dog was a gourmand.

It had taken Ansel a while to get used to her family. While he was growing up, meals were quiet affairs. You sat down, ate, and went back out to work again. In her family if you weren't quick, you lost your chance to talk, and people talked over one another. Someone had asked her once if they were Italian, but they couldn't use that as an excuse. They just liked to talk.

When it was Mom's turn she glanced at Olivia and said, "We fired Misty."

Dad's expression went bland. Jazzi knew that look. He wasn't going to comment one way or another. He never stooped to tell Mom "I told you so." Her dad was a sweetheart who gave an opinion and then left it alone. If a person agreed with him, fine. If not, that was fine, too.

"Misty's gone?" Jerod asked.

"And good riddance." Olivia stabbed a piece of salmon. "We couldn't figure out why she didn't bring in more money. We were *losing* money after we hired her. Come to find out, she was selling products from our booths instead of her own and pocketing the money. On top of that she was bringing in clients before and after the shop closed so she could pocket that money, too, and not put it on the books."

"Did Mom give her a key?" Jazzi asked.

"No." Mom sat up straighter in her chair, her shoulders squared. "Neither of us did. She must have made a copy for herself."

Even worse.

"She was a crook," Mom snapped.

Ansel frowned. "But didn't she have a great recommendation from the shop she worked at before?"

"The shop that didn't exist?" Olivia glared at her plate as though it offended her.

Ansel shook his head, confused. "What do you mean?"

"We looked up the shop online and called the number on their web page. They'd never heard of her. And that number wasn't the one she gave us. We called that number again, and a woman answered. I told her I was trying to find Misty about a hair appointment, and she told me Misty had moved to River Bluffs, that she'd left her last shop. 'Are you sure?' I asked, and she said she was Misty's best friend. She still kept in touch with her, and she was doing great at her new salon."

Gran put down her glass of red wine. "You got scammed."

"Big time." Olivia scooped up a bite of the pretzel salad and jammed it in her mouth.

"Did you get your key back?" Jerod asked. "Misty can't still get into the shop, can she?"

Mom nodded. "We got the key, but the man hasn't come to change the locks yet. And then no more new hires. We've learned our lesson. Our shop ran better when it was just Olivia and me working together."

The meal finished, Jazzi and Ansel stood to collect dirty plates and get ready for dessert. When Jazzi brought Gran a second glass of red wine she frowned at her.

"Chad's not the nice boy I thought he was. Don't let him fool you."

Jazzi stared at her, caught off guard. She and Chad had been engaged once, but it didn't go well. They hadn't seen each other since he'd remarried. Still, Gran had the gift of sight. And she'd mentioned him for some reason, though more often than not, she had no idea what that might be.

Gran looked upset, though, so Jazzi tried to reassure her. "Chad and I broke up a long time ago, Gran. I never see him anymore."

"You will soon," Gran told her. "But don't let him win you back. Stay with your Ansel. He's a keeper."

"Don't worry about that. I happen to love the guy." She glanced his way, and he grinned.

Gran smiled, satisfied, and they finished serving the orange pudding cakes Elspeth had brought. More coffee was poured, and at the end of the meal the men and kids disappeared into the basement and the women settled in the living room. As soon as Jazzi and Ansel placed the dessert plates in their deep farmhouse sink to rinse, they went to join them, Ansel carrying George with him.

For whatever reason the women always chose to sit in the seating area closest to the kitchen, the one with the butter-yellow sofas and chairs. Maybe so they could pop over to the refrigerator for more drinks when they wanted them. Jazzi poured herself a glass of pinot grigio for after-dinner chatter.

Eleanor, Jerod's mother, was excited about a cruise that she and Eli had signed up for. "We always spend every summer at our lake cottage," she told them. "But this year we're taking two weeks to go on an Alaskan cruise in early August. We've never taken one before, and Eli's always wanted to see Alaska, so we thought we'd give it a try."

Talk turned to trips and plans for the summer, and the women were still talking when the men came up from their pool table and video games to join them. A little after that everyone got ready to leave.

When the last car left the driveway Ansel looked at the clock. "They stayed longer than usual. It's almost six."

They finished cleaning up before going upstairs to change into their pajamas. Then they relaxed on their favorite sofas to watch TV and read. Tomorrow they'd start work on the new fixer-upper in Wildwood Park. The owners had retired and sold the house below market value so they could move to their condo in Florida as quickly as possible.

It wouldn't take Jazzi, Jerod, and Ansel long to paint, refinish floors, and repair the widow's walk at the top of the house. Nothing else needed to be done outside. The bricks were in great shape, and the trim was sparkling white. A quick job would be nice after the Dutch Colonial that had needed *everything* done to make it ready to sell.

At the end of the night, when they crawled into bed and Jazzi drifted off to sleep, a quick flash of Gran's words at supper popped into her mind. Gran had warned her about Chad. Jazzi hadn't thought about him for a long time. Why now? Gran's sight usually proved more confusing than helpful, even though it was always right.

Chapter 6

The next morning, Jazzi, Ansel, and Jerod pulled into the driveway for their new fixer-upper and stared up at it. A Georgian style, with an imposing main building, a wing off to the left and a sunroom to the right, it reminded Jazzi of something out of the history books for the Colonial period. Solid and brick, with black shutters and a white, columned entry to cover the front door and the steps leading up to it, it had five windows up, four down with a central door, and three dormers on the third floor. A widow's walk stretched between the two chimneys and a railing bordered the flat roof of the solarium. The house screamed status and wealth.

Jazzi grabbed the cooler out of the back of their work van and Ansel picked up George, then they started into the house. A white stairway topped with a wooden rail climbed at the end of the foyer, which was long and wide. Every room was huge but the kitchen. They'd decided to tear down the wall between it and the dining room. They'd have to install a beam because it was a load-bearing wall. But like many kitchens of that era, it was small, meant only for the cook to make food to serve in the monstrous dining room to the family and their guests.

They were going to gut the kitchen, too. It was dated, with white appliances. It wouldn't take long to cart them out on dollies and tear out the old cupboards because the space was so small. They strapped on their tool belts and got started. By lunch time the kitchen was bare and they'd knocked out the wall, leaving a few two-by-fours to support it. They stopped to eat the lunch Jazzi had packed—deli sandwiches and chips—and then got started on the new beam. That was heavy work, and it took them more time than they'd expected. But they stayed to gut the half bath off the hallway leading to the study. Then they all sat around the wooden table the previous owners used as an island to plan what they wanted to do with the kitchen, the sitting area arched off it, and the dining area they'd just opened up.

"I'd like to make this house more modern than we usually do," Jerod said, spreading pictures he'd brought across the wooden surface.

Jazzi looked at the sleek lines and stark colors, frowning. She liked warm and cozy, not being a fan of modern. And every house they'd finished had sold before it went on the market. Still, she didn't mind compromise. She pointed to one picture. "I could go with light wood floors like those instead of a warm color." She pulled out another magazine page. "And those white Shaker cupboards would look good with black appliances and granite countertops. We could do black, sleek hardware, too. Would that be modern enough—a black-and-white theme?"

They started serious haggling, and by the time they packed up to leave for the day, they'd mapped out their plans for the entire kitchen area. They'd made the kitchen bigger, so they decided to build a floor-to-ceiling pantry for more storage. Jerod had fallen in love with a white and gray, diamond-patterned backsplash to put behind the stove, so Ansel voted for a stainless-steel hood over it. Jazzi wanted those offset by narrow wooden shelves on each side of the backsplash to hold cookbooks and canisters for cooking ingredients. They were going to leave the wide archway that led to the sitting room, with its small, cozy fireplace and lots of windows to let in light. Bookcases were on either side of the fireplace. It would be the perfect place to snuggle to read in the evening.

"We can decide on the rest tomorrow," Jerod said, standing to remove his tool belt on the way to the door. "We didn't come up with much for the dining area. We should think some more about it, too."

Good enough for Jazzi. She went to get the cooler. Ansel hefted George onto his hip and reached for his hoodie with his other hand. They locked up and walked to their vehicles, then went in separate directions. Jerod lived south. They lived north.

"Want to grab something to eat on our way home?" Ansel asked. "That way you wouldn't have to cook."

She shook her head. "I always keep it simple on Monday. I bought a tube of pizza dough and everything I need to make a stromboli. I'm opening a bag of salad to go with it."

"Sounds good to me." Ansel loved food, but he wasn't picky. "I'll help make the salad."

She laughed. "You mean you'll open the bag?"

"I'll even put the salad dressings on the kitchen island." He grinned. The man was a champ. He parked the van next to her pickup in the garage and they walked to the house, side by side. When they stepped into the kitchen, the cats ran to greet them and twine around their ankles, begging for food. Jazzi laughed and bent to pet them, then noticed the answering machine blinking in the corner. They only used it for business, so she went to push the button to listen to the message.

"Sorry to call this number, but it's the only one I had for you, Jaz. This is Chad. Can we meet somewhere to talk? Maybe the coffeehouse on Anthony we used to like? Ginger and I are having problems. I blew it with you, and I thought you could help me so I don't blow it with her, too. I'd sure appreciate your take on it. Tomorrow night, if you can?"

Ansel stiffened ramrod straight. "I call you Jaz. He did, too?"

She shrugged. "What other nickname can anyone come up with for Jazzi? Did Emily have a nickname for you?" When a flush colored his face, her eyebrows flew up, and she grinned. "That good, huh? I'm a slouch. I only call you Norseman or Viking because of your coloring."

"And my parents are one hundred percent Norwegian," he added.

"What did Emily . . . ?"

He cut her off. "Don't ask. She was a nurse, obsessed with body parts."

"Really? Who knew? Did you play doctor?" She was enjoying watching him squirm.

He glanced at the answering machine again, and his humor faded. "Your gran warned you about Chad yesterday."

She gave him a look. "Not to go back with him. Like I ever would. I have you. I hit the jackpot."

His shoulders relaxed a little. "Are you going to meet him? He was a jerk the last time we saw him." They'd run into him at a restaurant when he was with his buddies at the bar. He'd stopped to say hi, but all he did was complain because he'd found out Ginger had an abortion when she was young and somehow it made it so she couldn't have babies. Chad had always wanted a houseful of kids. That was one of the reasons they broke up.

Jazzi studied him. "What would you do if Emily was in town and called you for help?"

Ansel's blond brows furrowed into a frown. He grimaced, and she knew his answer. "I'd meet her."

She went to wrap her arms around him. "I know you would. That's why I love you so much. You're so nice."

With a sigh, he dropped a kiss on her forehead. "Can you meet him early enough to come home for supper tomorrow so we can eat together?"

She nodded. "He can meet me on my terms or forget about it." She called Chad back and agreed to be at the coffeehouse at five thirty. When she hung up Ansel didn't look happy, but he'd come to terms with her going.

They put Chad behind them and went upstairs to take their showers and change into their pajamas. They could relax for the rest of the night. But as they made the stromboli and ate supper, Jazzi wondered how much Chad was willing to compromise. When they'd been together it was his way or the highway. Had he gotten smarter with Ginger? Only time would tell.

Chapter 7

They didn't even need sweaters when they stepped outside. The grass was green. Flowers were thinking of blooming and the air smelled fresh and clean. Jazzi loved warm weather. If nothing else, it meant her Norseman was back to wearing worn jeans and snug T-shirts, one of her favorite looks on him. They cracked their windows on the drive across town to Wildwood Park. George even sat up in the back seat of the van to look out the window.

At the house they found Jerod rubbing his chin, staring at the beam they'd installed the day before. "I think we should box it in and paint it white, like the walls, to give the rooms a more modern feel."

Not just white. Stark white. But Jazzi didn't mind. She liked the contrast between the black appliances and white walls. They got started and had finished pounding in the last nail when Jazzi's cell phone buzzed. She glanced at the ID. "Olivia."

Jerod frowned. "She never calls during the day. She should be at the salon doing somebody's hair by now. Maybe a client canceled on her."

If one did, she wouldn't get another appointment for a long time. Jazzi answered the call. "Hi, Sis."

"You aren't going to believe what Misty did now!" Olivia's voice was so angry, Jazzi blinked in surprise and put her on speakerphone. Before she could answer, Olivia went on. "Someone threw a brick through our back-door window and got inside to trash everything."

"How bad is it?"

"She smashed our mirrors, opened most of our products and squirted them all over the floor, made lipstick squiggles all over the windows. Do you want me to go on?"

No wonder Olivia was fuming. "Have you called Gaff?" Jazzi and Ansel had worked with the detective enough to think of him as a friend.

"He's been here and gone. The last tech just left. And Gaff's already checked on Misty. And can you believe this? Her lowlife friends all swore she never left the house after she got fired."

"Would anyone else trash your salon?" Jazzi asked.

"No! And bet you can't guess what kind of products her friends had at their house."

"Yours?"

"Bingo." Olivia stopped for a sharp breath. "They swore Misty bought them for them while she worked at the salon. Gaff said they all live in some run-down house off Broadway. They're probably as bad as she is. Mom and I had to cancel all our appointments for today to put the shop back in order, and we're going to be working late hours the rest of this week to get everyone in for their colors and cuts."

"You never installed a security system for the salon?" Jerod asked, coming closer to talk into the phone.

"Shut it, Cuz. We've never had to worry about security before, but we're having one installed as soon as the crew can get here next week. We're putting in a new steel door, too. Misty's so trashy, she might do this again."

Jazzi felt for her sister. "Are you going to be okay?"

"We have insurance, so most of the repairs are covered. But I can't believe what a tacky, sleazy girl we hired. Never again."

"Sorry, Sis." There wasn't much else to say. "How's Mom taking it?"

"She wants to drive to Misty's house and beat her with a baseball bat. You know Mom, not the martyr type."

Jazzi smiled. "Don't encourage that. Mom could end up in jail." Her mother's sister Lynda had hurt her enough when they were growing up, it had made her swear she wouldn't get hurt again. She'd often told them to be kind and nice, but not to take any crap off anyone. And she meant it.

Olivia snickered. "Never thought I'd be the voice of reason, did you?"

"You usually flare faster than Mom, but you get mad, then it goes away. Mom holds a grudge."

"Yeah, but there's not much we can do about this mess. No way to prove anything, so we might as well deal with it and be done."

"Sad but true. Hang in there."

When Olivia disconnected Ansel shook his head. "I never even thought of anyone being that vindictive."

"Misty has to have a screw loose," Jerod said. "The sooner they get the security system put in, the better."

They returned to work on the house. The floorboards needed to be replaced where they'd torn down the wall, and they had to lay new ones that they'd stain to match the others when they refinished them. Nail holes needed to be filled and sanded before they painted the walls, so they spent the day readying the room so they could sand the floors the next day.

There were two small rooms behind the kitchen on the way to the back door. They decided to make one a mudroom and the other a laundry room. The back door led to a deck. After lunch they took measurements and hunkered at the table to decide on plans for the rest of the first floor. Once those were drawn up Jerod looked at the clock and said, "Let's call it for today and leave a little early." He looked at Jazzi. "I hear you're seeing your ex tonight."

She wasn't going to sit through a lecture by her cousin, so she grinned. "I thought I'd interview him to join my male harem. He wasn't too bad-looking."

Jerod laughed. "Just don't feel too sorry for him when he gives you his sad story. If he's treating Ginger the way he treated you, he deserves to be kicked to the curb."

"You're not going to hear me champion him. When it comes to kids he has a bad case of tunnel vision." She went to get the cooler. "I'll bring my panini maker tomorrow. I'm ready to step it up with sandwiches."

"You haven't made soup for a while either." Jerod smiled when she gave him a dirty look.

"I'm going to have to step up my game. I wouldn't want you to starve and shrivel away."

They were still teasing each other as they locked up and left the house. The traffic wasn't as bad driving home because they'd left early and missed the rush-hour crowd. Jazzi had time for a shower, then changed into old jeans and a baggy sweater. It wouldn't do to doll up to see Chad. He'd take it the wrong way, and so would Ansel.

Her Norseman gave her a hug on her way out of the house. "Don't let him get to you."

She shook her head. "He already pushed all my buttons when we lived together. It won't happen again."

It took her half an hour to make a fifteen-minute drive. Cars had backed up on Coliseum Boulevard as usual at this time of night. Chad was already sitting at a table in the back corner, so she went to join him. The minute the waiter took her order he started in.

"Ginger's going to leave me. All the signs are there. I'm starting to think she's meeting someone on the side."

"You were always thinking I was seeing someone, too," Jazzi reminded him, "and I wasn't."

He scraped a hand through his dark hair. His pale blue eyes narrowed. The man was good-looking enough, nearly six feet tall and trim with a permanent tan, but he couldn't hold a candle to Ansel. "You were so pretty, and so many guys hit on you, it made me nervous. Ginger's pretty but no knockout. I think I'm right this time. I think she's having an affair."

The waitress came with her coffee and Jazzi took a sip to give herself time to think. "What if she is seeing someone? Would you forgive her and try to save your marriage?"

He let out a long breath. "The dumb thing is, I would. It's probably my fault anyway. I was such an idiot about the abortion and worse, about not being able to have kids. But when I thought I was losing her, I decided she was more important to me than any of that."

Jazzi stared at him, stunned. This was a Chad she'd never seen. "So how are you going to win her back?"

"That's why I called you. I don't know. We were happy when we got married, doing okay until I went off the deep end. And then I saw you at the restaurant, and you made me think. I eased up, and we started doing okay again. I'm probably still too controlling, but I'm working on that. But something happened, and now she's all weird and upset. I don't know what's going on with her."

"Do you let her know how much you love her? That you appreciate her?"

"I'm better at it now than I was when I first met her."

Jazzi frowned. "Is she away from home more than usual?"

He nodded, draining his coffee cup and gesturing for a refill. "She goes out to meet a friend I've never heard of or has to work a couple of hours later than usual." He shook his head. "She works at the school's food kitchen, making meals for them to ship out for lunches at the different buildings. She's never had to work late before."

Jazzi pinched her lips together. "Do you think she still loves you?"

"She says she does. I asked her. I asked her if she'd found someone who made her happier than I do and if she wanted to cut her losses."

"And?" She hadn't expected that. Chad really did care about Ginger. He'd turned vitriolic when she'd broken up with him, not wishing her well.

He shrugged his shoulders. "She said we'd had bumps, but she wanted to make it work with me. She thought we were good together."

She finished her coffee and decided to be honest. "I think you're right, that she's found someone else, but you've gotten yourself together and she's willing to give your marriage another try."

"That's what I think, too. So what do I do? Just sit and wait until she breaks it off with the other guy?"

"You don't have a choice unless you want to walk away. If you're willing to stick it out, just be good to her and let her work things through."

Easy for her to say. She didn't think she could do it. She wasn't particularly jealous, but if Ansel had an affair with someone else, it would break their trust, and she didn't know if she'd ever truly get it back.

Chad reached across the table and took her hands in his. "Thank you, Jaz. I know I didn't get anything right with you after we moved in together, and I wouldn't have blamed you if you told me to go rot when I asked for your help. But I really appreciate your coming tonight. Wish me luck, will you? I really want to make it work with Ginger."

"Good luck." She meant it.

He tossed enough money on the table to cover their bill and they walked out of the coffeehouse together. She thought about him all the way home. She was sure that he'd made Ginger miserable enough to see someone else, but he was trying really hard to fix things between them. She just hoped he hadn't waited too long.

Chapter 8

Jazzi lugged her panini maker to the Wildwood house the next day. She'd already brought the coffee urn she carried from job to job. She'd splurged on Gruyère cheese and deli roast chicken for lunch and brought a big bag of fresh spinach to add to them. After they got George comfortable in his doggy bed in the foyer they pulled on masks and started sanding the kitchen and sitting-room floors. Poor Jerod was dragging today. He had dark circles under his eyes, and she watched him struggle to hang in there as they worked. He gave a loud sigh when it was time to stop to eat.

"You okay?" she asked as they stepped outside to clear their lungs.

He took off his face mask and shook dust out of his hair and clothes before answering. "Pete's cutting molars. Poor kid's miserable. Keeps getting us up at night."

Ansel stepped out to shake off dust, too. "Want to call it quits early? Jazzi and I can work on the living room together and you can go home to take a nap."

"I can stick around 'til we finish the ground floor. The nice thing about having three sanders is the job won't take as long; then we can all head home."

He started back into the house, but the day was so pretty, Jazzi lingered in the yard a few minutes more. She wished there was a picnic table on the deck, but the previous owner had sold it. This was a beautiful older neighborhood where every house was different. She didn't know if it was a plus or a minus that it was pocketed between a highway on one side and two busy streets on the others. River Bluffs had built a high wall on those streets to keep out noise, so it was a fairly quiet neighborhood close to everything, but traffic flowed all around it. Finally, she couldn't put it off any longer and went back inside to get busy making paninis.

When she put one on Jerod's paper plate he bit into it and gave her a thumbs-up. "This'll be the best thing I eat today. I'm going to grab takeout on the way home. Franny's dragging as bad as I am."

Ansel glanced through the side door at the foyer and frowned. "What do we have in mind for that?"

Her cousin grimaced. "I don't know. The planks are wider than in the rest of the house, and they're cheaper wood. The floor's in worse shape, too."

"We should paint it," Jazzi said. She'd brought a notebook she kept house ideas in and flipped to a front page. "The foyer's wide and long, and the center staircase is beautiful. I think we should make them a focal point. We could stick with the white-and-black theme."

Jerod frowned until he saw the picture. The house's front door was painted black, and it opened into a hallway with a wooden floor painted white with black trim and big black diamonds painted in a pattern. "We've never done anything like that before. We'd have to measure everything off."

"It fits the house," Ansel said. "We could paint a protective coating over the whole thing."

"All we'd have to invest in it is labor," Jazzi added. "It would be time-consuming, though."

"But that's what makes it special." Jerod nodded approval. "You like it, too, Ansel?"

"Almost every room in the house only needs paint and refinished floors. Why not make this floor special? The only rooms we have to redo are the kitchen and baths."

"Inside. Outside, we need to replace the widow's walk," Jerod said. "The old wrought-iron is rusted. It's not safe. And the railing for the balcony over the solarium needs to be replaced, too, but that's wood, so it won't be as expensive."

Jazzi emptied her bottle of water. "I think we should make the widow's walk white instead of black to match the railing on the balcony."

"I can see that." Jerod finished his second panini and got up to throw away his plate. "I think we've got things figured out. If you guys are done eating, we can start sanding the living-room floor. Then we can clean it so we can stain it tomorrow and get out of here."

Even with all three of them working together, it took longer than they expected, the room was so big. They were walking to their vehicles when Olivia called again.

"You okay?" Jazzi asked.

"Misty hired a lawyer and she's suing us for defamation of character," Olivia said. "Can you believe her nerve? She's willing to settle out of court for ten thousand dollars."

"Ten thousand?" Jazzi almost dropped the phone, she was so shocked. "Dad has a lawyer, doesn't he? Someone threatened to sue his hardware store once."

"But we'll have court fees. Innocent until proven guilty is a joke. It's not cheap to go to court."

The more Jazzi thought about it, the less she worried. "Let her sue you. Any judge with a brain will throw out her case."

"You'd think, but you never know, do you? Mom thinks we should make a counteroffer and pay her off."

"That's what she's hoping for. If you cave now, why wouldn't she threaten you again?"

"Can she do that?"

"Maybe not for the same thing, but who knows what she could come up with next? Medical costs for an anxiety disorder?"

Olivia hesitated, and Jazzi gave her time to think. Finally, she asked, "What if the case drags on? What if her friends lie for her again?"

"Talk to Dad's lawyer, Livvy. If she loses the case, set it up so she has to pay the court fees."

Olivia gave a derisive snort. "With what? She doesn't have any money. The guy she hired must work for a percentage of whatever he gets. She can't afford a real lawyer."

"Promise to garnish her wages for the rest of her life if you have to, but don't just hand her money and let her get off easy."

Olivia's sigh sounded wrenched from her soul. "I wish she'd just die and go away."

"The world wouldn't miss her, that's for sure, but make her sweat. Don't let her scare tactics shake you."

"Easy for you to say. Have you ever been sued?"

"Comes with the territory. Someone's bound to swear our work isn't up to standard and try to cheat us out of money."

Another sigh. "Yeah, we get clients like that once in a while. They don't like the way their color turned out and refuse to pay."

"What do you do?"

"Threaten them with small claims court and promise to black ball them in any salon worth its salt."

"That's what Misty deserves."

"Yeah, I get it, but she sort of scares me. She's such a bottom-feeder, I've never dealt with anyone like her." Silence. And then, "Thanks for listening to me vent. I hope this is her last hurrah."

Jazzi hoped so, too. "Good luck, Sis." When she disconnected Jazzi explained what had happened to Jerod and Ansel.

Jerod shook his head as he started to his pickup. "Thank heavens we haven't met Misty. I wonder what Thane thinks about her. He gets a little protective of Olivia."

Ansel shrugged. "I'll see him tomorrow night for guys and girls' night out, but there's not much anyone can do. Hopefully, if Olivia and her mom tell her that they'll see her in court, she'll back down."

Jazzi wasn't so sure, but Ansel was right. There wasn't anything anyone could do at the moment. They batted ideas around on the drive home but let it drop once they started to the house. The weather was still so nice, it got her Norseman ready to fire up his gas grill and start cooking out, so she helped him set up the back patio and drag his grill out of the garage. Then, while he fussed more, she went in to start a stir-fry for supper.

When they'd first moved in together they'd ordered a lot of Chinese takeout, but she saw a cookbook on TV and ordered it to lower the sugar, salt, and carbs in their meals. They were young enough and did enough physical labor, they probably didn't have to worry too much about what they ate, but why not try to be healthier sooner rather than later? She couldn't believe how much healthier home-cooked meals were than restaurant food. So now she cooked her favorite takeouts at home, and Ansel actually liked hers better.

When he finally came into the house he glanced at her wok and grinned, then sniffed the air. Garlic. Ginger. Soy sauce. "Orange chicken?" he asked.

She smiled and nodded. "George and the cats already had some stir-fried chicken before I added the seasonings and sauce." Inky and Marmalade had a thing for chicken. When she made Mongolian beef they threatened to attack her for flat-iron steak.

"Lucky pets." He came to set up their plates and dinnerware at the island. "And lucky me." He brought a bottle of beer for him and a glass of wine for her.

When they finished their meal Jazzi shook her head. "I always think we'll have leftovers and we never do."

"Not with a stir-fry. It's too good." He helped her carry the plates to the sink to rinse and then handed them to her to put in the dishwasher. "Ready for the evening news?"

They watched a little TV before they went upstairs to shower and change into pajamas and then enjoyed relaxing for the rest of the night. Tomorrow was Thursday and they'd meet their friends after work. It was always fun, but it was also a long day. And Jazzi guessed neither Olivia nor Thane would be in the best moods. Olivia would be ready to vent. That's what family was for. To be there through good times and bad.

Chapter 9

Ansel slid pumpernickel bread into the toaster while Jazzi poured coffee for them.

"Where are you girls meeting tonight?" He spread butter and cherry preserves on Jazzi's toast, peanut butter on his.

"Dicky's Wild Hare. It's a short drive for me, but everyone else likes their barbecue enough to trek out north to meet there." She had a special fondness for their brisket. She and Ansel smoked a huge one every summer for a Sunday meal, but it always disappeared fast.

He came to sit on the stool next to hers, their knees bumping. "Was it your choice?"

"No, Didi's. She can finally eat barbecue without getting heartburn." Foods really affected her when she was pregnant, but now that Noreen was three months old, she could eat some of her favorites again. She still couldn't drink alcohol or coffee, though, because she was breastfeeding. Pure torture. Jazzi thought about that every time she thought about having a kid.

"I hope Thane's in a good mood tonight." Ansel grabbed a banana out of the fruit bowl. "Your sister's moodier than you are. She has a temper. I hope she's not taking Misty's drama out on him."

"He can take it. He's known her a long time. Her temper doesn't faze him much."

Ansel chuckled. "I guess you're right."

Jazzi stood to start packing ingredients to make more paninis for lunch when her cell buzzed. She frowned. "Who'd call this early?"

"Maybe Jerod's going to be late. Pete might have kept him awake most of the night."

But it wasn't Jerod on the phone when she answered it. "Jazzi, you have to come to the salon! *Now*. I don't know what to do." The connection went dead.

Jazzi stared at Ansel. "Something happened at the salon, and it must be bad."

They left George and rushed across town to the shop. When she called Jerod on the way to let him know what they were doing, her hand shook. Olivia sounded so upset. No, scared. Worry gnawed inside her.

"I'll meet you there. I'm on my way." Jerod hung up, too.

The minute they parked at the salon's back door Olivia raced outside. She was pale, her movements jerky. She grabbed Jazzi's hand and pulled her into the building.

"What did Misty do now?" Jazzi had tried to think of something horrible enough to panic her sister. A load of manure in each washbasin? It had to be something worse, far worse.

Olivia's face screwed up as she tugged her through the storage room, and Jazzi worried she was going to burst into tears or have a meltdown. What could have happened? Olivia was usually unflappable, squaring her shoulders and dealing with whatever came up. She'd never seen her like this.

Olivia opened the door to the shop and pointed.

Jazzi stared. She could feel the blood drain from her face. Misty was slumped in her sister's chair at the washbasin, her head resting on the edge of the sink and a pair of scissors jammed in her chest. Blood pooled on the rubber mat that surrounded the chair's base.

Olivia's voice wavered. "Those are my scissors. Someone used my scissors to kill her."

Ansel rested a hand on each of their shoulders. "Have you called Gaff?"

Jazzi blinked. Thank heavens her husband had remained stable. She'd lost it for a moment, too stunned to think.

"Gaff?" Olivia stared at him blankly.

Jazzi nodded, took her hand, and gently led her out the front door. She glanced at Ansel and he made the call.

"Can you remember if the door was locked when you got here, Livvy?"

Her sister took a shaky breath. She frowned, rubbing her forehead as if that would calm her tumbling thoughts. She visibly tried to concentrate. "I had to use my key. It had to be locked."

The front door had been, too, when she'd led Olivia outside. "Was a window broken? How did she get in?"

Olivia gave a slight shake of her head. "I don't know."

They stood there, waiting for Gaff, but Jerod got to them first. "Holy crap, you three look horrible." Ansel motioned to inside the salon, and he peeked through the front window, then grimaced. "Why here? Why couldn't Misty just crawl in a gutter somewhere to die?"

His words snapped Jazzi out of her numbness. Not very sympathetic about a murder victim, but Jazzi felt the same way. The girl was so nasty, she probably had a line of people who'd be happy to read her obituary.

Gaff pulled in the drive next, saw them, and came to park nearby. A team of techs pulled in beside him. He disappeared inside with them, and Jazzi, Olivia, Ansel, and Jerod moved to the corner of the building to wait for him.

Jazzi took a deep breath. "Have you called Mom yet?" she asked Olivia.

Her sister jerked, shaking her head vigorously. "She can't see this. She had trouble handling the vandalism. You can't let her come!"

Jerod wrapped an arm around Olivia's shoulders. "Calm down, Cuz. Everything's going to be okay."

"No, it's not! How can it be okay?"

Jazzi gently took her sister's hand. "Mom needs to call her clients to cancel appointments for the day."

"That's the first thing I did. A loop kept playing in my head where clients walked in and saw me standing next to Misty's body. I canceled them all. Then I called you."

"You called your clients before you called Gaff?"

She pinched her lips together. "I didn't want to see him without you." She looked like she was going to break down again, so Jazzi patted her shoulders.

"That's okay. I understand."

Olivia glanced at her watch. "Mom'll be here soon. I should call to warn her, but I just can't. Will you do it?"

With a nod, Jazzi punched in Mom's number and told her the news.

"She died in our shop? Wasn't destroying it enough? Just wait till I get there. That girl's going to wish she'd never . . ." Mom's rant stopped. "She'd dead, isn't she?"

"No pulse," Jazzi said. "You don't want to come here for a while, Mom. Olivia canceled your appointments, so there's no reason to. The techs aren't finished in the shop, and they haven't taken away the body yet." Olivia squirmed as she listened to the conversation. Finally Gaff came to question them, and Jazzi had to quit the call.

He took out his pen and notepad. "Was a door forced? How did Misty get into the shop?"

Olivia glanced at the shop's front door, looking bewildered. "Jazzi asked that, too. I don't know. She used a key when she worked here, but we took it away."

Gaff shrugged. "It would have been easy enough for her to make copies. Was anything else disturbed?"

She shook her head. "Those were my best scissors, though. They're expensive."

Gaff stared; then his tone changed, becoming gentler. "This looks bad for you, but you already know that, don't you?"

Olivia bristled, her dark eyes flashing. "I might have fought Misty in court. I might even have trashed her name to every shop owner I know, but I wouldn't kill her."

"I believe you," Gaff said, "but you know the ropes by now. You're a top suspect until we can rule you out. Don't leave town."

"In the middle of this mess?" Olivia scrunched her eyes shut, frustrated. She took deep breaths, then nodded. "I get it. You'll let Jazzi help find Misty's killer, though, won't you? She'll clear my name."

Gaff grimaced but nodded. "We're almost turning into a team. And this time around if I'm talking to Misty's roommates and friends, they might talk more to her than to me. That's what's happened before."

Olivia's shoulders relaxed and she turned to Jazzi. "You'll help me, won't you?"

Ansel nodded at the same time she did. "You're my sister. I'll do everything I can."

Just then, Mom's car pulled to the curb next to them. She got out and put her hands on her hips, glaring at Jazzi. "Did you really expect me to stay home when someone was murdered in our shop?"

Jazzi tossed Olivia a sympathetic glance. "We thought you might want to wait until they took Misty away."

"Well, I don't." Mom turned to Gaff. "You're going to find who did this, right? The faster, the better."

He'd worked with Mom before when Jazzi, Jerod, and Ansel had found the body of Mom's long-lost sister in the trunk in their attic. "Jazzi's going to help me," he said, trying to mollify her.

"Good." With a quick nod, Mom went to look in the shop's window. "That girl is nothing but a nuisance!"

An understatement but true. Ansel wrapped his arm around Jazzi's waist to offer her support, and Jazzi looked at him with a sigh. Another murder.

Chapter 10

Jerod walked to Jazzi's pickup with her and Ansel. "I called Thane, but he's working out of town today. Someone should stay with Olivia and your mom," he told Jazzi. "They might need you. Why don't we call today a bust and not worry about the Wildwood house until tomorrow?"

She nodded. "I don't think I'd be worth much anyway."

"None of us will." Ansel frowned. "Do you want to drive home with Olivia and your mom?"

But when she asked Olivia about it her sister shook her head. She seemed a lot more together now that Mom had arrived. "We're going to stick around here a little longer to see when we can hire a professional to clean the shop and open again. Can you come to my house after lunch? Mom's staying with me until Dad can leave the hardware store."

"I'll be there at one unless you call and need me sooner." Plans made, Jazzi left with Ansel, and Jerod drove back to his house to Franny and Pete.

Jazzi was too wound up to sit and relax. So was Ansel, so they drove to the lumberyard to buy what they needed to screen in their back patio. While they looked at roofing ideas for it, she convinced Ansel a striped canvas awning would be a good choice. Purchases made, they returned home and made a quick lunch before Jazzi had to drive across town again to her sister's house.

"What are you going to do while I'm gone?" she asked Ansel.

He grinned. "George is going to supervise on the patio while I dig the trench for a foundation."

"Sorry I won't be here to help." She tried to look sad, but he wasn't buying it.

"Yeah right. You love digging."

Jazzi ignored his sarcasm. He knew she'd help if she were home, but he was too excited to wait. The weather was good. He had a free afternoon and he had building materials. The die was cast. The project was simple except for getting everything square and plumb. Ansel was good at both.

And he was right. She *was* glad she was leaving him to it. She cracked her car window to enjoy the fresh air as she drove to the southwest side of town. Turning onto Hillegas, she glanced at the apple orchard on the corner. Too soon for blossoms yet, but when the trees burst into bloom they were beautiful. The owner had planted two rows of peach trees close to the road, and she reminded herself to stop for fresh peaches when they were in season.

When she got to Olivia's neighborhood she could hear children's voices drift from the nearby school. Their squeals and laughter always made her smile. Olivia's long, red ranch house sat near the back of the addition, bordering a golf course at the rear. The minute she pulled in the drive her sister hurried out to the pickup. Jazzi blinked. "Are we going somewhere?"

Olivia nodded. "Shopping. I need retail therapy, something to keep me busy. Mom's with Dad now, and I don't want to sit in the house alone."

"What are we shopping for?"

"Whatever interests us at Jefferson Pointe." River City's outdoor mall would be fun today, but it was too cold to walk from shop to shop in the winter.

Jazzi usually wasn't a fan of shopping, but she wanted Easter decorations for their big family celebration, so she drove to Jefferson Boulevard and headed toward the stores. She and her sister had to laugh at each other as they trudged from one end of the mall to the other, because Jazzi spent time in the bookstore and housewares shops, while Olivia dragged her into the women's clothing shops. Olivia loved fashion and Jazzi loved homes.

They didn't leave until an hour before Thane was due to be home, and then Jazzi drove Olivia back to her house and helped her carry in the new outfits she'd bought. "Are you going to skip girls' night out?" she asked.

Olivia shook her head. "I'd rather get together with everyone. If Thane and I stay home, we'll just hash over what happened today, and I don't want to yet."

Fair enough. Her sister was practicing avoidance, and why not? She needed a buffer before she sorted through everything that had happened. Jazzi gave her a hug. "See you soon." Then she drove home to spend a little time with Ansel before getting ready to meet their friends for supper.

When she walked to the house a trench lined two sides of the patio. Nice. Half the work was done. Less digging for her. Stepping inside, Ansel came to greet her, showered and dressed. He wore his good jeans that hugged his strong thighs and a tailored, light-blue shirt. Her man looked good! "Doggone. Where are you guys meeting tonight? You're all dressed up."

He grinned. "Walker picked Henry's, and we all dress up a little more when we go there."

They didn't have to, but Jazzi did the same thing. She thought of Henry's as a step up from their usual fare, even when she just ordered their chicken livers—which she loved.

He handed her a glass of wine. "I know you'll order a glass at Dicky's, but you've had a rough day. I thought you could use one."

"Thanks." She dropped onto one of the island's stools to sip it. "It looks like you got half the trench dug for the porch's foundation."

He sat next to her, nodding. "I hope I get some decent time to work on it this Saturday, but Radley called. He wanted us to help him and Elspeth pick up a washer and dryer and carry them down their basement steps this weekend. They found good used ones on Craigslist. A great chest freezer to put down there, too."

She shrugged. She was fine with helping family. "They've got to be pretty close to having the house finished, aren't they?" She hadn't envied them, renovating while they lived there. Radley had decided to keep his small apartment, though, for the times the house was too much of a mess. And that had helped.

"They're really close, hoping to move the last things in over Easter weekend. Which reminds me: They were wondering if we could help them the next Saturday, too. Her family has a lot of old furniture from her great-aunt that no one wants. Elspeth loves antiques. They're getting a double bed, two chests of drawers, and an armoire, along with some other, smaller furniture."

"Sounds great. Bet they're gorgeous." She and Ansel liked eclectic decorating, a mix of old and new. She finished her wine and glanced at the clock. "We'll give them the next two Saturdays, but I have to get ready now. If I go in jeans, Olivia will shoot me." Then she thought about the knife in Misty's chest and grimaced at her choice of words.

Ansel's eyebrows rose. He was obviously thinking about her sister, the suspected killer, too. He carried her wineglass to the sink and started for the door. "I'd better get going. I have a longer drive than you do."

Jazzi gave him a quick kiss, then started upstairs. "I don't have much time. I'm not going to look as nifty as you, but I'll make myself pass."

"Honey, you look good in anything, but your sister's a stickler. No use pushing her buttons tonight."

He left, and she hurried through getting ready. Dress pants and a lightweight sweater would have to do. Mascara, blush, and lipstick finished the deal, and off she went. She was the last person to arrive at their table.

Didi laughed at her. "You live the closest and you're the last to get here."

"That's my fault. I kept her busy all day." Olivia told them about Misty.

Elspeth stared. "Did the girl have a vendetta against you? Couldn't she have picked someplace else to die?"

Jazzi shook her head. "I doubt Misty planned to get killed at the shop."

"But why was she even there?" Didi asked. "Wouldn't she suspect you'd have a security system set up?"

"Not soon enough," Olivia said, scowling. "They're changing the locks and installing it tomorrow."

The irony wasn't lost on any of them. What rotten luck. One more day and a camera would have recorded whatever happened at the salon and an alarm would have gone off.

The waitress came for their orders. After she left Jazzi asked, "You worked with Misty long enough, Sis, you had to learn a little about her. What did she do outside of work?"

"She partied a lot. And she was always bickering with one person or another. She got in a fistfight with a girl at a nightclub because she accused Misty of trying to steal her boyfriend."

Somehow, that jibed with how Jazzi saw her. She wondered what Gaff had found out about her, if she had more enemies who might want her dead. And she decided to give him a call sometime soon.

Chapter 11

Jerod, Ansel, and Jazzi were sanding floors upstairs when the doorbell rang. Jerod stopped work, frowning. Tugging down his mask, he asked, "Could it be Gaff?"

Jazzi shrugged, dusted herself off, and went downstairs to see who was there. A tall, distinguished man with graying temples smiled when she opened the door. "I'm curious about the house. I've been living in an apartment since my divorce, but I'm ready to buy a place of my own. I have a friend who lives in this neighborhood and he told me about this place. Would you mind if I walked through it?"

"No problem at all. Let me get my cousin. He'll be happy to show it to you." She called up the steps for Jerod.

When her cousin saw a potential customer in the foyer he plastered on his best smile and came to greet him. Jazzi left him to do his thing. He was the salesman of their group. And sure enough, by the time the man left, the house was sold.

"He wanted to buy it early so that he could have a say about the rest of the finishes," Jerod told them. "He liked most of the plans I showed him, but he wants the sitting room painted butter yellow. He said with all the windows, it would make the room look sunny."

Ansel nodded. "Easy enough, but you said he liked *most* of our plans. What else does he want to change?"

Jerod pulled a list out of his back pocket. "He wants the master bedroom and bath to keep the black-and-white theme of the rest of the house. He wants beadboard, painted black, put on the wall behind the pedestal sink in the master bath, and he wants charcoal tiles on the floor."

Masculine. He wanted the rooms to have a masculine feel. "Anything else?" Jazzi asked.

Jerod went to the next item. "He wants shiplap on the master bedroom walls."

"All of them?" Ansel asked. "People usually just want one focus wall."

"All of them," Jerod said.

She nodded, starting to like the picture forming in her mind. "We can paint it white and give him a black, modern chandelier and a black, wrought-iron bed frame."

"That'll work." Jerod scratched his head. "I couldn't picture how to do black in a bedroom."

"Anything else?" Jazzi asked.

"Nope, that's it." Jerod returned the list to his pocket.

The man's ideas wouldn't make that much extra work for them. A little, but not much. The other three bedrooms were larger than usual, but only needed paint, and they'd already sanded their floors. The second bathroom was large, too, but he'd liked it, so they only needed to give it a fresh coat of paint. Nothing extravagant.

Ansel looked out the upstairs window at the old trees that dotted the neighborhood. "This is the fastest we've ever sold a house. I mean, we've barely gotten started on the renovations."

"I hope this housing market never quits," Jerod said, "but I know it will. It sure has made it nice for us, though."

And they'd better enjoy it while they could.

They decided to stop for lunch before finishing the rest of the floors. Jazzi had made Buffalo chicken dip with chips and pita for lunch. She was tired of sandwiches. She thought she had enough to take leftovers home for tomorrow, but she was wrong. What was it with men and Buffalo chicken?

After lunch, when Jerod and Ansel went upstairs to work, she lingered behind to call Gaff. "Any news?"

He let out a long sigh. "Misty caused so much trouble for so many people, I'll need to use a Ouija board to narrow down suspects."

"Anyone in particular look like a possibility to you?"

"I've visited three of her sometime friends, but more often enemies, and they all clammed up the minute they saw me. They hate cops. Care to come with me on Monday to talk to her roommates? They might open up more for you."

She'd hoped he'd ask. "What time will you pick me up?"

"After lunch? That will give me time to clear up some things at the station first."

"I'll see you then."

When she went upstairs to help with the sanding she told the guys what Gaff said.

Jerod used his sleeve to wipe sweat from his forehead. They'd opened the upstairs windows to circulate air in the rooms, but the sanders were heavy equipment. It took effort to use them. "The sooner you clear Olivia's name, the better. She'll get grumpier the longer she chews on what happened."

Who wouldn't? No matter how hard Jazzi tried to push the murder to the back of her mind, she couldn't. But work helped, and it was time to get back to it.

Before they left for the day they all pulled on knee pads and stained the kitchen wood floor a light color. It could dry over the weekend before appliances arrived. Cleanup took longer than usual before they finally locked up the house to leave.

Jerod stopped at his pickup. "What are you guys doing this weekend?" When Ansel told him about starting to screen the back patio and helping Radley and Elspeth, Jerod laughed at them. "Bet you two will be happy when the rest of us finally are finished with our houses and you don't have to help us anymore."

"We've done our share lately," Ansel admitted, "but I think Radley's the last one."

Her cousin grinned. "What are you going to do when he decides to move somewhere bigger in a few years?"

"He's on his own."

"Right." Jerod gave him a knowing look.

Ansel grimaced, and Jazzi knew he'd have trouble turning down his brother if he needed help again. He shrugged, admitting the obvious. "What are you doing on your days off?"

"Franny and I are taking the kids shopping for Easter clothes. A lot of people don't dress up for church anymore, but when my wife goes she wants us to look good."

Jazzi nodded. "I haven't gotten used to jeans at church either. I'm not against them. I just feel funny wearing them. And let's face it, none of us attend very often."

Gran called them "part-time Christians," and she was right. Or rather, part-time churchgoers. Jazzi considered herself a Christian whether she went or not.

On the drive home she and Ansel stopped at the meat market to buy steaks and a bag of salad. Her Norseman had a movie he wanted to rent, so they were going to clean up, change into their pajamas, and eat a quick supper. Then they'd make popcorn before hitting the couches.

George loved it all. By the time the movie started he'd had tidbits of Ansel's steak, and now he sat beside him begging for popcorn. The cats loved it, too, but for different reasons. They batted it around the wood floors. This Friday night was fun for all.

Chapter 12

Jazzi and Ansel hurried to give the house a quick clean before they left to pick up Radley and Elspeth. They left George home this time. They'd be in and out too many times, and George wouldn't like it. Since Ansel had moved in with her, the pug didn't mind being left as much as he used to.

When they reached Radley's apartment they all climbed into Jazzi's pickup, the men in front, the women in back, then drove to pick up the washer and dryer Radley had found. The couple selling them lived on the west side of River Bluffs in an apartment. The southwest side of town had built up so much since she'd grown up there, it sprawled farther and farther, creeping toward County Line Road, one new subdivision after another. Thankfully, the apartment complex was close to Jefferson Boulevard.

"We bought a house," the husband explained when Radley knocked on their door, "and the appliances came with it, so we don't need ours anymore."

They were white, without any fancy buttons, but they worked, and they'd be in the basement. No one would see them. Elspeth and Jazzi stayed out of the way while the men rolled them to the truck. Then they drove back to the house on Wilt Street, and once again the women stayed in the kitchen while the men maneuvered dollies with the appliances down to the basement and hooked them up.

That done, they set off to get the chest freezer. This time they headed east out of the city limits to a farm with a rutted driveway. They bumped their way down a washed-out, gravel lane to a house that hadn't seen paint in a long time. Radley and Ansel went to knock at the front door, and a burly man, still in his bathrobe, cracked it open.

"We came about the chest freezer," Radley told him.

The driver's window was down, and Jazzi heard the man say, "Oh, yeah. It's in the barn. You can pay me for it now. I'm going back to sleep."

Radley shook his head. "I want to see it first."

"Whatever." The man closed the door.

Ansel drove the truck to the barn, and he and Radley went inside, then came out empty-handed. They got back in the truck and Radley turned to Elspeth, in the back seat with Jazzi.

"The barn was full of mice," he told her. "If they chewed on the wiring, the chest wouldn't last long, might even be dangerous to use."

Elspeth wrinkled her nose. "It's probably filthy anyway. We'll keep looking."

On the drive back to the street Radley called the man's cell to tell him they didn't want it, but he didn't pick up. Radley left a message and shook his head. "He knew we wouldn't buy it after we saw it."

On the way into town Ansel stopped to order Chinese takeout for lunch. Jazzi wasn't hungry until the aromas of the food filled the truck for the rest of the drive. By the time they reached Wilt Street and settled at Radley and Elspeth's new kitchen island, they were all starving.

Elspeth went for paper plates and Jazzi nodded approval of the new stainless-steel appliances Ansel had talked Radley into buying. "Your place looks great."

The kitchen island sat where the wall that separated the small kitchen from an all-purpose room used to be. They'd helped knock it down, along with another wall behind it, and installed beams to create a huge dining area. An open door on the side led to a study-guest room. She and Ansel had helped move a half bath to create that space. Now, the bath opened off a back mudroom instead of the kitchen.

Elspeth handed out silverware and they all dished up. She gave a satisfied smile. "Radley and I would never have thought of this layout on our own, but it's perfect for entertaining. We love it."

"Is the upstairs completely finished now?" Ansel asked between bites of Mongolian beef.

Radley nodded. "Will be once we get the furniture here. The only work I still need to do is to refinish the stair railing, but that can wait."

They finished the last of the egg rolls and crab Rangoon, and Jazzi and Elspeth divided the rest of the Cantonese chicken. Radley ate the entire carton of sweet and sour pork by himself.

The meal finished, Jazzi and Ansel stood to leave, and Ansel patted his brother on the back. "Looking good. You guys have done a great job."

Radley, grinned, putting his arm around Elspeth. They both looked proud of themselves. And they should.

Curious, Jazzi paused on their way out. "I almost forgot. You told me you had an idea for the wall behind your couch," she told Elspeth. "What is it?"

Elspeth grinned. "I'm sewing a quilt to hang there."

"Brilliant! It will look perfect with your family's antiques." Elspeth was an expert seamstress and often sewed little presents for people to surprise them. Presents that had to take a lot of time to make. She'd sewn costumes for her and Radley for the last Halloween party. They went as aristocrats. Jazzi couldn't imagine how much work those had been.

"If you like it, I could make one for you," Elspeth said.

Jazzi shook her head. She couldn't ask anyone for something that time-consuming. On the drive home Jazzi tried to picture what kinds of colors Elspeth would use for her quilt, but Ansel drummed his fingers on the steering wheel, anxious to move on with their day. "Have you already made your grocery list? We're getting a late start for the store. It's going to be busy."

"I'm ahead of you. It's on the fridge, and I'm making an easy supper tonight. Mac 'n' cheese and a big salad."

"Your spicy mac 'n' cheese with pimiento cheese sauce?"

When she nodded he grinned. Once they pulled into their drive he waited in the pickup while she ran inside to get the list. She should have put it in her purse when they left that morning, but she didn't realize how long it would take helping Radley and Elspeth. George stood to come to her, saw her grab the long note from the refrigerator door, and sagged back onto his doggy bed, pouting. Even the cats looked unhappy. There'd been no lunch today, but she'd buy them a package of diced ham at the store to make up for it.

They flew through the store as fast as they could and had just finished loading the groceries into the back of the pickup when Chad called. Bad timing. They were already behind but, frowning, Jazzi answered it.

He sounded frustrated. "Ginger's left me. I had to work today on a big landscaping project. This is our busy time. When I got home she was gone."

"Did she leave a note?"

"Nothing, but her car's gone and she won't answer her cell phone."

"Are her clothes in the closet?"

She heard footsteps and a sliding door. He sounded even more upset. "They're all here. So is her makeup in the bathroom. Something's wrong."

"Why do you think that? She probably just went somewhere and it took longer than she expected."

"No. She always leaves a note. Always. She never stays away this long. She'd have called to let me know. She's thoughtful that way. Something's wrong, I tell you."

"Have you called her friends?"

"Yes, when I thought she'd left me. I wanted to talk to her, but no one's seen her. Or at least they won't tell me they have."

"Don't panic yet. Maybe there was some kind of emergency."

Ansel was listening to her end of the conversation, frowning. He didn't look upset about the call. He looked worried.

"If there was an emergency, she'd still have called me. This isn't like her."

"You told me something's been bothering her lately. Maybe something caught her by surprise."

"She'd still have called!" He sounded frustrated, scared. She tried to calm him down, but he cut her off. "I have to go. I'm calling the police. I'm worried about her."

Jazzi let him go but doubted the police would look for Ginger this soon. They usually waited until a person was missing for twenty-four hours. It wasn't like this was a situation for an Amber alert. Still, part of her liked it that Chad was so worried about his wife.

Ansel gestured for them to get in the pickup and waited until he was on the way home to ask, "How bad is it?"

Jazzi explained and he shook his head. "I'd be worried, too."

She took a deep breath. "So would I, but there's nothing Chad can do right now. I hope I hear from him soon."

Chapter 13

Jazzi made a big pot of mac 'n' cheese and every bit of it was gone.

"My mom always made the box kind," Ansel told her. "Bain, Radley, and I thought it was the best thing we'd ever eaten...until I had yours."

The man was wonderful for her ego. She loved to cook but knew her limitations. Fortunately, his mother's cooking was so bad, anything she made tasted good in comparison. Jerod's wife, Franny, did as little in the kitchen as possible but was a whiz at restoring furniture. And her mom and sister only visited the stove occasionally.

She stood to carry their dirty dishes to the sink and bent to kiss the top of his head. It was the only time she could reach it—when he was sitting and she was standing. "Feel like cooking a little more? We can make the Sunday meal ahead of time tonight so we won't have to rush tomorrow."

"What's on the menu?"

"We're doing chicken Seville and boiled baby potatoes. Didi's bringing a seven-layer salad and Elspeth's making banana cream pies."

"Chicken Seville?" He puckered his brow, trying to remember. "Have we ever had that before?"

She shook her head. "I don't make it very often, but Jerod loves it. It has artichoke quarters, black olives, and roasted red peppers with the chicken in a sauce."

He looked uncertain. "If Jerod likes it, I probably will."

She laughed at him. "If you don't, you can make yourself a deli meat sandwich."

"Not nice." He went to help her get what she needed from the refrigerator, and forty minutes later the food was ready. He blinked, surprised. "That went fast."

"I told you I was keeping the Sunday meals quick and easy until Easter."

He got a clean spoon to take another taste of the sauce. "It doesn't taste like a quickie meal."

"Thanks, but half of the ingredients come out of a jar or can. I like recipes like that." She put a lid on the pans and left them to cool, then they headed to the living room. They were settling on their couches when Chad called again.

"The police won't look for Ginger until she's been missing twenty-four hours." Jazzi could have told him that, but he wouldn't have believed her. He needed to make the call to satisfy himself he'd done everything he could to find his wife. "They've agreed to watch for her car, though. That's the best they can do, but I'm going nuts with worry. She'd have called me by now, no matter what."

Unless she *had* left him. But then, why hadn't she taken her clothes? Her makeup? Something was off about her being gone, and Jazzi understood why he was worried. Jazzi glanced at the clock. Almost eight. "Does she have any relatives who were sick or might have had an accident whom she'd rush to?"

"None she mentioned. She wasn't close to her family like we are."

She bit her bottom lip. She'd met his parents and younger sister when they'd been a couple and they were all close. They probably hated her for leaving him. His dad had been as controlling as Chad became. Maybe that was why Chad thought it was normal. She'd loved him once, but he'd bludgeoned that to death. She had to ask, "Did you try to control Ginger like you did me?"

"No. I was stupid with you, but I learned from my mistake. I couldn't get it when you left me, couldn't understand why. A guy I work with finally spelled it out for me. I did better with Ginger until I wanted babies."

"You nagged her all the time?"

"And I was horrible when I found out about the abortion. I made her cry." His voice tightened, full of shame. "She didn't deserve that. Her parents wouldn't help her. She couldn't raise the baby alone."

Jazzi agonized for him. He really was trying to change, but she didn't know how to help him. "Did you have an argument before you left for work today?"

"No, like I told you, we were doing better than we ever had. Things were looking good for us."

She didn't know what to tell him. "There's really nothing you can do now, Chad. I know it's hard, but you just need to hang in there. Maybe you should go to your parents' house, stay with them a while."

"No, if Ginger comes home, I want to be here."

She let out a frustrated sigh. She hated waiting. So did he. "If you hear something, let me know, will you?"

"Promise. And thanks for listening to me, Jaz. I swear, if she ever comes home, I'll never rag on her again. About anything."

She knew him. He'd never be able to keep that promise. Maybe he'd made Ginger mad and didn't even realize it. If she left because she was angry, maybe she'd stormed out of the house intending to come back but hadn't worked through her anger yet. Either that or . . . She didn't want to think about it.

When she put down the phone Ansel came to wrap his arms around her. "It's hard to know he's so miserable, isn't it?"

She nodded. "He deserved it when I left him, and he might even deserve it this time, too, but it doesn't sound like it. I don't blame him for thinking something's wrong."

Ansel tightened his hug, holding her close. "If I ever leave you, I'll give you lots of advance warning."

She sputtered and pulled away to see the evil grin on his face. He gave her a quick kiss. "I'll never leave you, and I hope Ginger calls Chad soon, but you've done all you can."

He'd helped to lighten her mood, but she couldn't completely shake it off.

"Come on. I know something that will lift your spirits." He grabbed her hand and tugged her toward the stairs, looking at the pets. "Later," he told them.

They knew what that meant.

Chapter 14

Bless his dear empty stomach, Jerod was the first to walk through the kitchen door on Sunday. Instead of the usual cheeseball, Jazzi had made spinach and artichoke dip because they were having chicken Seville with artichokes for lunch. Franny brought her usual veggie tray and Ansel spread out an array of crackers and pita chips. For a little variety, Jazzi had made an onion dip, too, with potato chips.

Jerod went to the fridge for a beer, then filled a small plate. He ate so much, Franny smacked his shoulder. "Leave some for everyone else."

He grinned and reached for more chips, but Jazzi went to the oven and pulled out more of the dip. Her cousin had a thing for artichokes. "Oh, you care," he teased when she put it on the kitchen island next to the first one.

Jazzi rolled her eyes. He was so full of himself. "You're family. I'm stuck with you."

Franny laughed, putting chips on plates for Gunther and Lizzie. The kids wrinkled their noses at the other offerings. "Nothing else until after you eat your lunch," she warned.

Walker came in next, cradling Noreen in one arm, with Didi following, holding River's hand. River saw Gunther and Lizzie and ditched her. Franny threw a few chips on a plate for him, too, and Ansel opened the basement door to let them zip down to their play area. Before Pete could crawl to the open door, he shut it.

Pete tugged on Ansel's jeans to pull himself to his feet and screamed in frustration. Ansel reached down to swing him off the floor, surprising him. He gulped down his tantrum and stared at her Norseman. Ansel tossed him in the air and caught him, and he laughed. "See, buddy, it's not so bad," Ansel told him. "We bought you a new toy."

Jazzi motioned to a plastic shopping cart for him to hang on to and push. It was full of different plastic food replicas—fruits, vegetables, and pizza slices. When Ansel set him back down he crawled over to check it out. They'd bought a kid-size stove and refrigerator for the basement. When the guys went down there after the meal Pete would have something of his own to play with.

Jerod shook his head. "If that would work at home, I'd buy him something new every day."

"No, you wouldn't." Franny crossed her arms over her chest. With her long, carrot-colored hair and freckles, she made Jazzi think of Pippi Longstocking, and she was usually smiling. But not now. "He's not going to be spoiled."

Jazzi grimaced. "Good luck with that. If we ever have a kid and he's a pill, I'm going to have to sit him in one corner and Ansel in the other so he doesn't try to rescue him."

Ansel chuckled, not denying it. "Discipline's going to be hard for me."

The rest of the family gushed through the door in one clump. Jazzi hurried to hang Gran's jacket on the coat tree, then went to the fridge to pour her a glass of red wine. Gran liked hers cold. Coat free, Thane and Olivia were drawn to the dips. When Jazzi joined them, Thane shook his head at her. He hadn't pulled his wild auburn hair back in a ponytail today, and the spring breeze had blown it in different directions. He wore a black T-shirt with his black jeans that had a baby chicken hatching out of an egg with the words "I Love Chicks" emblazoned over it.

"I can't believe you and Ansel had to clear my name when Darby was murdered, and now you're trying to help Olivia. She's so mad about Misty being killed in her shop with her scissors, I don't think she realizes how bad it looks. She's so sure you'll clear everything up, she's not worrying about it."

Jazzi blinked. "I'm not Sherlock Holmes or Miss Marple. I only tag along with Gaff."

Gran pursed her lips and her eyes took on a glazed look. Jazzi held her breath. Had Gran had another vision? Staring at her, unseeing, Gran said, "That girl cheated the wrong person. She thought she could get away with anything." Then she shook her head and took another sip of wine.

Jazzi glanced at Ansel, who shrugged his shoulders. "That might help you rule out the girl who threatened to kill her for stealing her boyfriend."

"Maybe. Unless she tried to steal her boyfriend *and* cheat her out of money, which I wouldn't rule out."

Jerod dragged himself away from the dips and threw away his paper plate on his way to get another beer. "I'm glad you're going with Gaff tomorrow. Maybe you'll get the lowdown from Misty's friends."

"And enemies, if she tried to cheat them, too," Ansel pointed out.

The conversation came to an abrupt halt when Radley and Elspeth arrived last with her banana cream pies. The men's focus shifted to the mounds of whipped cream on top of each of them. Franny turned a stern look on Jerod so that he wouldn't whisk a finger in one as it passed him.

Too much temptation. Jazzi and Ansel loaded the hot food on the kitchen island with Didi's seven-layer salad and encouraged people to grab plates and get in line.

They avoided talking about Misty during the meal. Instead, Radley told everyone that all their house needed now to be finished was the furniture they'd pick up next Saturday, and then they could start hosting some of the meals. Walker talked about a big project his cement company had been hired for. "It will keep us busy for a month and it's close to home, so I'll be able to spend more time with Didi and the kids."

When Didi talked about what a sweet baby Noreen was Mom frowned. "I'm curious. Jazzi might have told me, but I forget. How did you choose her name? I've always liked it."

"It was Brooklyn's middle name," Didi said, "and we wanted to share Brooklyn's memory with River."

River glanced at Gunther and Lizzie, proud of that. Jazzi had to give Didi and Walker credit. The boy had lost his mother and they'd done a wonderful job of helping him adjust.

Franny had stopped feeding Pete for a minute to listen, and he grabbed the spoon of potatoes she'd scooped up for him and threw it across the floor. Jerod sighed. "I'll clean that up in a minute. I'm glad someone here has an easy baby."

Ansel laughed and shook his head, pointing. "Don't worry about it." George was faithfully following the trail of potatoes, licking them up.

Dad looked across the table at Jazzi. "What about you two? Anything new in your lives?"

She didn't want to tell them about Chad and Ginger. When she finally broke her engagement with him, her family had had nothing good to say about him. She'd appreciated how they'd rallied around her, but they wouldn't be kind to him now either. She glanced at Ansel to save her. He started to tell them about the new fixer-upper they were working on when Gran pointed her fork at Jazzi.

"That boy isn't lying. She didn't leave him."

Dad frowned and Jazzi grimaced. "Gran's talking about Chad." When every expression went dark, even Jerod's parents, she explained about how he was trying to be a better husband to Ginger, but she had disappeared.

Mom's eyes flashed. "And he asked you to help him? He has some nerve."

Dad didn't trash Chad, though. He shook his head, looking worried. "Too many women have been on the news lately because they've disappeared. It's horrible. I hope they find her safe and sound."

Gran shook her head. "She shouldn't have gone with him. It's sad."

"Is she dead?" Jazzi asked.

Gran blinked. "What?"

The thought was gone, whatever it had been. Gran's visions came and went. But it worried Jazzi. "Sad" had an ominous ring to it.

To change the mood, Ansel told them about screening in the back patio.

"What kind of roof are you putting over it?" Walker asked. "I've been thinking about adding a porch onto the back of our place."

The talk turned to the pros and cons of peaked roofs or awnings. After dessert the men went out to look over Ansel's plans and building supplies. The women grabbed more drinks and settled in the living room.

"What have you girls decided to make for Easter?" Mom asked, always ready for a celebration.

"I usually make a big Ossian ham," Jazzi said.

Mom wrinkled her nose. "I know, but we have ham at Christmas, too."

Jazzi rolled her eyes. Why was it the people who didn't cook were always the pickiest? "Ansel's been talking about adding a prime rib."

"Now that sounds wonderful!" Mom smiled. "We'll throw some extra money in the jar to help you cover it. What else?"

Didi said, "My grandma always made broccoli and rice casserole, a fruit salad, and deviled eggs. She's been gone a while now, but I thought I'd follow in her footsteps."

That sounded like a great tradition to Jazzi. When Mom looked at Elspeth, she said, "My family makes lemon meringue pies and carrot cake. I'll bring those."

Wonderful. Jazzi raised her eyebrows at Olivia. Her sister grinned. "Mom and I will bring plenty of wine and beer."

"And I'll bring homemade bread," Gran said. "Samantha helps me make it."

Samantha nodded with a smile. Gran's fellow widow was a wonderful roommate for her. Quiet and steady, they all loved her, thinking of her as part of the family.

When the men came back inside people got ready to leave. Dads had to drag kids out of the basement to go home, but by six the house was empty.

Jazzi glanced at the clock and Ansel pinched his lips together. "You were hoping Chad would call with some news. I'm sorry, Jaz."

"It's been too long," she said. "I'm starting to think something bad happened. Gran made me think Ginger's dead."

"And that Chad's telling the truth. Will his family help him handle it if they find her body?" He helped her carry dishes to rinse and load in the dishwasher.

She gave a long sigh. "His dad's a jerk, but he loves Chad. His mom's wonderful. So is his sister. They'll help him through whatever happens. They were there for him when I left him."

"Do they bad-mouth you like your parents badmouth Chad?"

"Probably worse."

He chuckled. "My wife, the heartbreaker." When they finished cleanup he glanced outside. "It's a beautiful day. Want to go downtown and spend some time on the Riverwalk?"

"Not tonight. I'm not in the mood."

"Want to rent a movie?"

She gave him a sideways glance. "A chick flick?"

"If it helps."

She hugged him. "You're the best. You know that?"

"I kind of suspected it." He laughed. "Come on. Let's change into our pajamas, I'll make popcorn, and you can pick what we watch."

"I love you."

"I love you, too, but I can't make anything better about this mess. I can just be here for you."

"That's enough." She slipped an arm through his and they went to change for the night.

Chapter 15

Jazzi packed plain old, deli sandwiches and chips for lunch on Monday. Plain sounded good after all the rich food they'd had lately. Ansel grabbed George and she took the cooler as they trekked to the work van. The cats had been extra-bothersome this morning, so she'd not only fed them, she gave each of them a small pile of shredded cheese. She didn't treat them with it often, but they knew they were being spoiled when she did.

Inky had jumped on the countertop by the sink before she left to chew the heads off the flowers in the pitcher—his way of letting her know he hadn't had enough attention lately. He was a brat, but she adored him. She'd have to drag a string around the house for him when they got home tonight.

Jerod was already at the house when they got there, scattering drop cloths all over the kitchen floor. They were going to paint the kitchen ceiling and walls before the cupboards and appliances were delivered. It wouldn't take them long because they were making everything the same shade of white.

They finished before lunch, ate quickly, and the truck backed into the drive with their deliveries at the same time Gaff pulled to the curb in front of the house. Jazzi ran out to go with him to interview Misty's roommates and the men went outside to help unload the truck.

It was cooler today, so they'd needed hoodies, but the air was crisp and clean. The grass was starting to green and crocuses bloomed under the maple in the house's front yard. They'd listened to the weather forecast on the drive to the house and snow was predicted later in the week. Indiana weather. March bobbed up and down.

As Gaff turned onto Taylor Street, he told her, "Misty lived in a house off Broadway with four other girls. It made the rent cheap. Each time I've stopped there they've clammed up. They aren't cop lovers. I'm going to let you do most of the talking today. Maybe they'll share more."

The street off Broadway was so narrow, there was only parking on one side. Jazzi glanced up and down the block with dismay. The houses were so close together, if you opened a window, you could touch your next-door neighbor's siding. She wasn't sure a person could squeeze between the buildings. Misty's front porch was sagging on one side, propped up by an unpainted two-by-four. The yard was mostly mud. There was a small, fenced backyard that had never been mowed. A window in front was broken, with plywood nailed over it.

She glanced at Gaff. "Is the inside any better?"

"Not that I noticed." He knocked on the door and waited.

Finally, yawning, a girl in flannel pajamas and big fuzzy slippers, her blue-black hair pulled up in a ponytail that sat on her head like a topknot, opened the door. Tattoos covered her arms and neck. She led them into the living room, where two people were sleeping on broken-down couches. She kicked one girl's leg, dangling over the edge of the couch to the floor.

"The cop's here again. Wake up."

The girl pushed herself up to lean against the back of the couch. Lank, greasy hair hung to her shoulders. Thin lips curled down in an angry expression and she stared at Gaff unhappily. She wore a once-white T-shirt and panties. With a grimace, she pulled her blanket around her waist. "What now?"

The girl across from her had fallen asleep in her clothes—a plaid flannel shirt, jeans, and work boots. She yawned and propped her head up on her elbow. "Do you know who killed Misty?"

"Not yet," Gaff said. "That's why we're back. We'll keep coming back until we get some answers that help us solve the case."

The girl made a face and heaved herself into a sitting position, her elbows on her knees, her head cradled in her hands.

The girl who'd let them in pursed her lips. "I'm Georgie. I'll get Trina." She walked to the stairs and yelled, "Get your fanny down here! The cop's back."

A girl with blunt-cut, reddish-brown hair and bangs came down the steps, dressed in a long, chenille robe. "Has he started asking questions yet?"

"Not yet." Georgie dragged a wooden chair from the dining room next to the couch to sit on. So did Miss Blunt Cut. Georgie nodded at each girl in turn. "Miss Sour Puss is Brittany, Lumber Girl is Val, and this is Trina." She narrowed her eyes, studying Jazzi. "Who are you?"

"Jazzi Herstad." She'd finally gotten used to saying that. It had taken a while to use her married name instead of Zander's. "Misty got killed in my sister's beauty shop."

Brittany snorted. "Bet that made her day."

"Nothing about Misty made Olivia happy."

Georgie barked a laugh. "Our friend was consistent, I'll give her that. She was a pain for everyone she met."

Jazzi frowned. "I thought she was your friend."

"Friends don't welch on their share of the rent every month," Brittany snapped. She pushed a strand of greasy hair behind her ear. "She was a two-timing backstabber."

"Are you the girl whose boyfriend she tried to steal?" Gaff asked.

Georgie snorted. "If you can call him a boyfriend. He was a trucker who stayed at one of the motels she cleans rooms for out north. He only buys her a meal at the truck stop and expects favors when he's there for a couple of nights."

Harsh words. Jazzi couldn't hide her surprise. Did these girls like each other? Or did they just need to share rent money?

Brittany glared at her. "At least my boyfriend buys me a meal. Your guys only buy you a few cheap drinks."

Georgie shrugged. "I don't call them boyfriends. They're one-night stands."

When Brittany's face screwed up and she leaned forward to spew more vindictive words, Gaff held up a hand. "Ladies, please. We're only interested in Misty and trying to find someone who might have wanted to kill her."

Lumber Girl entered the conversation. "You mean besides us?"

Jazzi blinked. Which one was she? Val. The girl's lips turned down as she went on. "If Misty could cheat us out of her share of the rent she did, at the same time she ate the food the rest of us brought in. If she could sneak a few dollars out of your purse when you weren't in the room, she did."

"Then why did we take her in?" Trina demanded. "None of us liked her."

Georgie nodded toward Val. "Because her car needed a new fuel pump and we needed a little more money coming in. Misty could put on the dog when she needed to, and she paid ahead for her first month's rent. She fooled all of us, even you."

Trina grimaced. "Yeah, she was all types of wonderful for the first week or two. We should have kicked her out the minute she didn't come up with her share of the money."

"Easier said than done. Look at what she did when they fired her at that salon." Val shook her head. "She could be downright mean."

Gaff gave a subtle nod for Jazzi to keep the conversation going. She asked, "Did any of you know the girls she invited to the hair salon early so she could pocket the money and sell my sister's products cheap?"

Georgie, whose hair was blue-black, said, "She dyed my hair there once, then charged too much but slipped me a bunch of free products."

"I wouldn't trust her with my hair," Brittany said.

Jazzi didn't know how to respond. It didn't look like the girl even washed her hair, let alone styled it. "Where did she get her clients?"

Val rolled her eyes. "At bars. She hung out at one on Brooklyn Avenue a lot and invited people in for special deals."

"How do you know that?" Brittany demanded.

"Because I went there with her once and she stiffed me with the bill."

Trina nodded. "I know the bartender there, but I only go when I think Misty won't be there." She stopped and shook her head. "I guess I don't have to worry about that anymore, do I? Anyway, he told me that Misty did a lot of business there."

"I always suspected there was something going on between them," Val said.

"Something romantic?" Jazzi asked.

Val snorted. "More like something to do with money. Misty got a lot more turned on by dollar signs than romance."

They talked with the girls a while longer but didn't learn anything new. Finally, Gaff rose to leave, handing each of them one of his business cards. "Thanks for helping us, and if you think of anything else, give us a call."

Georgie raised an eyebrow at him. "Are you really going to keep coming back until you find out who killed her?"

"Probably. Sometimes people remember something after the fifth or sixth time I knock on their door."

The girls grimaced in unison. "If we think of anything, we'll tell you," Val said.

"I appreciate that." When he pulled away from the curb he grinned. "We got a little more information this time."

"Are you done for the day?" Jazzi asked.

He shook his head. "Thought we'd stop in to visit the trucker Misty tried to steal from Brittany. He sounds like a real prize, doesn't he?"

A booby prize, but Jazzi didn't comment. If he knew anything that would solve the murder, she wanted to see him.

Chapter 16

The trucker stayed in a motel on the north side of town, close to a truck stop and diner. It was two stories high with rows of doors on both levels and faced a busy highway. A busier highway bordered its side. The sound of traffic was constant as they climbed the stairs to the man's room.

He opened the door on Gaff's fifth knock. It looked like he'd hastily tossed on jeans and a hoodie. The bed was unmade, and empty chip bags and soda cans littered the top of the dresser. The TV was on, but muted.

"Yeah?" His brown hair was flat on one side and mussed on the other. Stubble covered his cheeks and jaw. He glared at Gaff's badge, then turned a narrow gaze on her.

Gaff tucked his badge away. "Pierce Somers? I need to ask you a few questions about Misty Morrow. You spent time with her a few days before she was killed."

Pierce motioned them inside. There was one rickety chair near a desk in the corner and the bed. No place else to sit. Gaff and Jazzi planted their feet to stand.

Pierce went to sit on the edge of the bed. "Just met her, and don't call me Pierce. My nickname's Wheels. Everyone calls me that." Covering his mouth, he yawned, then asked, "Who's the blonde? Don't tell me she's your partner out of uniform."

"I've brought her along as a consultant. She knows some of the people involved."

"Right." The man ran his hands through his hair, scratching his scalp as if it itched.

Jazzi noticed a wedding band on his third finger. So did Gaff.

"You're married?" he asked.

"What of it? Don't go getting no ideas my wife got jealous and came after Misty. She don't care if I play around when I'm on the road as long as I don't come home with no disease."

"Did you play around with Brittany?" Gaff asked.

"Me and every other trucker who looked at her sideways." He reached for a pack of cigarettes on the nightstand, took one, and lit it. He inhaled a deep breath, then purposely blew the smoke between Gaff and Jazzi.

"Don't," Gaff warned.

"Or what?"

"I'll ask you questions at the station."

Wheels stabbed out his cigarette and crossed his arms. "So get with it already."

"What can you tell me about Misty?"

He shrugged. "That girl was a little prettier than average, don't you think?" He looked at Jazzi for an answer.

"Not by much. She did the most with what she had, though." When Jazzi saw her, she had royal-blue streaks in her dark hair and wore too much makeup. Not exactly pretty, but dramatic-looking.

Eyes glittering, he looked her up and down. "Not everyone can look like you, doll. She caught your eye and looked like a good time, but she'd empty your wallet when you were sleeping if you didn't hide it. I locked mine inside my truck when she was in the bathroom." He raised an eyebrow at Jazzi. "Were you a friend of hers?"

"Hardly. She was killed in my sister's beauty salon, where she worked."

Wheels shook his head. "Such a waste. We weren't done having fun yet. Did Brittany kill her?"

"Her roommates swear she was at home asleep when it happened," Gaff said.

Wheels barked a laugh. "They would, wouldn't they?"

"We checked on it, and she was at work cleaning rooms all that morning." Gaff gave him a level look. "Where were you last Thursday morning?"

"Here, but I didn't catch the lady's name I was with to let you check on that." He winked at Jazzi. "I could teach you a few things, doll. Is your husband the jealous type?"

"We both are," she told him, and that seemed to intrigue him more.

"What do you think, girlie? Did your sister kill her?"

He was trying to provoke her. He must like to poke at people to get a rise. "Not her style. She'd trash her reputation instead. Misty would never work in another high-class salon."

"Are you like your sister?"

"Neither of us put up with much crap." It was her turn. "Did you taunt Brittany to let her know you slept with Misty? Were you trying to start trouble?"

His lips lifted in a slow smile. "I didn't have to start nothing. The trouble was already there. I just fanned it a little."

Yup, he would. And he'd think it was funny. "Did it backfire on you? Did you get Misty all up in arms, in your face?"

"Enough to make me kill her?" He huffed in disdain. "That girl wasn't worth the bother."

"How long will you be in town?" Gaff asked, glancing out the front window at his rig, parked at the side of the lot.

"I leave this afternoon, but I'll be back on Thursday. I split my time between here and Chicago. No over-the-road routes for me."

"Do you find girls at every stop?" Jazzi asked. "Are any of them the jealous type?"

"Doll, I'm good, but the women I meet on the road know what's up."

"Did Misty ever talk to you about anyone who hated her enough to kill her?"

"Not everyone hated her, but not many liked her. She knew that and didn't care. Had plenty to say about your sister, though. None of it good."

"It wouldn't be. She and Olivia bumped heads, and Olivia won."

He rubbed his chin. "She did talk about a bartender she seemed to pal around with a lot."

Gaff caught her eye and nodded. "Her roommates mentioned him."

Wheels glanced at the clock. "Any more questions? I gotta hit the road soon."

Gaff shook his head. "I might have more later. If you think of anything, give me a call." And he handed him one of his cards.

"Will you bring the blonde with you if I do?"

"Depends." Gaff started to the door. Once they were back in his car, he asked, "Mind if we stop at the bar on Brooklyn next? I'd kind of like to talk to this bartender. He got along with Misty. Maybe he knows more about her than the others."

"Mind if I get some onion rings while we're there?" She'd only eaten half a sandwich for lunch and had climbed up and down ladders all morning to paint. She was hungry.

Gaff grinned. "Let's hope they're not greasy." And he headed south into town.

Chapter 17

On the way to the bar Jazzi asked Gaff about missing persons and told him about Chad's wife, Ginger.

Gaff pressed his lips together and shook his head. "The husband's always the prime suspect in a missing wife's case. But you already know that. It's been long enough, somebody's started looking into things by now, but it usually takes a while to find someone when they disappear, because if they walked out they don't want to be found. Either that, or whoever buried them doesn't want their body found."

Jazzi grimaced. "Would you check on it for me? See if they've made any progress?"

Gaff nodded. "But don't hold your breath."

Traffic was snarled on Wells Street, so Gaff took side streets to get to Fairfield. It was busy, too, but at least, traffic was moving. It was after three by the time they reached the bar on Brooklyn. It was emptying out when they walked in. Workers were heading to jobs and the next-shift customers hadn't arrived yet.

The bartender eyed them suspiciously. "Never seen you here before."

Gaff took out his badge to show him, then took out his notepad and pen.

The aroma of burgers, pork tenderloins, and fries hovered in the air. Jazzi looked at the menu. "Can I get an order of onion rings and a glass of pinot grigio?"

The bartender turned to the window and said, "Did you hear that, Sammy?" When the cook answered he nodded. "They'll be right up. Now, what's this all about?"

"I'm investigating the murder of Misty Morrow," Gaff said. "And this is my consultant, Jazzi."

The man studied her, shaking his head. "I've heard that name before. From Misty. You came in for a haircut when your sister caught Misty in the shop."

Jazzi nodded. "My sister wasn't very happy. Misty wasn't supposed to have a key. And you are?"

"Rick. I own this place. Misty came in a lot. I didn't hassle her about trying to drum up customers here." The man was big, not as tall as Ansel but massive. He had long hair and a beard and wore an earring in his left ear. He handed Jazzi her wine and she took a sip.

"Were you friends?" she asked.

"Do I look stupid? Misty was no one's friend. But she was always passing out coupons here for good deals. I'd have put a stop to it, but my customers liked it."

"Did she offer you anything?" Gaff asked.

Rick laughed. "She tried. I don't swing that way."

That was probably safer with a woman like Misty. "Did she confide in you about anything?" Jazzi asked.

The cook brought the onion rings to the window and Rick got them for her, along with Ranch dressing. "She said she'd met some new guy and was going to be rich. She didn't come in as often as she used to."

"Any idea who he was?" Gaff poised his pen hopefully.

"She met him here one time, not sure if it was coincidence or she'd planned it that way. He was a suit, wore an expensive watch and drove a fancy car. Paid with cash. Never gave his name."

There were no customers besides them, so the cook left the kitchen for a break and took a stool at the far end of the bar, sipping a Pepsi. He was thin with graying hair and studied them curiously.

Gaff reached over to steal one of her onion rings and nodded. "Good." He turned his attention back to Rick. "Did you notice the make of the car?"

Rick gestured at his cook. "Sammy went outside for a smoke that night, remember, Sammy? Did you get a good look at it?"

"A black BMW, latest model." Sammy grimaced. "The guy didn't mind flashing cash around. Pulled out a wad of bills to peel off one. Told me to get him some pull tabs."

"While you were on break?" Rick looked peeved.

"Guy like that don't care 'bout someone like me," Sammy said. "Got 'em for him. He went through all of 'em. No winners. So he tossed me another twenty for more."

"How much did he burn through?" Gaff asked.

"A hundred bucks. Won ten back."

Jazzi finished her drink and Rick went to refill her glass. She was going to change to water but then looked at the clock. By the time she got back to the house, Jerod and Ansel would be ready to leave. She nodded her thanks and reached for another onion ring. Sammy made good food.

Gaff eyed her basket and she pushed it toward him to offer him another one. He smiled his thanks. "Anything else?" he asked Rick.

The bartender frowned. "Surprised me that the guy was hanging out with someone like Misty. I got the idea he was the brains and she was going to be his front man. That doesn't always turn out well if the business is a little shady, and it would surprise me if his was legit. I tried to warn Misty about it later, but she blew me off."

Gaff raised his eyebrows at Jazzi. "Anything I'm forgetting to ask?"

"Do you remember the names of any of the women Misty talked into coming to my sister's salon?"

Rick nodded. "Most of them are regulars here. I feel for your sister. I don't know what story Misty came up with to get hired by her, but Misty used to laugh and tell me how much she was ripping her off."

Anger did a fast burn through her, but she shook it off when Rick pulled a napkin to him and began writing a list of women's names on it. "These are good people," he said, pushing it to her. "They thought they were getting a special rate."

"I don't blame them." Jazzi finished the last of her food and reached for her purse. When Rick started to shake his head, she said, "Sammy's worth his weight in gold. These were some of the best onion rings I've had for a while. I'm happy to pay for them." Sammy gave her a grin, and when Rick told her a price, she added more for a tip.

When she and Gaff stood to leave Rick said, "I hope you find whoever killed her. She was nothing to brag about, but she didn't deserve a pair of scissors in her chest."

He was probably right, but Misty had sure pushed her luck and gotten away with it longer than most people would have.

Gaff handed him a card. "If you think of anything . . ."

"I'll ask around," Rick told him. "See if I hear anything new."

"I appreciate that." With a nod, they left. Gaff drove her back to the Wildwood house and asked, "Mind if I come in? I always like to see your work."

"We're making the interior more modern than usual this time." She led him inside. When they reached the kitchen the guys were still installing the cupboards. The top ones were all hung and looked great, but Jazzi didn't like the white on white.

Jerod looked at her expression and nodded. "Yeah, my idea didn't quite work. It looks like a freaking hospital, doesn't it?"

"It's pretty sterile." There was a large expanse of wall behind the sink with no window to break it up.

"So how do we fix it?" Ansel asked.

"We can put the same tile backsplash on that wall as we do behind the stove."

Jerod grinned. "I brought a lot of pictures of samples. We can decide on a few that will work, then send them to the buyer and let him pick his favorite."

Ansel turned to Gaff. "What do you think of it? We're going to install a pantry, but we won't get to that until tomorrow."

"It's a lot of white," Gaff said.

Jerod grimaced. "That was my idea, but we're going to have black granite countertops and appliances." He walked to the boxes that had been delivered in the morning and ripped off an upper corner for the refrigerator to show Gaff.

"I like the black and white." Gaff still sounded doubtful.

"We'll have you back when the kitchen's finished," Ansel told him. "Maybe Jazzi can make something special for lunch for us."

"For our favorite detective? I'll give it my best shot." She already knew what she'd make—Philly cheesesteak sandwiches. Gaff loved a good steak.

"You've got to see the rest of the place," Jerod told him. "Come on. I'll show you."

When they returned Gaff walked to the back door, past the mudroom and laundry room, to check out the backyard. "This place is huge. Only one man's going to live in it?"

Jerod nodded. "He has a friend close to here and I think he entertains a lot."

Gaff shook his head. "Annie would complain about how much time it would take to clean all these rooms."

Jerod laughed. "Rich, divorced men don't clean. They hire someone. Might even hire people to do the catering and lawn, too."

"Must be nice." Gaff started to the front door, then paused, looking at Jazzi. "It'll take me a while to look up the names the bartender gave us. When I find them want to drive along with me when I visit them? They're all women. They'll feel more comfortable talking to you."

"The ones who came to Olivia's salon for cheap deals? Yeah, I'd love to hear what they have to say."

He nodded. "I'll give you a call. And this place is classy. I can see why it's already sold."

When he left Jazzi went to hook on her tool belt to help with the last of the cupboards. "If we get these installed, we can start on the pantry tomorrow, right?"

"That won't take long, but then we have to put up the backsplash and hook up all the appliances," Ansel said. "Oh, and install the countertops."

With the three of them working together they were making great progress, and she'd be at the house all day tomorrow. They might get everything done.

"Tell us what you and Gaff did while we worked." Jerod snorted when she told them about Wheels and all his women, and he looked thoughtful when she explained about Misty and the rich guy.

"Sounds like she got in over her head," he said.

"That's what the bartender thought. He tried to warn her, but she didn't listen."

Ansel frowned. "And the only clue you got was that the guy drove a new BMW?"

"Not much, huh?" Jazzi screwed in the last screw to hold the final cupboard in place and dusted her hands on her worn jeans.

While she and Ansel cleaned up the workplace, Jerod reached for his phone. "I'll let the guys know they can deliver the black-granite countertops tomorrow."

That done, they sat around the kitchen table for Jerod to show them the backsplash brochures he had. They picked out three they thought would work and Jerod e-mailed their pictures to the new owner. Five minutes later, while they were locking up, he replied, and Jerod grinned.

"He picked the gray-and-white tiles I wanted. I'll order those, too."

On the drive home Ansel glanced at her. "You have to feel like you're starting to get somewhere on Misty's murder. Sounds like you and Gaff found a pretty strong lead. That should make your sister breathe a little easier."

"I'd sure love to find out who the new guy in her life was. I hope somebody can shed some light on him."

"It sounds like he didn't *want* people to know him. It's not going to be easy to track him down. I'm surprised he met her at the bar, to be honest."

"So am I, but Misty might have insisted on it. She could be stubborn."

Ansel turned onto the road their house sat on. "He probably thought the bar was so small and no-account, it didn't matter, and he used cash."

When they got home and walked inside their conversation ended. The cats ran to twine around Jazzi's ankles, meowing more than usual. She glanced at the pitcher that held her flowers, and only stems protruded from the water. Every bloom lay scattered across the stainless-steel countertop. She raised an eyebrow at Inky, who returned a steady stare. There was no shaming her black cat, but then, he felt as though he were perfectly justified in being ticked with her.

Marmalade rubbed her chin on Jazzi's leg and purred. What a sweet feline. Jazzi caved and fed them their favorite wet cat food before filling George's bowl. After she put the cooler away she opened the kitchen drawer that held the cats' string. Inky's head went up and he ran to play. Where Inky went, so did Marmalade. She pulled the string all around the house, letting them pounce on it, before moving to a new spot. And then she and Ansel went upstairs to shower and change. The cats sprawled on the bed, an invitation to pet them before returning downstairs, so she spent time doing that, too.

By the time she and Ansel went to the kitchen to start supper, she'd redeemed herself as a cat mother.

"What are we eating tonight?" Ansel asked, going to look inside the fridge.

"It's Monday. Something easy. Brats, hash browns, and a salad."

"Sauerkraut?"

"If you want some. There's a can in the cupboard. You like it with a touch of brown sugar and caraway seeds."

He smiled. "You always think about what I like. It's nice."

Why wouldn't she? She loved the man. They'd eaten and cleaned up and were each snagging their spots on the couches when Chad called.

Jazzi pressed her lips together, bracing herself, giving herself a moment before answering the phone. "News?"

His voice was strained. "They found Ginger's car in a field on the west side of town. Her purse was on the front seat, but other than that, it was empty. The cop who came to ask me questions thinks Ginger's hurt or dead. He thinks I did it."

Exactly what she'd dreaded. Hope flushed out of her. She could feel it move down her body and disappear. She didn't know what to say. Finally, she asked, "Are you all right?"

"I'm with my family. They're helping me, but it looks like . . ." His voice choked to a stop. After a minute he said, "It looks like Ginger might be dead."

If her purse was still in her car, it didn't look good. At first Jazzi thought she might have driven there to meet somebody and left with him, but she would have taken the purse with her. "I'm sorry, Chad. Is there something I can do?"

"Help find who killed her. Please, Jaz. The cops think it's me, but I have to know. I have to know what happened."

"I'll try," she promised.

"Thanks." And he disconnected.

She looked up at Ansel. He winced. "Have they found the body?"

"Not yet."

"They will. Maybe Gaff can help you find out who killed her."

"You don't care that I promised to help Chad?"

"How could you turn him down? The man just lost his wife. Worse, he's the top suspect. Just like your sister."

She wrinkled her nose. "I don't think Olivia's at the top of the list anymore."

"But she's still on it." He sagged against the back of the couch and ran a hand through his white-blond hair. "We've been trying to stay away from murders and now we have two. At the same time. Life isn't fair."

She didn't say it. Both of their parents had given the same answer to that. "Who said life was fair?" her mother often quoted. She took a deep breath. "Want to watch the news?"

They both needed a distraction, but they switched off the TV when the news anchor reported about a local woman's disappearance, stating that her car had been found in a farmer's field.

"A movie?" Ansel asked.

"*The Thirteenth Warrior.*" She watched it whenever her emotions were in too much turmoil. Seeing Vikings battle a fireworm and hordes of enemies held her attention enough to push gloomy thoughts away for a while.

Ansel nodded and slid it into the DVD player. Then he went to sit with her. Having a Norseman to lean on helped make her feel better, too. But it was still a long, upsetting night.

Chapter 18

They were working on the pantry at the Wildwood house when Gaff called.

She picked up the phone. "You heard?"

"You still don't think your ex killed her?" he asked.

"No. We had some serious fights, but he never raised his hand to me. It never crossed his mind."

"You weren't married," he pointed out. "If you asked for a divorce, you wouldn't be entitled to keep the house or ask for a settlement."

"They don't have any children. Would she get support?"

Gaff hesitated before answering. "Probably not, but she might get the house."

"I don't think Chad would lose it over that. I don't think he'd hurt her."

"You still care about this guy? I've heard Jerod talk about him. He doesn't have anything good to say."

"We had a messy ending. Chad was a jerk, but I still don't think he's a killer."

"Do you know how many wives, parents, and neighbors say that?" Gaff asked.

"Too many?"

Gaff's sigh came over the phone. "I hope you're not one of them, but you've done me plenty of favors. I'll ask around to see what I can find out about Ginger. Maybe something changed lately that will give us a clue."

"Thanks, Gaff."

His tone changed to all business. "I got the information on the bartender's regulars and their addresses. Can you go with me tomorrow to talk to them?"

"Wednesday's open. No problem. Can you make it in time for lunch?"

"You're feeding me?"

"Why not? All of us have to eat."

He chuckled. "Should I consider this a bribe? To encourage me to dig a little deeper?"

"I'd never bribe a cop. Unless it was you."

He chuckled. "I'll see you tomorrow for lunch. We can both get a few things done in the morning, and I know you'll make something good."

"See you at twelve thirty."

When he disconnected Jerod said, "He's not grabbing you today? Whisking you off somewhere?"

"Tomorrow."

Her cousin frowned, studying her. "You doing okay? There was a time I wanted to pound Chad, but you feel sorry for him now, don't you?"

"He was trying to make it work with Ginger. I never even met her, but she sounded so nice, it bothers me that someone might have hurt her."

"Then she's where you should start," Jerod said. "Chad said she'd been acting funny lately, didn't he? That sounds like something was up, something that got her in trouble."

"Something that probably got her dead," Ansel said, his voice flat.

Jazzi let out a long breath. She didn't want to think that. "I'm still clinging to a small hope that Ginger got in a car with someone at a secret rendezvous and ran away with him."

"Without her purse?"

Doggone him! Ansel would have to remind her of that. She grimaced, pushing that thought away and turned to Jerod. "How's Pete doing with his teeth?"

It was an abrupt change, but she didn't want to talk about Chad anymore. Jerod and Ansel exchanged glances and got the message.

"The last tooth finally broke through the skin," Jerod said. "Pete has diaper rash and diarrhea, but he's a lot easier to live with now."

"Diarrhea?" Ansel glanced at George, lying in his doggy bed. "Dogs are sure easier than kids. When we have ours, we're hiring a nanny when they cut teeth."

Jerod laughed. "Yeah, keep telling yourself that."

While the guys worked on installing the pantry, Jazzi started on the backsplash for the two walls. Jerod had stopped on his way to work to pick up the tiles this morning. Installing them would go fast. There was no intricate pattern. Each tile was a vertical rectangle, white with a gray design in the center. It was just a matter of spacing them.

She was still at it when Jerod and Ansel finished the pantry and they came to help. With three of them working, they had both walls done before lunch. She'd brought ham and cheese to make paninis, so the guys were happy. So was George, who plopped down at Ansel's ankle to beg for tidbits.

After lunch they worked together to install the island, then Jerod called to have the countertops delivered. Heavy work. It was late afternoon before the three of them finally connected the stove, refrigerator, and farmhouse sink with a garbage disposal.

They ran out of time. "Ansel and I can put up the hood tomorrow morning and you can put all the hardware on the cabinet doors and drawers," Jerod said. "Does that sound all right?"

There were a lot of cabinet doors. She frowned, but nodded. "I should be able to get those done before Gaff gets here."

Jerod reached in his back pocket to take out another picture. He looked at her and grimaced. "You're not going to be too fond of this one."

She raised an eyebrow. "Did you print this off the Internet?"

"Not me. The new owner sent it to me. He found it on Pinterest."

Ansel glanced over her shoulder and frowned. "A mirror over the sink? And open shelves on both sides of it?"

"And light fixtures on each side, too." Jerod pointed to them. The shelves and lights were glossy black, and the mirror was framed in black, too.

She shook her head. "Every time he goes to the sink, he's going to see his reflection in the mirror." She thought of how her hair exploded to twice its size every time she cooked in a steamy kitchen. She didn't want to see herself then.

Jerod shrugged. "The owner's a handsome guy. Maybe he wants to check himself out when he has guests."

She hoped his reflection made him happier than she felt when she saw hers in a mirror.

Jerod patted her shoulder. "This wasn't my idea. It's his house."

"Whatever." She handed the picture back to him. "The good news is, we should finish in here tomorrow. Did you buy the big hanging lights for over the island?"

Jerod pointed to a stack of boxes in a far corner. "Ansel and I can tackle those jobs while you're with Gaff."

"Then we're set." Ansel went to pick up George. "We can call it a day."

Jazzi nodded, grabbing the cooler to follow the guys out the door. "When Gaff brings me back he'll get to see the kitchen when it's done. Let's hope he likes it better than last time."

"He will. It's all coming together." Jerod locked the door and they walked to their vehicles. "I'm not crazy about a mirror over the sink, but it looks good in the picture."

Ansel put George on the back seat, then slid behind the van's wheel. Before starting the engine, he tugged his cell phone from his pocket. "I forgot. Someone tried to call earlier today when Jerod and I were wrestling with the pantry, and I didn't check the message." He pulled it up and frowned. "It's from Radley. He wants to know if we can help him pick up the couch and chairs they bought today."

Not one bit of her wanted to. She'd been looking forward to going home and doing nothing tonight. But his brother was probably counting on her pickup. With a sigh, she nodded.

Ansel didn't look enthused either. "He should have given us some advance warning."

"It was probably a spur-of-the-moment thing. A lot of the stores give you cheaper prices if you don't need them to make a delivery."

"Yeah, that's what we did. Loaded your truck with our stuff to save some money."

"If they bought the furniture today, they probably have to pick it up today, too."

He nodded but grumbled, "We're giving them one more Saturday, then they should be done." He made the call. "When do you want us to meet you and where?" That determined, Ansel disconnected.

"Do they want us now?" Jazzi asked.

"No, they're going to meet us at the furniture store in an hour. That'll give us time to drop George at home, feed the cats, and take quick showers." He glanced at her as he turned to drive past Lindenwood Cemetery on their way home. He was taking the back way to avoid downtown traffic. "Want to eat out tonight?"

She shook her head. "I'd rather grab takeout and chill at home."

Once they walked through their door they rushed to get everything done before starting out again. They meant to let George veg at home, but he hurried to go with them. He stood at the door and whined. Jazzi stared. "He doesn't want to be left behind."

Ansel shrugged. "Let's take him. He can stay in the pickup with you while Radley and I load and unload furniture." He scooped up the pug, leaving an unhappy Inky and Marmalade behind. She'd be glad when they finished screening in the back patio. She could leave the cats out there on nice days.

It took longer to get the furniture and carry it into the house on Wilt Street than they'd expected, and by the time they carted in the last chair and coffee table, Jazzi's stomach was growling.

"Thanks for everything," Elspeth told them. "You guys go get something to eat. Radley and I are going to our storage unit to load all our kitchen stuff to bring here. I want to empty it out before we have to pay for another month. Then, after the antiques on Saturday, everything's moved in."

"Everything?" Ansel glanced at Jazzi and she nodded. "Jaz is okay with it, so we'll help you with the storage unit, and we'll stop to buy Coneys again for supper, if they sound good to you."

"We should buy them for all the work you've done," Radley argued.

"It's our housewarming present to you. Enjoy it while you can," Ansel said.

There were a lot of boxes in the storage unit and it took an hour to empty them out. By the time Ansel stopped to pick up the Coney dogs, the aroma filling the truck was too much for her. She opened the box and scarfed one down before they made it to Wilt Street, reaching back to share a few nibbles with George.

By the time they carted all the boxes into the house, Jazzi was exhausted. As soon as they finished their late supper, they drove home.

"Sorry," Ansel told her. "This ended up being a bigger project than I thought."

"Life happens." She shrugged, but she was so happy when they got home, she wanted to kneel down and kiss her kitchen floor. They went straight upstairs to change, and when they came down to watch a little TV at first Inky snubbed her. Her black cat had strong opinions about how a cat should be treated, and his standards weren't being met. But when he saw Marmalade lying next to her, getting all the love, he couldn't stand it and jumped up to press next to her, too.

Mollified, the cats raced ahead of them when they climbed the stairs to bed. Ansel and Jazzi flopped inelegantly onto their sides of the mattress, turned, facing in opposite directions, and dropped to sleep. When Jazzi woke to the alarm the next morning she blinked, surprised. She'd been too tired to lie awake thinking about Chad and Ginger last night. Maybe being dead tired had been a good thing.

Chapter 19

Jazzi and Ansel dragged while he made breakfast for them and she sautéed the ingredients for the Philly cheesesteaks for lunch. Why had she volunteered to make something special today? But at the time they hadn't planned on working so long at Radley and Elspeth's house. With a sigh, Jazzi felt relieved that Saturday would be the end of it, that Ansel's brother and his fiancée would be completely moved in.

She wrapped the slivers of rib eye, onions, and peppers in foil, then placed them in a special carrier to keep them warm. Once she'd packed the rest of the meal Ansel grabbed George and they left for work. This morning the guys were installing the stainless-steel hood over the stove while she installed the hardware on the cabinet doors and drawers. They'd decided on simple black pulls.

While they worked, Jerod regaled them with the news that Lizzie was going to be in the school play before Easter. "She's memorized every single one of her lines already, and she has a whole lot of them. Mom and Dad are going to come to watch her with us."

"You'd better be careful," Jazzi warned. "This might give her the acting bug."

He chuckled. "She already goes around the house singing into a wooden spoon, pretending it's a microphone."

"What about Gunther?" Ansel asked. "Does he like to perform, too?"

"Nah, he's a tinkerer, likes to tear things apart and then put them back together again. And he loves to help Franny in her woodworking shop. The kite he made in art class flew the highest at Field Day yesterday. He brought home a ribbon for it." The man was proud of everything his kids did. Jazzi got a kick out of it.

The closer it got to lunchtime, the harder they worked, trying to get everything done before Gaff came. He walked through the door a little later than planned, giving them time to finish. While he stopped to admire the room, Jazzi popped the steak and veggies in the new microwave they'd installed, adding cheese on top. Once the cheese melted, she assembled the sandwiches.

All three men went back for seconds. No surprise: when steak was involved they never turned down extra helpings. Ansel collected the dirty plates to toss in the trash, and Gaff asked, "Are you ready?"

Jazzi grabbed her purse and a sweater. The mild temperatures had dipped last night. "When we get back the kitchen will be done," she told him.

"You're doing more? It looks great now."

And it did. They'd moved the long work table off to the side to make the room an eat-in kitchen. It looked surprisingly good. When the owner had guests over for a more formal meal he could seat them in the dining area.

On the way to his car, Gaff said, "Rick gave me half a dozen names, but we shouldn't need to stay long anywhere. I'm thinking our visits will be in and out."

"Where to first?" Jazzi asked.

"A subdivision close to State Street, not far from here." They drove past the cemetery again and past the University of Saint Francis. Jazzi always looked to admire the old Bass house the school used as a library now. The college decorated it for Christmas every year and let people tour it. She and Ansel had walked through it twice, and each time they were impressed by the old woodwork and opulence of yesteryear.

The subdivision was across the street from the school, and soon Gaff was pulling into the woman's drive. She lived in a trilevel house in immaculate condition. Its roof was new, with textured shingles that matched the color of the shutters, and the gutters were new, too. The woman opened the door to greet them before they knocked.

"You're late." She turned to lead them into a formal living room. She was tall with short, steel-gray hair and gray eyes. No makeup.

"This morning got busy." Gaff reached for his notepad and pen. "You went to Misty's salon for a bargain cut?"

Leading them inside, the woman made a face. "Worst haircut I ever had. She was surprised when I refused to pay for it."

Her hair was layered to perfection. "How long ago was that?" Jazzi asked.

"Two weeks ago. She meant to make a scene when I didn't pay, but then she glanced at the clock and let it go. She didn't want the shop to open and have customers hear us arguing." She smirked. "I dislike paying for shoddy work, and that seems to be common these days."

She went on to tell them how she did her best not to pay for the new roof and gutters she'd had done either. Jazzi had admired both on her way in. She decided the woman made a habit of complaining and trying to get money off everything she had done. When she and Jerod had first started renovating houses they'd worked with a few people like her. That was why they'd found a good lawyer.

By the time they left the house they hadn't learned anything new about Misty, but Jazzi had learned that she really didn't like this woman.

Once in the car, Gaff shook his head. "She wasn't any help." They drove to the second house closer to town, and that woman—young, with three kids running in and out of the room—was upset when she called the salon and learned Misty wasn't there anymore.

"I was going to make an appointment with the owner, but she charged too much."

"How much for a haircut?" Jazzi asked.

"Twenty-five dollars. And the half-price sale on hair products was over, too. I went to a walk-in shop instead."

Jazzi could tell, but decided with young children, money was probably tight.

At a third house, in a well-kept neighborhood farther east, the woman invited them inside and offered them coffee. When Gaff demurred she settled on the couch across from him. "How can I help you?"

He poised his pen. "We were hoping you could tell us something about Misty when you went to her salon."

Books were scattered on the end table, and a newspaper lay open to the comics section on a recliner. She wore exercise pants and a loose top and pulled her legs up under her to get comfortable. "Misty did a good-enough job, but there was something about her I didn't like. She was too friendly, if you know what I mean. It felt fake. I would never have gone to her, except my beautician moved away. I was looking for someone new and Misty was passing out coupons at the bar I went to. Like I said, she did a good job, but I got worried when she told me that I'd get ten percent off if I used my debit card instead of cash. I mean, wouldn't that worry you? I told her I left my card at home and only brought money, but she wasn't happy about it."

Gaff locked gazes with Jazzi. "Did you notice anything else?"

"She had me come in really early, said that she was booked up for the holidays, but I got the idea she wanted me out of the shop before the owners came in."

"What made you think that?"

"I went to get highlights. My hair takes longer to process than a lot of people's, and she kept glancing at the clock. The closer it got to opening time, the more nervous she got."

Jazzi nodded. "My sister didn't know she was taking early customers. She never gave Misty a key to the salon."

The woman's eyebrow rose and she gave a knowing nod. "That's what I wondered."

Gaff thanked her for her time and left his card with her. Then they drove to the fourth house. The woman who greeted them there was older, with beautiful, white hair.

"I got a permanent," she told them. "My hair's getting so thin, I need the lift. Misty had me come in really early. I can understand why the girl was booked all the time. She did a good job."

Gaff leaned forward on his elbows. The woman was a little hard of hearing and he wanted to make sure she heard him. "Did you have any problems with your credit card after going to her?"

The woman's pale blue eyes went wide. "How did you know? I made a few stops before I went home that day, but someone stole the information off my card and I had to cancel it. Do you think it was that nice girl?"

"That girl wasn't very nice, and it wouldn't surprise me," Gaff told her.

"Oh, my, she seemed like such a dear. Is that why she's dead?"

Gaff closed his notepad and put it away. "We aren't sure yet, but thank you for your help."

The next two women had had similar experiences. They'd used their debit cards to pay Misty, and then the banks had called to report fraud and cancel their cards.

"Bingo," Gaff said as they headed back to the fixer-upper. "Now we know what Misty and her new guy were up to. Misty stole information from each card she processed."

Jazzi would call her sister tonight to let her know. Olivia wouldn't be happy. When they reached the fixer-upper she invited Gaff in to see the finished kitchen, and when he looked at it he gave them a thumbs-up. "This one's a winner."

"You like the mirror over the sink?" Ansel asked.

"It's better than looking at a blank wall."

When he left Ansel asked, "Well, what did you learn?"

She told them about the credit cards and Jerod shook his head. "Misty just keeps getting better and better."

When it was time to leave they gathered at the archway to the sitting room to study their work.

"This might not be my style," Jazzi said, "but I have to admit the kitchen's a stunner."

Chapter 20

On the drive home Ansel told Jazzi that Bain had called to tell him that their dad tripped over a hose in the barn and fallen. "He broke his wrist. He can't milk, but Greta's been filling in for him. Dad's fine now with it plastered up, but Bain says he's fallen a few times lately."

"Has Bain taken him to a doctor?" she asked.

"He's tried. Dad won't go."

Typical of Dalmar. How Ansel's parents had produced four decent children was beyond her. "Then tell him you're paying for a doctor to come to him."

Ansel chuckled and punched in Bain's number. It made Jazzi nervous when he talked on his phone while driving through heavy evening traffic, but at the moment they were stopped at a red light. When he told Bain what Jazzi had said his brother laughed. "That'll set him off, but it might work. I'll let you know how it goes."

By the time traffic flowed again the call was done. When they got home the weather was so mild, they decided to work in the flower beds for a while. The temperature had climbed enough, she didn't even need her sweater. The weatherman predicted a warm day tomorrow, too, and then snow. It didn't seem possible, but Indiana weather was like that. And spring temperatures could bounce up and down, day by day.

Jazzi glanced at the woods behind their house. Light green leaves covered the tree limbs. She took a deep breath. She loved the smell of growing things. George sprawled on the cement patio, supervising, and the cats hunched at the French doors, watching.

"It'll be nice when the screen porch is done and they can come out with us," Ansel said.

Jazzi glanced at Inky, his tail twitching back and forth. "Let's hope that makes them happy and they don't have a fit to be outside in the open."

"The ground's so nice, it feels like we could plant some early flowers," Ansel said.

Jazzi shook her head. "Gran's rule was never to plant annuals until Mother's Day. Then you don't have to worry about frost."

"That's almost two months away."

"And the weather's unpredictable until then." She sat back on her heels to inspect the clean bed.

"What if I grill the pork chops we thawed for tonight?" Ansel asked.

"I'll make two vegetables to go with them."

He pushed to his feet. "How about a glass of wine on the patio?"

She was nodding when he cracked the French door and Inky flew out of the house. She grabbed for him, but he was too fast. He sped across the yard, heading to the trees at the back of their property.

"The coyote still lives there. I've heard him a few nights." Ansel ran after him and Jazzi joined him, but they lost Inky before they reached the tree line.

"I should have been more careful . . ."

Before Ansel could blame himself Jazzi shook her head. "He's been waiting to make an escape. He would have managed eventually. All we can do now is to call for him."

But Inky ignored them. Jazzi got more and more irritated with the furry brat. "Even if we find him, he won't let us catch him. We'll just have to wait until he comes home."

"What if he doesn't?" Ansel frantically scanned the area.

Jazzi laid a hand on his arm. "We're going to hope for the best. There's nothing we can do."

They reluctantly walked back to the house. When they went inside to get the pork chops Ansel said, "Maybe the smell of food cooking will bring him back."

Jazzi doubted it but didn't say so. She'd fed the cats when she came home. Inky wouldn't be hungry and he'd stay away until he was.

They ate supper at the kitchen island, and Ansel dropped down bits of pork for George, but his gaze kept drifting to the French doors. When they finally went to watch TV he got up at every commercial to check outside and call for the cat.

Before going upstairs to bed, they both went outside to stand on the patio to call. And lo and behold, a black cat sauntered toward them, looking thoroughly pleased with himself. Ansel gave a low growl, but Jazzi bent to scoop up the cat. He wiggled and she carried him inside, where he jumped down and went to his food bowl. Empty. She'd filled Marmalade's but not his. He turned his head and gave a sharp meow. She raised her eyebrows at him. "You weren't home for your bedtime snack. Hope you're plenty hungry in the morning."

She turned and started upstairs, and Inky looked surprised. He looked at Ansel and meowed. Her Norseman glared at him. "You made me worry so much, you're lucky she's going to feed you in the morning. I feel like locking you in the basement for a few days."

The cat was too smart for his own good. He knew he was in trouble and went to rub against Marmalade. For the first time his sister hissed and batted him away. He jerked back and stared. Then he went to George, but the pug's growl stopped him.

"You're in disgrace," Jazzi told him. "You have to earn back the perks you took for granted."

Inky sat and raised a paw to start washing himself. He was playing it cool, as if he didn't care if he was scorned. But when they reached the middle of the stairs he raced after them.

"Good idea." Ansel's voice was harsh. "Or we'd close the door and you'd sit in the hall all night."

He couldn't possibly have understood what Ansel said, but he recognized the tone. He raced ahead to slink into the room before they reached it.

With everyone cuddled in bed, Inky pressed against her calves and Marmalade stretched against Ansel, Jazzi's thoughts roamed as she fell asleep. The stupid cat had upset her more than she cared to admit. If she and Ansel got this anxious over a missing cat, what must poor Chad be going through now? No one had found Ginger yet. He was probably clinging to hope that she was still alive but fearful she wasn't. She was glad he was staying with his family, that he had support. That he wasn't alone.

When she and Ansel had first moved in together and he'd driven to Wisconsin to help his dad and Bain with their barn roof, she'd been surprised by how lonely the house felt with him gone. That was why she'd adopted the cats. If she hadn't known where Ansel was, if he was alive or dead, she couldn't imagine how horrible it would be. She hoped they'd hear something soon, good or bad. The not knowing was horrible.

Chapter 21

Jazzi couldn't believe it was Thursday again. The days had sped by recently. They had so many projects going on, she could hardly keep track of them, and Easter would be here soon. This Saturday, after they helped Radley and Elspeth, she wanted to decorate the house for the holiday. She hadn't even begun to bake and decorate sugar cookies or make candy yet. She usually sent home a plate of nougats, caramels, and fudge for each person as a parting gift on Easter. And this year she wanted enough new matching dishes to serve everyone.

She complained to Ansel on the drive to Wildwood Park. "I want to make sugar Easter eggs with scenes inside them for the kids, but I'm running out of time."

"You have two weeks to go, and I'll help you."

"Right. You'll be working on screening the porch. I know you."

He grinned. "Only on Saturdays. My evenings will be all yours. How do you make sugar Easter eggs anyway?"

"You have to use a mold. I signed up for a candy-making class with Gran when I was in high school and learned how to do it there."

He glanced at her. "You and Gran took a class together?"

"Two of them, at Country Kitchen. We took cake decorating, too. Gran's the one who taught me how to cook. Mom would let me spend a weekend at her house and we'd make all sorts of things."

He smiled. He had a soft spot for her grandma. "Did she have the gift of sight back then?"

"I think she was born with it, but it was as hit-and-miss as it is now. It always takes a while to figure out what her visions mean."

"And you two made sugar Easter eggs together. Do you still have yours?"

She shook her head. "I kept it for years but finally pitched it when I moved to our house."

"You wanted new Easter pillow covers for the couches, didn't you? Did you order them yet?" She'd shown them to him on Amazon, and he'd liked the idea of changing their pillow covers for every season.

She nodded. "I want to buy new dishes, too."

That excited him. "I've seen some really nice ones. My mom didn't like to cook, let alone worry about how the table looked. Once I met you, I realized how pretty a house could be."

"I want stoneware. It goes from the table to the oven, freezer, microwave, or dishwasher. And they're hard to break. With as many people as we feed, that's important."

"Do they make pretty ones?"

"Gorgeous."

He turned into Wildwood, took a left, and parked in the fixer-upper's drive. Jerod's truck was already there. When he reached for George he said, "It would be fun to do an Easter egg hunt for the kids this year. We could hide eggs inside and outside the house." He frowned. "Do they make Easter piñatas?"

"Probably." She grabbed the cooler to carry inside. "Are you going to fill one with Easter candy?"

His blue eyes sparkled. "And we should buy sidewalk chalk. The kids can decorate our patio."

She stifled a groan. Her Norseman sure enjoyed entertaining kids. Who knew what he'd come up with next?

When they walked in the house Jerod was stirring white floor paint for the foyer. "First we have to paint the boards to get our white background. Then, after the paint dries, we can tape off the design. And then we can paint the black border and diamond shapes. Even with us all working together, this is going to take us two days."

If they didn't take any breaks. It took them until lunchtime to finish painting the white coat that was the base for the design.

"Did you bring anything wonderful for lunch?" Jerod asked, sounding hopeful.

She gave him a look. "You're getting spoiled, but I made tuna salad for today. I'm tired of deli meat."

That made the men happy, but George pouted. She handed Ansel a small baggie of deli turkey. "I didn't forget your little buddy."

Grinning, he tore off little pieces to sneak to him.

The floor wasn't all the way dry when they finished lunch, so they went outside to work there until it was ready. It was cool enough that they pulled on their hoodies to inspect the yard. It was in good shape. Jazzi thought about Chad and his landscape business. This was his busy season. She wondered how he was holding up.

They carted their ladder to prop against the back of the house and climbed to the roof to look at the rusted widow's walk. The previous owners had taken good care of the house, but they hadn't replaced the ornamental walk when they had the roof redone. Maybe they were nostalgic about it for some reason. It was in too bad shape to keep, though.

Without houses to block the breeze, it was cooler on the roof. Their cheeks and noses turned red as they worked, and Jazzi had to yank her hair tighter in her ponytail to keep it from blowing in her face.

"We might as well start taking this thing down," Jerod said.

They tossed pieces to the backyard to scrap later and completely get rid of before going back inside the house. The warmth felt good. Jazzi tossed her hoodie over a kitchen chair and sighed. Her skin didn't feel as tight in here. The paint was finally dry, so they strapped on knee pads and began to tape off their measurements. That took them the rest of the day.

Even with the pads on, Jazzi's knees were sore. Jerod grunted when he pushed to his feet and scowled at their finished work. "We can paint in the black tomorrow, but it's going to be time-consuming. Whose idea was this anyway?"

"Wait 'til you see it when it's done." Jazzi hoped it looked as good as the picture.

Ansel patted her shoulder. "It's going to be a showstopper. Anything that's this much work has to be."

Jerod grumbled as he went to leave through the back door. "When we finish it we need to put a protective coat over it. We don't want it scratched up and ruined for a long time."

He had a point. Jazzi grabbed her cooler and followed him out the kitchen door with Ansel carrying George behind her. They locked up and walked to their vehicles.

"Are you going to be able to enjoy yourself tonight at the restaurant?" Jerod asked her. "You'd better take a couple of aspirin to get rid of your aches."

Better yet, she was going to take a long, hot shower. Ansel, who was two years younger than they were, laughed at them. "You guys are getting old. I feel great."

"Good, you can bend to feed the pets tonight," she told him.

He groaned. "I didn't say I felt wonderful."

"I'm going home to chase kids," Jerod said, gingerly sliding behind his truck's steering wheel. "Think of me."

They waved goodbyes, then drove in separate directions. "Where are you girls meeting tonight?" Ansel asked her on the ride home.

"Henry's. And I'm starving. You?"

"Everyone's coming to our place to look at the porch project. I'm grabbing wings and fries for all of us."

The news surprised her. "Are they as excited about the porch as they were the basement?"

"Not even close, but Walker wants to add a sunroom on the back of his place. He wants to see what we're doing."

Walker's house was in front of his cement company, so he had plenty of room to add on. She remembered that he loved to grill on the back patio, and his mom had often grilled burgers and brats for the men who worked for them, driving trucks. "He'd enjoy a sunroom, and Didi could sit out there when she worked."

"He's talking about getting River a puppy." Ansel turned on their street to head home.

Jazzi shook her head. "Dogs are a lot of work. Mom has to let her dogs in and out all the time." Mom's backyard was fenced in for Ebbie and Lady, her two labradoodles. Then she looked at George. "Maybe he should get a pug."

Ansel chuckled. "I don't know if all of them are like George."

They reached their driveway and turned in. When they walked through the kitchen door Inky and Marmalade ran for their dinner and attention. Inky was so sweet tonight, weaving around her ankles and purring, Jazzi gave in and fed them herself while Ansel fed George. Then they hustled upstairs to shower and change.

She let Ansel take the first shower so that when it was her turn, she could stand under the hot water longer than usual. She felt her muscles relax and sighed with relief. Then she took care with her hair and makeup. Olivia wouldn't care if they'd crawled on the floor all day. If Jazzi looked dowdy, she'd let her know.

When they were finally ready Ansel drove to pick up his wings and she drove to Henry's. It would be nice for the pets to have the men at their house tonight. All of them slipped them bits of food and spoiled them.

She was smiling as she passed a wood on her way into town, and then she thought about Chad and Ginger. Instant guilt weighed her down about going out and having fun tonight. Chad had to be hanging onto hope and dreading the worst. Her stomach knotted every time she thought of him, but there was nothing she could do. She forcefully tried to push those thoughts out of her mind but only partially succeeded. She was grateful when she walked inside the restaurant and saw that Elspeth was already there—a smiling Elspeth. Good. She needed smiles tonight.

Starting to the table, Donna—their longtime waitress—called, "Pinot grigio?"

When Jazzi nodded she went to get her the wine. The minute she sat down, Elspeth beamed. "We got every box you helped us take out of storage unpacked and put away. If we're lucky, we can host Thanksgiving this year. The only worry is that we don't have the parking space you guys have, but maybe people can ride together when they come to our house."

Jazzi waved that worry away. "We'll think of something. My family loves food. We'll all get there."

Elspeth laughed. "The other worry is that we don't have a basement to entertain the men and kids."

This time Jazzi rolled her eyes. "The men survived for years without their toys, but the kids are trickier. If you stick a TV and game system in a guest bedroom, you could shoo them up there."

"There won't be any chairs."

"They're kids. They can sit on the floor."

Elspeth looked relieved, and then her smile grew wider. "We're making the second bedroom into a sewing room."

Jazzi had never met anyone who loved sewing as much as Elspeth did. "What are you working on now?"

"Quilts for each of the beds in our house. Sunbonnets for a girl and trucks for a boy."

Wow. She and Radley were thinking ahead. "I've never seen a quilt with trucks."

"I know. I designed it myself." She looked pretty proud of herself.

Didi slid into the third chair just as Donna brought Jazzi's wine. Before Donna could ask she said, "Just soda for me." With a nod, Donna went to get it, and then Didi pushed her cell phone out for Jazzi and Elspeth to see. "Walker got all excited when he heard that Jerod bought Easter clothes for his kids, so we went shopping and found this suit for River." She showed them a picture of River, standing straight and proud, wearing a navy suit.

"Does he need a suit?" Elspeth asked.

"No, but we're going to do something fancy so that he has someplace to wear it." She flipped to another pic. "And look at the dress we bought Noreen."

The baby looked so adorable in a ruffled pink dress with a huge pink flower on her headband that it almost made Jazzi want a baby. Almost.

Olivia came to join them last. She ordered a glass of red wine and sighed. "Mom and I finally got everyone caught up on appointments. I hope Misty's happy. She sure made our lives miserable lately."

Jazzi shrugged. "I don't think she meant to die in your salon."

"Any news on her?" Didi asked.

Jazzi told them that she and Gaff had learned she'd been stealing info off credit cards to commit fraud.

Olivia's drink came and she gulped down a swallow. "The world's better off without that girl. Have you got any good news for us, Sis?" When Jazzi grimaced Olivia sighed. "Does it get worse?"

Jazzi told them about finding Ginger's car.

Didi flinched. "But you don't think Chad killed her, do you?"

"No, but it looks bad for him."

They batted ideas around until Donna came for their orders. And then they made a point of changing the subject. Their girls' night out was to lift their spirits, not dampen them. Still, when they left to go their separate ways each of them looked a little more unsettled than when they'd come.

Driving home, Jazzi passed the wood again and wondered how soon it would be before Gaff called her to tell her they'd found Ginger's body. Was it lying in the cold, damp earth right now? She shivered when she remembered finding the shallow graves near Olivia's house. How many bodies were buried where no one would find them? And what had happened to Ginger?

Chapter 22

When Jazzi looked out the bedroom window Friday morning snow was falling. The daffodils that bordered the garage were stooped with white caps. The crocuses struggled above the thin, white blanket to spread their cheer. Early tulips circled a tree trunk, looking cold and droopy. But the snow wasn't supposed to last once the temperatures rose again the next day.

Ansel came to stand behind her and wrapped his arms around her. "A good day to hibernate. I'm sure glad I don't have to trudge out every morning to milk cows anymore."

"Your dad and Bain love it."

He nodded. "They really do. I'm glad Bain's going to try more markets this year, though. The last time I looked, milk prices were dropping. Some dairy farmers aren't going to make it. I feel for them. They didn't do anything wrong."

She leaned back against him, enjoying his closeness. "It's sad to see any business go under. People put so much time and hard work into them. We've been lucky that the housing market's been so good for so long. And Chad got lucky when he started his landscaping business. It just grew and grew."

He gave her a gentle squeeze. "I hope he hears something soon. The worry has to be driving him nuts."

Inky looked at them from the open door to the master bath and meowed. They weren't keeping their regular schedule. Ansel chuckled and went in to get ready first. The cat liked to bat at the running water in the sink. When it was her turn she washed up and dressed quickly, adding only mascara and pulling her hair into a ponytail before going downstairs. Ansel was pulling the pumpernickel toast out to butter it, so she poured them each coffee.

After breakfast she left Ansel to feed the pets while she ran to the basement and took a gallon of chili out of the freezer. It was cold enough today, it would taste good. She grabbed her instant pot and added cheese and crackers to the cooler, then they set off.

Jerod had already started the coffee urn when they walked into the fixer-upper. His gaze immediately slid to the carton of soup she took out to thaw. "Is that the last one from your freezer?"

She nodded. "It'll be warm outside soon. Thought I might as well finish it up."

He looked outside and grimaced at the snow. "Mother Nature just had to give us one last hurrah before spring comes. The dress we bought for Lizzie has shorter sleeves. I hope it warms up for Easter."

So did she. Her family always dressed up for holiday meals, and her spring dress had shorter sleeves, too. Olivia bought a new dress each year, but Jazzi liked the one she had and was happy to wear it again.

Jerod glanced into the foyer. "You ready?"

"Not really." Ansel started tugging on his knee pads. "But it needs to be done."

They kept the front door locked today so that no one stepped inside on the fresh paint, and they got busy painting the black border and diamonds on the floor. It was slow progress, and they were all ready to quit by lunchtime for a break. Jazzi was dishing up the chili when Gaff's car pulled into the drive.

She ran to the back door to call him inside. "We didn't expect to see you today. Come in this way because . . ." The words died on her lips. When she looked at his face she knew he hadn't come with good news.

He walked to the back of the house and came into the mudroom, glancing at the filled bowls on the table in the kitchen. "Sorry about the bad timing, but we found Ginger's body buried in the woods a mile from where they found her car. Thought you'd want to know."

Jazzi rubbed her arms. "A shallow grave?"

He nodded. "Just like the bodies you found near the wetlands."

"Could you tell how she died?"

"It looks like someone strangled her in her car, then dragged her to the woods. One of her shoes was missing. We looked everywhere for it but couldn't find it. We're not making that public, so keep that under your hat."

"Will do." Ansel motioned him farther inside. "Can you stay for lunch? We have plenty."

"Thanks, but I can only stay for a minute. Too much to do today. I'll grab something on my way to the station."

He probably didn't want to be around them after he delivered the bad news. She didn't blame him. She hugged herself. Suddenly, the house felt cold.

Gaff scraped a hand through his short, salt-and-pepper hair. "I know you don't want to hear this, but it looks even more like her husband lost his temper and killed her."

She shook her head. "He's been too worried when he couldn't find her. Chad's never been good at hiding what he thinks or feels."

"I hope you're right, but it doesn't look good for him."

Gaff started to the door but stopped when she asked, "How did he take it when you told him the news?"

"He's a mess. We brought him in for questioning, but we don't have any evidence to hold him. My money's on him, though, and I'm sorry for that. We grilled him pretty hard. He went to spend the day with his family after we let him go."

Jazzi felt horrible for him. She felt sorry for Ginger, too. It was a good thing Chad had family. And it made her think. "Did you notify Ginger's family?"

He nodded, looking unhappy. "They live in Peru, Indiana, but they aren't the warm, fuzzy type."

"Peru?" Jazzi frowned. "Elspeth's family lives there, too."

"Why doesn't that surprise me? How do you always know someone connected to everything I find?" Gaff leveled a gaze at her. "You're going to grill your friend about them, aren't you?" When she nodded he said, "If you learn anything interesting, will you pass it on?"

"Sure. Someone else did this, not Chad. All you have to do is find out who really killed her."

Gaff rolled his eyes. "You'll tell me even if it makes Chad look bad, right?"

She made a face but nodded. "Fair is fair. You share with me."

Nodding at the bowls on the table, he turned to leave. "Your lunch is ready. Try to enjoy it. It smells wonderful." Then he ducked out the door. He must really be busy, not just avoiding them.

When they sat at the long wooden table to eat George came to beg but only ate a couple of nibbles of cheese before slowly walking to his doggy bed, disappointed.

Jerod watched him. "Your dog should win an Oscar for his suffering."

Ansel glanced at George, head down, eyes sad, and shook his head. "He has no idea how real dogs live. If he were a working dog, he'd probably run away."

"Waddle, you mean." Jerod had set the tone, avoiding the topic of Chad, and she was grateful. They didn't talk about it during lunch or after, pushing themselves harder than usual to finish the foyer before they left for the day. When they'd painted the last diamond pattern they pushed to their feet with groans. This had been a more involved project than usual. Time-consuming. But when they stood back and looked at the finished floor Jerod let out a low whistle and grinned.

"This is really something."

It had been worth the extra effort. Ansel narrowed his eyes with a thoughtful look and Jazzi shook her head. "I love our foyer just the way it is."

He grinned. "Am I that easy to read?"

"This time you were."

Jerod started into the kitchen to clean their brushes and work materials. Jazzi and Ansel joined him to help. They hadn't mentioned Chad or Ginger once, but when he pulled on his jacket to leave he said, "Today's been a crappy way to end the week. When I get home I'm wrapping Franny in a bear hug she'll never forget, and then I'm grabbing supper so that we don't have to cook. I want to have a special night with her. Tomorrow I'm calling to have a security system installed."

Jazzi understood his need to keep his family safe. She'd had a system installed when she'd first moved, alone, into her stone cottage, before Ansel had moved in with her. The house was so isolated, no one could see if someone tried to break into it.

Ansel looked at her. "We're going out tonight. I don't want to sit at our kitchen island thinking about Chad and Ginger. It's too depressing."

She nodded as they walked to their vehicles. She needed some cheering up. Once they started for home she said, "Let's go someplace nice and then go shopping. We haven't done either for a while."

"A night out." He smiled. "I like it."

George gave him a sad look from the back seat. The pug knew they were going to leave him tonight. He was too smart for his own good.

"I'll bring you home a hamburger," Ansel promised, and the pug perked up. He could be had with bribes, and they often went out on Friday nights. It had only been lately that they'd been so busy, it was nicer to stay in. Besides, Jazzi's high school BFF was very pregnant and too tired for her and her husband to meet them someplace.

Jazzi and Ansel weren't in any hurry when they got home, so they fed the pets and spent extra time playing with them. Even the cats knew that meant they were leaving them for a few hours. By the time they dressed in nice slacks and sweaters, the pets ran to the kitchen island to make the most out of their hardship, hunkering at their food bowls for extra goodies. And for once it worked. Ansel gave George a few extra pieces of deli ham and Jazzi gave both cats some shredded cheese. When they finally walked out the door the pets had settled down to wait for them to come home later in the evening.

"We never go to Henry's together," Ansel said as he backed out of the driveway. "I think it's time we did."

Jazzi licked her lips. "The seafood bar is open on Fridays and Saturdays."

He smiled. "I know. And I know you love the scallops there. I'm going to have the fish special."

"Whatever sounds good to you. We're going to enjoy tonight."

The restaurant was crowded when the hostess seated them at one of the last open tables. Jazzi could feel herself relax the minute she walked in the room. She loved its wooden ceiling and stained-glass side windows. The bar had an old, classy vibe.

The man at the seafood station offered fresh oysters, huge shrimp, and smoked salmon. Best of all, he changed the recipe for the fresh scallops he cooked to order each week. Tonight he was cooking them in a cream sauce. Jazzi ordered french fries to go with them. To her, the two made a perfect meal. Ansel ordered the Friday all-you-can-eat fish. Lord help them. The man could put away a lot of food.

They ordered beer and wine and let the sounds of the restaurant engulf them. This time of night Henry's was full of voices and laughter combining into background noise. It was known for its atmosphere, good food, and good drinks. Jazzi and Ansel took their time enjoying themselves, and when they left they were in the mood for more fun. They headed to the shops off Jefferson.

They hit lots of them, and Ansel bought so many plastic Easter eggs, Jazzi decided they'd have to fill some with candy instead of filling them all with quarters, like he'd planned. They found more Easter decorations than they needed. She was disappointed she didn't find any dishes that excited her but decided to shop online for them. Ansel wanted plain white, but that didn't inspire her at all. At the end of the night they'd visited the bookstore and bought a stack of new books—one of them a cookbook with more exotic flavors than she usually used and two mysteries. They had plenty of sidewalk chalk, Easter baskets, and a piñata, but no dishes.

When they got home the pets attacked them. As promised, Ansel had bought two junior hamburgers, one for George and one to split between the cats. He fed George and she fed Inky and Marmalade, then petted them even more. Finally, they climbed the stairs to change into their PJs and settle in the living room. Ansel handed her the laptop. "Want to find dishes you like and order them?"

He turned on the TV while she searched. When she gave a happy sigh he got up to look at them. "Nice. White for me, some color for you."

The stoneware dish sets had white centers and blue-and-white-striped borders. There were matching bowls, casseroles, and platters that went with them. "They can be here before Easter."

"Order more than we need now," he said. "We'll probably need them eventually."

So she did. Satisfied with the evening, they watched the news they'd recorded, then flipped to Acorn TV to watch an old *Poirot*. Her Norseman loved Agatha Christie as much as she did. Halfway through the show, her phone buzzed. She glanced at the ID and braced herself.

"Chad," she said.

Ansel paused the TV and she answered the call, putting him on speakerphone.

"I'm sorry it's late," Chad said in a rush. "And this is asking a lot, but I have to see where they found Ginger. My family thinks that will only bother me more, but I have to see it. Can you go with me tomorrow evening to find it? I have to work during the day. I mean, I could call off and let someone else do it, but I need to work, to keep busy. Could you pick me up at four? I'll be done by then."

She glanced at Ansel and he nodded. She hesitated. Going with him was going to be miserable. She'd be lucky if she didn't break down, but if something happened to Ansel, she'd want to see where it occurred, too. "I'll be there," she told him.

He let out a shaky breath. "Thanks, Jaz. I owe you one. More than one."

"You'd do the same for me."

He grunted. "You wouldn't call me. And I get that. But I would."

When they hung up she slumped back on the couch. "Going with him is going to be awful."

He nodded. "There's nothing easy about losing someone you love. I'm glad you can be there for him. And when you come home I'll be here for you."

He would be, too. She thought about her to-do list for the day. "We're helping Radley and Elspeth tomorrow morning. Then I'm going with Chad. It'll be late by the time we can go to the store to shop for the week."

"No problem. Make out your list and I'll go by myself. I know where everything is by now. I shouldn't screw up too much."

She smiled. He was trying to cheer her up. "You'll do fine. You'll get everything we need. And thanks."

"Good, then that's settled. And when you get home everything will be put away, and if you want to cook, I'll help with that. I'll make this as easy for you as I can."

That's why she loved him.

By the time they climbed the stairs to bed they'd both resigned themselves to the fact that tomorrow was going to be a tough day, but together they'd get through it.

Chapter 23

Saturday morning was a bit of a struggle. Jazzi couldn't stop thinking about what lay ahead. Ansel must be, too, because there was no lively chatter at breakfast. Even the pets sensed their moods and were more subdued than usual.

They went through the motions of a quick cleanup of the house and then drove to Radley and Elspeth's. Those two were so excited to be doing the final thing to finish their house, their happiness was infectious. Even when Jazzi told Elspeth about Ginger's parents living close to where Elspeth's family did, she didn't get as depressed as she had yesterday.

Elspeth's eyes widened at the news. "My little sister, Hillary, knew a Ginger. I just didn't put that together with Chad's wife."

"She's the sister who's pregnant, isn't she?" Jazzi asked.

Elspeth nodded. "I'm twenty-six. She's only twenty-two. I'm the only sister who's waited to get married and have kids."

"Nothing wrong with that." Jazzi caught Ansel's gaze in the rearview mirror. He was smiling, the crinkle lines showing at the sides of his eyes. "Did you know Ginger at all?"

Elspeth shook her head. "She was too far behind me in school, but I've heard plenty about her family. They live outside of town, a rough crowd."

"Gaff hinted they weren't easy to work with."

"They avoid most people and most people in Peru avoid them," Elspeth said.

The drive there took over an hour. It was a beautiful day for it. Highway 24 was hilly and curvy. In early May all the redbud trees would be in bloom, but it was too early for them now. The drab hills had greened up, though, and Jazzi admired the beauty of spring.

They visited while Ansel drove. "Your sister's baby is due next month, isn't she? I know you're probably making something for her. What are you working on?" Jazzi asked.

"An embroidered baby blanket with teddy bears and blocks around spaces for the baby's name and date of birth, and I'm crocheting lots of hats and booties and more blankets."

"Everything pink?" Jazzi asked.

"Most of it."

"There's no way the ultrasound tricked you and the baby's a boy, is there?"

Elspeth laughed. "I sure hope not. I'd have to save everything and hope someone has a little girl."

Chuckling, Radley turned in his seat to join in. "Franny found an antique cradle and refinished it for us to give to Hillary. It's beautiful, and she should have charged us more for it, but she wouldn't budge."

Jazzi smiled. "Franny can be stubborn. She has to be to live with Jerod."

Elspeth reached forward to affectionately rub Radley's shoulder. "We're both so low-key, it's nice. We don't get too bent out of shape about anything."

Jazzi studied Ansel. "I guess we'd be sort of in the middle, not that mellow but not that high-maintenance either."

"A perfect balance," Ansel teased.

Radley snorted. "Maybe now with Jazzi, but get you around Dad and Bain and you can get your hackles up."

"That didn't happen 'til they kicked me out of the house," he pointed out. "I tended to resent that."

"I can see how that might do it." Radley turned to put in a new Keith Urban CD when the one they'd been listening to started to repeat the first song

Jazzi looked out the side window to watch a hawk plummet into the middle of a field. She grimaced. Some small animal just died, but as Gran had often told her, hawks had to eat, too. Gran loved hawks and owls, but then, she had a barn with too many mice. Jazzi looked at Elspeth. "You were close to your grandma, like I am to mine, weren't you?"

"You and I have a lot in common." Elspeth's hand went to a chain with a birthstone on it. "Granny gave me this. She's the one who taught me to sew."

"My gran taught me to cook."

"See?" Elspeth smiled. "My mom and granny are both good cooks, but Granny's the one who loved to bake."

The sign for Peru was ahead, so Ansel turned left at the next road. It took another few minutes to reach the town and a few more to reach Elspeth's parents' house. They'd crossed railroad tracks and passed a restaurant before turning into their drive. A man and woman hurried out to meet them.

"My mom and dad," Elspeth told Jazzi and Ansel. "Larissa and Donald."

Her mom was short and stocky with graying hair, her dad tall and lanky. He pushed his glasses higher on his nose to see them better.

Elspeth flew into her mother's arms and Radley went to shake hands with her father. He turned to introduce them. "This is my brother, Ansel, and his wife, Jazzi."

"Welcome." The couple led them into their Cape Cod–style house. It had a large living room on one side and a kitchen and dining room on the other. The carpet was well-worn and the couch's cushions sagged in the middle, well-used, but it was spotless.

"Did you have a good trip?" Larissa asked.

"We yakked the whole way." Elspeth sat on the couch beside Radley and her parents took two straight-backed chairs so that Jazzi and Ansel could have the comfortable ones.

"It's going to take a while to haul everything out of the basement," Donald said. "Do you want to get started? Then we can visit over something to eat."

Great aromas were coming from the kitchen. Elspeth inhaled and smiled. "Is that lasagna?"

"Your favorite." Her mom looked pleased. "There's plenty for all of you. We're so happy you two came to help load Granny's antiques for our daughter and Radley."

Elspeth's dad led them into the basement, where antiques were packed in the center of the room—a walnut bedframe, two chests of drawers, and a monstrous armoire. Jazzi and Elspeth carried the bed's headboard together and the men took the heavy furniture. They struggled with the armoire. Jazzi and Ansel had one in their bedroom, but it wasn't as big as this one.

It took them a while to load everything into her pickup and fasten them securely. By the time they were finished Jazzi was ravenous. The scents of tomato and garlic had followed her everywhere she went every minute they worked.

Elspeth led them into the dining room to a large cherry table. "Make yourselves comfortable. I'll help Mom carry things to the table."

Besides the lasagna, there was a huge tossed salad, garlic bread, and banana pudding. Every bit of it was delicious.

They were quiet for a while as they emptied their plates, then they relaxed and talked over dessert. When there was a lull in the conversation Elspeth said, "Jazzi's friend just lost his wife, Ginger, one of Hillary's friends in high school."

Her mother's lips pinched together at the name. "I felt sorry for that girl. She was nice, but people stayed away from her family. She and her brothers pretty much raised themselves."

Her dad frowned. "She was younger than you. How did she die?"

Elspeth made a face and glanced at Jazzi. "Someone killed her," she explained.

"No!" Larissa's hand flew to her throat.

"Did she have any enemies in Peru?" Jazzi asked.

"Ginger?" Elspeth's mom gave her head a quick shake. "The girl stayed in the background whenever I saw her in town, almost cowered, afraid if someone noticed her, they might pick on her."

Donald frowned. "Come to think of it, I saw her a couple of weeks ago at our grocery store. She looked stronger, happier. Leaving Peru was good for her."

"You saw her here?" Elspeth asked, surprised. "She doesn't come back to visit her family, does she?"

"Why would she?" Her mother shook her head. "Her brothers moved away, too. Only her parents live in that ramshackle house outside of town, and they don't appreciate visitors."

That made Jazzi wonder. "Then why do you think she came back? Does she have close friends here?"

Elspeth pursed her lips, thinking. "Sorry, I just didn't know her that well."

When Jazzi looked at her parents, they shook their heads, too. The atmosphere grew gloomy.

"Sounds like you've reached a dead end." Radley stood to gather dirty dishes to carry to the sink. "But we came here to collect our furniture and we did. It's beautiful. Thank you for keeping it for us," he told Elspeth's parents. "And thanks for the great meal, but we'd better get going."

"Can we help you with the dishes before we leave?" Ansel asked.

"Lordy, no. You've helped our daughter enough." Larissa stood, going to hug each of them before they left. "It was a pleasure meeting you."

They stayed to talk a little longer before making the drive back to River Bluffs. Jazzi would be covering the same territory soon when she drove this way with Chad. On her way to pick him up, she meant to call Gaff to let him know Ginger had been back in her hometown for some unknown reason before she was killed. For now, though, she switched gears to enjoy the people she was with on the ride back.

She and Elspeth talked about Easter. "I thought you'd be driving to celebrate it with your family," Jazzi said. "I'm glad you're spending it with us this year."

"Radley and I decided to take turns between my family and his for Easter, to spend Thanksgiving with you guys and Christmas with my folks in Peru."

Jazzi nodded. "That makes sense. It gets tricky once you're a couple."

"Do you and Ansel ever go to see his parents?"

Jazzi raised an eyebrow. "You met them when we drove to Wisconsin for Bain and Greta's wedding. We plan to drive there once in a while to see those two, but Ansel doesn't want to spend the holidays with them, and Bain's thinking about driving here once in a while."

Elspeth grew thoughtful. "When you go to see them can we tag along? Radley's not excited about visiting his parents either, but he feels guilty about that. It would help if we went with you guys."

"That would make it more fun for us, too."

They moved on to another topic. "Are you making anything special for Easter this year?" Elspeth asked.

Jazzi told her about making the sugar Easter eggs with peepholes, and Elspeth got excited. "Can I make them with you? I'd love to give one to my sister's little girl when she's born."

"What about your other sister?" Jazzi asked.

Elspeth smirked. "She has three boys—rowdy ones. They'd probably use the sugar eggs for batting practice."

Jazzi thought of Jerod and laughed. "Yup, that's what my cousin would have done."

When they reached the house on Wilt Street the guys carried the antiques upstairs to the bedrooms, and when they were finished Radley called down to Jazzi, "Come on up and see how everything looks."

She stopped in the door of the master bedroom and gave a satisfied sigh. "It's beautiful."

They'd painted the walls a soft apricot color, and Elspeth had sewn white, country curtains for the two windows. She'd made a quilt for their bed, too.

Ansel nodded his approval. "It's so relaxing. It feels like an oasis."

Elspeth leaned into Radley, beaming. "Thank you."

The second bedroom was painted light, sage green, and they'd made it into a sewing room. It had plenty of room for Elspeth's projects. And the last bedroom was butter yellow, with a huge, shaggy rug in its center, dotted by beanbag chairs facing a large-screen TV. A gaming system and controllers were stored under it. A perfect place for kids to hang out.

On their way back downstairs Radley asked, "Can you stay for a while?"

Ansel shook his head. "We still have to go to the store and get a few things done tonight." On the drive home he glanced at Jazzi. "I didn't think you'd want to talk about going with Chad. You didn't bring it up, so I didn't either."

"Thanks. You're right. I'm not looking forward to it."

Once home, they were hurrying through their grocery list one more time when Bain called. Ansel put his phone on speaker.

"I got Dad to the doctor and he has high blood pressure, really high. He has to start medicine, and he's grumbling about that, but the doctor gave him the 'silent killer' lecture and he settled down a little. The doctor also told him it was time he let me run things more, so that he didn't get so upset and worried, that he needed to let go of some of the stress."

"How did he take that?

"He agreed in the doctor's office, then told me it was never going to happen on the way home. He said he'd drop over dead first."

Ansel laughed. "Sounds like Dad."

"I told him I was planting an orchard, starting beehives, and growing produce for a farmers market whether he liked it or not, and he let that go."

"Good. Greta excited about that?" Ansel asked.

"She's already ordered a lot of heirloom seeds and started tomato plants in Radley's old bedroom. Lots of them. She wants to sell jams and jellies, apples and apple cider, and honey besides produce."

"Ambitious." They talked a little more. When they finished Ansel grinned at her. "It's nice to hear Bain sound so happy."

"It's nice to have all you Herstad boys happy for a change." She glanced at the clock. "I'd better get ready to go."

"We're doing a one-dish meal for Sunday?" Ansel asked.

She reached for her purse. "Chicken Divan. I'm going to use rotisserie chickens as a shortcut this time, but I need fresh broccoli."

"That's it? That's all we have to make?"

Jazzi smiled. "That, and baked sweet potatoes. Didi's bringing a Waldorf salad and Elspeth's making a cherry cobbler."

He grabbed the list on their way out the door. He let her back up and drive away first, and then he left for the store. She called Gaff on her way to Hillegas Road.

He sounded aggravated. "I knocked on lots of doors in Peru and not one person mentioned seeing her there. Thanks for passing this along."

"No problem."

"If I go back there, care to come with me?"

"Count me in."

It had been a long time since Jazzi visited Chad's parents, and once she clicked off her phone, she had to concentrate to remember exactly how to get there. Their subdivision was off Highway 14, southwest of town. When she pulled in the drive Chad walked out to get in her pickup.

Jazzi smiled. "Glad you didn't make me come in. I'd have felt awkward seeing your family again."

"I'd feel the same way seeing yours."

She drove back to 24 and headed toward Peru again. From the directions Gaff gave her, Ginger's car and body were found closer to another small town, only a short distance from where she grew up. There wouldn't be a sign for the turn off, so once they passed the road for Salamonie Dam, they squinted to read each street marker.

"There." Chad pointed, and she made the turn. Ten minutes later she slowed, watching how many miles she'd gone before pulling onto the side of the road. "According to the directions, they found Ginger's car here."

It had been towed away as evidence, so she hoped she had the right spot. They got out of the truck and looked around. No houses anywhere nearby. Open fields and woods in the distance.

Chad frowned. "Why would Ginger come here to meet someone? There had to be some place better than this. There's nothing."

"Maybe that's why they picked this spot. Who was going to see them?"

His face pinched, he ran a hand through his black hair. "I've kept telling myself she wouldn't have an affair, that it had to be something else, that maybe she was trying to help some ex she thought I'd be jealous of, anything but . . ."

She laid a hand on his shoulder. "She loved you. You told me you two were doing better lately. Maybe she came here to break it off. Maybe that's why she's dead."

"Oh, man." He shut his eyes for a moment, then took a deep breath. "Let's find where she was buried."

They started across a plowed field. Trees clustered in the distance, and when they entered the woods it took them a while to find the yellow police tape that marked where her body was found.

Her grave was even more shallow than the ones near the wetlands, but then the ground hadn't thawed yet. It would have been work to bury her at all.

Chad jammed his hands in his pockets, pinching his lips in a tight line. He turned to gaze in all directions. "Couldn't get much more secluded."

Jazzi didn't even see a farmhouse in the distance. "It doesn't look like anyone ever comes here. If whoever killed her had moved her car, no one would have found her."

Chad blinked and pinched the bridge of his nose. "That would have been the worst, never knowing. I'm surprised they found her anyway."

"Gaff said they used dogs."

He nodded, spreading his legs to stand more securely, obviously planning to stay a while. Jazzi didn't hurry him. A squirrel started down a nearby tree, saw them, and scampered higher. It had been warm enough earlier that she hadn't worn a sweater, and now she regretted it. Standing still, doing nothing, made her notice the air's bite more. The earth, under the trees, was cool, the chill creeping into her toes.

They stood there a long time until Chad finally said, "Let's get out of here and go home."

She turned to start back to the truck. The ride home was quiet, Chad lost in his thoughts, his expression brooding. It wasn't until they were close to his parents' house that he said, "Thanks for going with me, Jaz. Somehow, seeing where it happened made it more real. Gave me a little more closure."

"Are you going to be okay now?"

"The police are still dogging me, and I'll do better if they catch her killer, but I can function. I'll probably just go through the motions for a long time. My mom said a year, my dad said longer."

She nodded and pulled in his drive. "Take care, Chad."

"You're still working with Gaff to find her killer?"

"Whenever he lets me."

"Thanks for that, too." He saluted and walked up the sidewalk to the house.

Jazzi sighed with relief on the drive home. Visiting Ginger's grave had been depressing, but it could have been worse. Then her mind shifted to her sister and Misty's murder. Gaff hadn't said much about that case lately. She'd have to call and bug him about it next week. Once she pulled into her own garage, though, and walked inside their stone cottage, she pushed thoughts of murder away. She was ready to enjoy what was left of their Saturday night.

Chapter 24

Before people came on Sunday she and Ansel slid the casseroles in one oven, the sweet potatoes in another, then started setting the table and stacking dishes on the kitchen island. While the food cooked, they put up the Easter decorations they'd bought. Seeing the white rabbit on the fireplace mantel, the spring pillow cases and the basket-shaped candy dish made it feel like Easter was near. Last year she'd put a small, white tree on the farmhouse kitchen table to hang tiny Easter eggs on, but she'd had to give up on it after only a week. Inky thought all of those hanging ornaments were toys for him to bat around.

This year, before she put the tree on it again as a centerpiece, she gave the cats new toys to divert them. One of them had feathers hanging from slender, flexible rods, and every time a cat batted them, they twirled. Inky loved it, batting them over and over again. Marmalade played for a while, then carried one of the new felt mice, stuffed with catnip, to the deep window in the sitting area. She stretched in the sun to watch Ansel hang a spring wreath on their red front door. As usual, George supervised from his doggy bed.

By the time Jerod and Franny walked in with their kids the kitchen smelled wonderful and the house looked cheerful. He took a deep breath, then looked around and smiled. "Your place looks great. Now we can start the countdown to the Easter feast."

The rest of the family filtered in quickly. Only Radley and Elspeth were late. Standing around the kitchen island, snacking on the cheeseballs and crackers, laughing and talking, they caught up with each other. People were dressed more casually than usual today. Walker and Didi wore jeans and button-down shirts, Mom and Dad, Dockers. Jerod's parents wore jeans and dressier knit shirts, but Eleanor came with a burp pad to throw over her shoulder before she reached for baby Noreen. That woman couldn't keep her hands off babies. Even Olivia wore a tunic top over leggings. And Thane, in his usual style, wore jeans and a T-shirt with a pitcher of beer printed in its center. But Gran and Samantha wore dresses.

"Lookin' good," Jerod told them. "What's the occasion?"

Gran patted her snowy white hair, framing her wrinkled face like a fuzzy halo. She beamed at Samantha. "We went to a baptism this morning. One of Samantha's friends invited us to her grandson's ceremony."

Radley and Elspeth came to join them as Samantha explained, "I was the dad's godmother and watched the boy grow up. I'm glad I got to see him celebrate his first baby."

Gran took a sip of the red wine Jazzi brought her, then shook her head. "It's too bad Chad can never have kids. He wanted them so much."

At the name Chad, Elspeth turned to Jazzi. She'd pulled back her long, light-brown hair in a headband today, accenting her oval face. "I've been trying to figure out why I didn't connect Chad's wife, Ginger, with Peru a lot sooner, and then I realized that when I heard her last name, it was her *married* name, and I didn't recognize that. I've been thinking about her, though, and remembered that she used to date a boy from another town all through high school."

"Another town?" Jazzi had been walking to the refrigerator to get herself a glass of pinot grigio but stopped to listen.

"If I remember right, he only lived one town over." Elspeth spread cheese on a cracker and handed it to Radley. Smiling, she said, "We didn't have much for breakfast this morning."

Jazzi returned to Ginger's boyfriend. "How did Ginger meet him if he didn't live in Peru?"

"Oh, that's easy. Our small high schools consolidated into one huge school, so kids from all over the area were bused there. Parker and Ginger clicked in their freshman year and were a couple all four years, but he kept getting into small-time trouble, so when he graduated, his parents talked him into joining the army. The rumor was that Ginger didn't know she was pregnant until after he shipped out."

Ansel frowned. "Did she tell him she was pregnant?"

"He was sent overseas and she didn't want to go. People gossiped that he planned to be a lifer, and she didn't want to be an army wife. She aborted the baby really early and moved away."

"Is he still overseas now?" Jerod asked.

She had everyone's attention and shrugged. "A rumor started that he got in a little trouble in Germany, so he didn't sign up again this last time. He came home instead, but I don't know if that's true or not."

Jazzi thought through the timeline Chad had told her. "Do you know when people said he came back?" She wondered if it was the same time Ginger started acting strangely.

"Sorry. I didn't pay much attention."

Ansel turned to Jazzi. "Do you think he got back in touch with Ginger?"

"It's something to check in to."

"Not until later." Jerod patted his stomach. "I'm close to running on empty."

Not a very subtle hint to put food on the island so people could eat, but he was right. Jazzi got her oven mitts. "Everything's ready."

She and Ansel loaded the butcher-block counter with the casseroles, sweet potatoes, and rounds of crusty bread, along with the Waldorf salad Didi had brought. "Grab your plates," Ansel announced.

They didn't have to say it twice. As usual, once everyone was seated, they made small talk while they ate. Jazzi and Ansel cleared the table and brought the cobblers for people to dish up and then he got out gallons of ice cream. Lizzie had just finished telling them about her school play when Gran looked at Jazzi.

"She was pregnant when she died."

"Who?" Jazzi stared. "Ginger?"

"The girl with the auburn hair."

Jazzi rubbed her forehead. "She was sterile, Gran."

Gran waved that away. "No, Chad was." Then she blinked. "Can I have another scoop of ice cream and more wine?"

Ansel got up to get them, and Jazzi asked, "Do you know who got her pregnant?"

Gran frowned. "How would I know that? I'd never ask anyone something that private."

Jazzi shrugged. The vision was gone. "Thanks, Gran."

Gran scowled at her but brightened when Ansel gave her another glass of wine. She liked to start dinner with wine and finish it with another glass.

A short time later Jazzi and Ansel cleared the table again, stacking dirty dishes in their deep farmer's sink. Then the men and kids disappeared into the basement and the women relaxed in the living room. People started for home sooner than usual, though, and Jazzi was relieved. It had been a long week. She was ready to have a quiet night.

As she rinsed dishes and Ansel loaded them in the dishwasher, he said, "Easter's only two weeks away, but I hope both your murders are solved by then."

"I do, too." Lately she'd been focused on Ginger and Chad, though. It was time to ask Gaff about anything new on Misty's case. Before they went upstairs to change into their pajamas, she called Gaff and told him what Elspeth and Gran had said.

"She was pregnant?" She could almost hear Gaff shaking his head. "I'll look into both things. I was thinking about interviewing more people about Misty's death on Tuesday. Can you go with me?"

"Tell me a time and I'll be ready." Maybe they could make some headway on clearing Olivia.

"I'll get back to you," he said. "And thanks for more leads."

"No problem." As they climbed the steps to their room, Jazzi pushed clues and what-ifs out of her mind. Ansel wanted to watch a basketball game tonight and she had a book to finish. It was going to be a nice night.

Chapter 25

When they walked into the Wildwood house on Monday the foyer floor looked great.

"It still needs a protective coat," Jerod said. "That should go fast, but we'll have to wait to do it until the end of the day so we can walk on it now."

"What have you got planned for today?" Ansel asked.

"Painting the rest of the rooms down here. We have to go through the foyer to get to the living room. "

Jazzi frowned. "We still have the sitting room and study and the laundry and half bath to do. There's no way we can finish them all today."

"Yeah, but by the end of the day tomorrow the ground floor's finished." Jerod jammed his old white hat with a brim on his head. He looked like he was ready to visit a rain forest, but it worked. It kept paint splatters off his hair and face.

"We'd better get to it." Ansel reached for the baseball cap he wore when they painted and Jazzi wrapped a scarf over her hair. They decided to work together on each room rather than tackling them individually. George avoided them as much as possible. He didn't like the smell of paint fumes.

By the time they broke for lunch the sitting room was a warm butter yellow with a crisp white ceiling and trim. Jazzi kept food simple on Mondays—deli sandwiches and chips. The deli meat tempted George from his doggy bed and Ansel tossed him small bites now and then.

While they ate, Jerod told them the new owner had called him last night, asking if he could move into the house by Easter.

"What did you tell him?" Ansel asked.

"I said we'd do our best, but I couldn't promise it would be finished. We should be able to get the inside done, but we might have to come back to do the widow's walk railing and the railing for the balcony."

"Was he all right with that?" Ansel finished his can of soda and tossed it in the recycle trash.

Jerod nodded, standing to clean his part of the table, too. "The upstairs isn't going to take too long. Our biggest project is the master bath; then we only need to sand floors and paint."

"Only." Jazzi made a face. "The rooms are all big."

"Piece of cake!" Jerod told her. "We're pros. We'll make them all sparkle in no time."

"If you say so." He was spreading it on thick.

They decided to paint the study next. It was a small room, to be used as an office. She painted the ceiling and walls white while the guys painted the bookcases and the wood trim black. They'd built a rectangular table to use as a large desk and painted it black, too. The two colors made for a dramatic contrast. She'd ordered a black-and-white throw rug for the floor, and once the painting was done Jerod rolled it out in the center of the room, under the desk, only letting the edges of the wood floor show. It tied everything together.

He grinned. "You done good, Cuz."

High praise from him. Before starting on the huge living room, they looked at the picture they'd chosen for inspiration. They'd decided on a white ceiling with soft, cream-colored walls and white trim. The owner wanted this room and the sitting room to have an English manor house feel. She'd chosen two Oriental rugs to achieve that, one for each room.

They had to stay an hour later than usual to paint the protective coating in the foyer. But when they walked out of the house all they had to do the next day was finish the laundry room, the half bath, and the mudroom—all white with black counters and shelves. But those rooms would take a while; the laundry room had so many shelves.

"For once, the only bathroom we have to gut is the master," Jerod said. "That feels like a miracle."

It hardly ever happened. They should rejoice while they could. Locking up, they called it a day and headed for their homes.

Once there, it was so nice outside, Ansel pulled the riding lawn mower out of the garage to fiddle with. "I want to make sure it starts. I'll probably have to mow soon."

Jazzi rolled her eyes. The man mowed the grass when it was a fourth of an inch longer than usual. She left him to it and went inside to shower and change and start supper. She was browning bulk sausage, adding mushrooms, onions, diced green peppers, and tomato sauce for sausage rolls when he joined her inside.

"Mmm, I'll be right down to help." He didn't fool her. He wanted to make sure she added enough shredded mozzarella before she sealed the pizza dough. Then they worked on a tossed salad together.

They were enjoying a quiet Monday night when Gaff called.

"What if I pick you up after lunch tomorrow?"

She smiled. "Why don't you come to the fixer-upper at noon? I'm making Reuben paninis."

His voice perked up. "I love corned beef."

"Then you should like these. We like sauerkraut and Thousand Island on ours, but I can make yours any way you like."

"I want the whole shebang, and thanks. I'll see you at noon."

She called Jerod to let him know she'd be leaving work early, and he was happy to hear it. "I'm glad he's working on Misty's murder again. I'll be glad when that one's behind us."

She and Ansel would be, too, but it didn't feel like they were even close to finding whoever had done it.

"We'll worry about clues and witnesses tomorrow," Ansel told her. "That's soon enough. If it's a nice night tomorrow, I might try to get some more work done on our screened porch while you make supper."

"Works for me." And they enjoyed the rest of their night. They went to bed early enough to wake before the alarm clock went off the next morning. Inky bounced right out of bed with them, but Marmalade opened one eye and ignored them. Their orange tabby enjoyed her beauty sleep. She didn't move until Jazzi and Ansel started making the bed.

Even though Jazzi had organized everything to make the paninis and they got to Wildwood before starting time, Jerod was already there and had a sawhorse set up in the backyard. "Ansel and I can work on the half bath and mudroom while you're with Gaff. Let's try to get the mudroom done before you have to leave."

They worked at building and installing shelves and a long seat with storage beneath it on one wall, then adding another wall on the end to box them in. Once it was all put together they sanded and painted. When they finished she stared at their work, surprised.

"I think this is the best mudroom we've ever done."

Ansel nodded. "Painting the end wall black ties it in with the kitchen. I really like it."

He had that tone in his voice, and Jazzi knew he was trying to decide if they could do something like that in their house. There wasn't a good way now, but if he added a garage onto the side of their cottage, he could put something like this between the kitchen and garage door to connect them. She'd wait to mention that, though, until he finished the porch.

They were cleaning up their mess when Gaff's car pulled into the drive.

"You can start lunch," Jerod said, "while we finish up."

She went to assemble their sandwiches.

When Gaff walked in the back door Jerod asked, "Where are you two off to this time?"

Gaff went to grab a few chips out of the bag on the wooden table. "I want to visit more people Misty knew to track down the mystery guy she was working with, probably on credit card theft. I'm taking another look at the trucker, too; I interviewed him this morning. I didn't want Jazzi around him. Turns out another woman was stabbed to death when he was in a town west of here on a special delivery—a waitress who worked at a truck stop."

Jazzi put the paninis on the table and they all took a seat. Ansel piled chips on his paper plate, frowning. "It's hard to believe no one saw anything the morning Misty died. The shop's in a strip mall with other businesses."

Gaff shook his head. "Cops went door to door, but no one was open for business yet. Misty was killed before Olivia got there at nine."

Jerod reached for another sandwich before Jazzi had even started hers. "Well, Thane's ready for you to lock someone up. He says Olivia's been moody ever since she found Misty's body in her wash chair."

"She's pretty much cleared now," Gaff told them. "The lab looked at her clothes and there were no blood splatters on them. One of her neighbors saw her leave the house that morning at eight forty. There was no way she could've been there when Misty was killed."

"It still bothers her." Jerod went for another can of soda. "She told Thane it's hanging over her head until you make an arrest."

Gaff huffed. "If only it were that simple. We'd have hurried it up for her if I'd realized that."

Jerod laughed. "Right. Well, good luck today, you two."

When they finished eating, the guys cleaned up so she could leave. Once on Jefferson, Gaff said, "I thought we'd start with the supply shop where Misty bought her stuff for the salon."

"You mean she bought something on her own?" Jazzi asked.

"No more than she had to. The shop's on the south side of town. The owner likes to gossip. Should be an interesting interview. She wasn't too keen on seeing a cop, but I think she'll have plenty to say to you."

Jazzi hoped so. The more information, the better.

Chapter 26

On the drive to the supply shop, Jazzi asked, "How did the interview go with the trucker?"

He grimaced. "Not very well. When I told him a waitress had been stabbed to death at one of his stops, he shrugged and said, 'Oh? What's that got to do with me?'"

"Maybe you should have taken me along with you. He loves to brag, to let me know what a catch he is."

"Or to shock you." Gaff shook his head. "No, it wasn't a pleasant interview, and he clammed up about anything important. I get a bad vibe from him. I don't want you around him."

Come to think of it, she didn't want to be around him either. They passed through town on Calhoun, drove under the underpass, and kept going. She watched as the Saigon Restaurant, the Oyster Bar, and Welch's Ale House slid past her window. Eventually, they reached the strip mall with the supply shop. The entire mall needed an update. It wasn't in bad shape, it just needed a fresh look.

Beauty products lined the front window of the shop, just a few doors down from a corner liquor store. When they walked inside, the owner was with a customer, so Gaff waited. That gave Jazzi time to study her. The name on the tag pinned to her flowered smock said Trudie. An older woman. Maybe in her sixties. A minimum of makeup—mascara and blush. Eyebrows so thin, they looked like she'd drawn them on with a pencil. Not what Jazzi expected from a woman who sold beauty products.

When Trudie finished ringing up the order she smiled at her customer. "Take care 'til I see you next month." She had a hoarse, smoker's voice, followed by a smoker's cough. The customer left, and Gaff stepped closer to display his badge. She wrinkled her nose in distaste, then glanced at Jazzi.

"She's consulting with me on this case," Gaff told her.

That brought a smile. "You have beautiful hair, gal. Is it natural?" When Jazzi nodded she let out a sigh. "You have no idea how lucky you are. Me? I have diabetes, and my hair's so thin on top, you can see through it in bright sunlight."

Jazzi looked at it more closely. It was sparse. "Is there something you can take for it?"

"I've been trying primrose oil, but I can't tell much difference. It worked for my friend, though."

Gaff cleared his throat. "Sorry, ladies, but I came here to ask about Misty Morrow. I've been told she bought her supplies from you."

Trudie made a face and turned back to Jazzi. "Funny thing about that girl. She didn't buy half the supplies other hairdressers need."

"That's because she was borrowing from the other people in the shop without asking and without repaying them," Jazzi told her. "She worked in my mom and sister's salon."

"Is that so?" Trudie's eyes lit up. Gaff was right. She loved gossip. "I could see her doing that. She was always trying to tell me the price on one of my products was wrong so she could get it cheaper." She snorted. "Like a trick like that would work on me. I've worked here so long, I have them all memorized."

"Did Misty ever come in here with someone else?" Gaff asked.

She started to answer, then had to turn her head to cough. It took a minute to stop before she could talk again. "Nah, she was always alone and always in a hurry. She tried to use a credit card from her shop the last time she came, but I couldn't accept it. Didn't have a valid ID for it."

Gaff scribbled that in his notes. "Do you happen to remember the name on the card?"

"No one I knew, so I didn't pay attention." She reached for a bottle of water under the counter and took a sip.

Gaff dug one of his cards out of a pocket to hand her. "Thank you for your time, and if you think of anything else, give me a call."

"Sure thing, hon." She smiled at Jazzi. "Hope you let that beautiful hair down once in a while. It looks great in a ponytail, but men love hair like yours."

"My husband sure does."

Trudie laughed, and they left her in a good mood to return to Gaff's car.

"That went well." Gaff patted his notepad. "Interesting that she tried to use one of the stolen credit cards. I thought she'd have given it to her partner."

"Maybe she thought she'd charge something on it first."

"Sounds like something she'd do." Gaff glanced at her. "Are you up for visiting Misty's roommates again?"

"Whatever you want to do." She was just a tagalong, hoping to find new information so Olivia wouldn't have to think about Misty ever again.

Only she and Val were at the rental when Georgie motioned them inside. Her blue-black hair was as messy as it was last time, pulled into a topknot at the top of her head. She was sporting a new tattoo on the only skin that had been visible the last time they'd come.

"Sorry, I worked late last night, just got up." She motioned toward Val. "She has the day off because construction hasn't started on the steel building they're doing. Earthmovers are leveling the dirt today."

Regardless, Val was dressed in a flannel shirt, a red one this time instead of blue. It must be her uniform of choice.

Gaff took out his notepad. "I'll make this quick, but I wondered if you could tell us Misty's favorite restaurants and bars, any place she might meet people or friends."

"She didn't have friends," Val said, "but she liked hanging out and flirting for free drinks."

The two women gave him a list of places to try. He thanked them, and they left. One restaurant was just a few blocks from their house down Broadway. He drove there and parked in Trubble Brewing's lot. The lunch crowd had trickled to a few customers, and Gaff snagged the one waitress covering the dining area now and showed her his badge.

"I'm investigating the death of Misty Morrow and I was hoping you could tell me about her."

The girl's dark hair was pulled into a high ponytail like Georgie's, but somehow she made it look cool and stylish. "Misty? She usually came in here with Jameson. All of us were shocked when we saw her obituary in the paper."

"Is Jameson his first name?"

She laughed. "No, it's his nickname. He likes his whiskey."

"Any idea what his last name is?" Gaff asked.

"Kruper. He plays in a band. Keyboard. That's how they met. Misty was in the night he came to play. They got pretty close. Her death sort of threw him."

That was a first. Most people were happy she was gone. "Were they friends?" Jazzi asked.

She scrunched up her face. "Not exactly." She looked up when a group of people walked in. "Sorry, I have to get their orders. They come in for a late lunch and only have an hour."

Gaff thanked her and, as usual, handed her a card. When they left he said, "Let's drive to see Kruper." He looked him up and headed to his apartment.

Kruper rented the upstairs of an old house off Sherman. Jazzi used this route to visit River Bluffs's zoo each summer. It wasn't a terrible neighborhood, but it wasn't a great one either. They climbed the outside stairs to knock on his door.

Kruper staggered to pull it open when Gaff knocked, half asleep and half dressed. He was in pretty good shape. Not all muscle like Ansel, but fit. Medium height, he was attractive in that rocker-type way—lots of hair, tattoos, and a careless sexuality. He winced when Gaff introduced himself.

"Sorry, hangover." He turned for them to find their way inside and flopped back down on the sofa. "What do you want?"

Gaff went through the whole Misty spiel. When he finished Kruper tried to focus on him, rubbed his eyes, then looked away.

"Misty had a way of making enemies," he told them. "Sometimes I hit it off with her. Sometimes I didn't. We'd been shaky lately because she met someone new. It never lasted long. Most guys wouldn't tolerate her, put up with her crap."

"But you could?"

Kruper shrugged and turned his attention to Jazzi. He tilted his head to study her a moment. "We never asked much of each other. Didn't expect it to go anywhere. That worked for both of us." He frowned. "You're pretty. Who are you?"

Gaff introduced her. "Jazzi's my consultant on this case."

"Jazzi?" He smiled. "I like it. Did you know Misty?"

"She worked at my sister's beauty salon and stole from her."

He threw back his head and laughed. "Yup, that's Misty!"

Every time someone said that it irritated her, as if stealing was all right because, oh yeah, it was Misty. "Do you have any idea who the new guy was she was seeing?"

He rubbed his eyes again, trying to focus. "Someone out of her league. He runs some kind of travel agency in town, not sure which one. Misty thought he'd take her on a tropical vacation someday." He snorted. "Get real. He was just using her."

Gaff nodded, satisfied. "Anyone else we should know about? Someone else who might want her dead?"

Kruper blinked at the word "dead." He lowered his face in his hands. "I can't believe someone jammed scissors in her chest."

Gaff tried again. "Anyone else we should question?"

Shoulders slumped, he shook his head. "I wouldn't know. When Misty showed up that was fine. When she didn't, that was fine, too. Neither of us asked too many questions, you know?"

They were losing him. He was sinking lower and lower on the sofa. Gaff stood and thanked him for his time, laying his card on the coffee table where he might see it once he sobered up.

When they walked out the door they pulled it closed behind them and heard it lock. Then Gaff drove to the two other restaurants Misty's roommates had told them about and another bar, but they didn't learn much.

Finally Gaff dropped Jazzi at the house on Wildwood. "Thanks for going with me. People talk more when you're with me. I'll check out travel agencies around town. There aren't that many. Maybe I'll get lucky."

When she walked inside the fixer-upper the guys were finishing painting the laundry room. Everything was white, but they were installing a black granite counter over the washer and dryer and black shelves over that. She started painting the shelves, and together, they installed the counter. When they walked out of the house the first floor was finished.

Chapter 27

Wednesday was a labor of love. They decided to paint the handrail for the stairs black and repaint all the rails white. Intricate work. It would take them all day. They were all working on different parts of it when someone pounded on the front door. Not a knock. A belligerent fist on the door.

Jerod was at the bottom of the staircase and went to answer it. He yanked the door open, scowling.

A woman with brittle, white hair, bleached within an inch of its life, stared up at him. She looked to be five-four, with a pear-shaped figure. Her jeans could hardly contain her bottom. "Are you friends of Elspeth from Peru?"

Jerod crossed his arms, blocking her access to the house. "Who are you?"

"I'm Tanya Yorke, Parker's new girl. I heard you came to Peru and was asking about my man."

Ansel came to stand next to Jerod. "What if we did?"

The woman turned a shoulder and pushed between both men. The only way to stop her was to grab her and push her outside. They might eventually, but not yet. She stared up at Jazzi. "You! You're the one. I heard you came with Elspeth and was asking around about Parker and that prissy girl, Ginger. I want to make this clear: Parker's with me now. So lay off."

Jazzi raised her eyebrows, unimpressed. "How long have you known him?"

Tanya lifted her chin. "That doesn't matter, and it's none of your business."

"Just what I thought."

Tanya glared. "What does that mean?"

"You knew Parker would ditch you in a minute for Ginger. Did you kill her?"

"You've got the nerve!"

"No, *you're* the one who came to us, remember?" Ansel had heard enough. He stepped between her and Jazzi. "Do you have any information that will help us find Ginger's killer?"

"Why would I? I'm glad she's dead."

"You're a real winner. Get out. You're wasting our time."

She stared. "What are going to do? Throw me out?"

Ansel looked at Jerod. "You take one side. I'll take the other."

"Don't bother. I'm leaving, but if you're smart, you'll take my warning seriously." She stomped to her car, parked out front.

Jerod watched her speed away and gave a low whistle. "I'd say someone's a little insecure."

"I'd say if Parker settles for her, he's an idiot." Ansel shook his head. "She's staked her claim, Jaz. You'd better not go after her man."

Suddenly serious, Jerod said, "You should call Gaff and tell him about her. She's just crazy enough, she might have killed Ginger if Parker even looked at her."

Jazzi couldn't picture that. She thought Tanya was all talk, no action, but she made the call anyway. Then she joined the guys to finish the stairs.

Detail work like the spindles always made her impatient, so she was grateful when they finished them by the end of the day.

On the drive home she teased Ansel. "You don't have any old girlfriends who are going to come to yell at me for taking their man, do you?"

His blue eyes twinkled. "None that you can't handle."

Darn right. Women like that pushed too many of her buttons.

When they pulled into their drive and started toward the house, she stopped to look at his porch project. "If we order in a pizza tonight, I can help you with whatever comes next."

"Really? After a full day's work at Wildwood?"

She patted his arm. "This is our house, our project. The cats will love it when it's finished."

He reached out to hug her. "You're just being nice to me, but I'll take it. I'll order in the pizza and we can get busy."

She went inside to feed the cats while he ordered delivery for seven, then they got busy. The porch wasn't going to be attached to the house to avoid stricter building codes, so she helped him tamp gravel into the trenches he'd dug, then secure treated timbers on the gravel base. Next, they predrilled holes and nailed the corners together with long spikes.

That done, they got started on the kit Ansel had bought. They'd cut and notched the vertical posts for the horizontal framing before they had to quit for the night.

Ansel looked pleased at what they'd accomplished. "Thanks, Jaz. You've given me a great start."

"That's because I like you." She patted his fanny as she walked into the house. Hurrying upstairs, she showered and changed before the deliveryman came with their pizza and breadsticks. George almost pranced to the kitchen. He was a fan of pepperoni.

Because they ate later than usual they had less time to relax before heading to bed. But it didn't matter. They were both so tired, they fell asleep when their heads hit the pillows.

Chapter 28

A cold drizzle fell on Thursday—terrible weather for girls' night out. Olivia called to cancel before they left for work.

"I'm going to the salon today, but I'm skipping going out for supper. I'm starting to get a cold and I'm dragging. I took meds that are supposed to get rid of it, so I hope they kick in soon."

"Then I'm glad you're staying home tonight. Hope you feel better before Sunday."

"If I don't, I won't come to the family meal. I don't want to give this to anybody. None of us want to be sick at Easter." She had to stop talking to sneeze. "I'm wearing a mask at work so I don't give this to my customers."

"Have you thought about canceling for the day?"

"Can't. I'd never get everyone in before the holiday. I've called all of them and warned them, and they're all coming anyway."

Another sneeze. "Hang in there, Sis. And good luck."

"I'll need it. Hope to see you on Sunday."

Ansel frowned as Jazzi closed the call. "Your sister's sick?"

"She sounds miserable. She took one of those meds that are supposed to stop a cold if you take it soon enough, and her customers are still trooping in for cuts and colors even though she warned them."

He raised his eyebrows, surprised. "I don't think having your hair look great is worth getting sick over."

"Neither do I, but some women must."

On the way to the fixer-upper Didi called. "I can't make it tonight. I caught River's cold. It's going around at his school."

"Hope you feel better soon." Jazzi disconnected while coughs sounded on the other end. Then she called Elspeth to let her know it would only be the two of them tonight.

"Would you mind calling it off this week?" Elspeth asked. "Radley and I are leaving town tomorrow night to drive to my parents' place for the weekend. My sisters are coming, too. We're doing an early Easter and I have to make a few things to take. I was going to talk to you about missing the Sunday meal when we got together tonight."

"No problem. Have fun with your family and see you soon." This time when she disconnected Ansel was frowning.

"Did everyone cancel on you?" When she nodded he said, "You could come out with us tonight. None of the guys would mind."

She smiled as they pulled into the drive at Wildwood. "That's sweet, but I won't mind sitting a Thursday out. I can use a night to relax."

He went to grab George out of the back seat and she got the cooler. Nothing special today, just plain sandwiches and chips. On their way inside he nodded. "You might enjoy some time alone. I get it. Do you want to grab something to eat on our way home so you don't have to cook?"

She hadn't thought that far ahead. "That sounds great." It would be nice to have a to-go supper while she finally got to make cookies for Easter. Not that she was telling him that or he might want to stay home to help her. Which was nice. But so was alone time.

Jerod pulled in the drive behind their van and came to walk in with them. "Ready to paint the rooms upstairs today?"

They decided to start with the three kids' bedrooms. They were large but not huge, and they each had two windows, crown molding, and wide trim. Those always took more time. They'd be lucky if they each finished their room by the end of the day. If they did, they could work on the master bedroom and second bathroom the next day. That bath had recently been remodeled. It had a ceramic floor that looked like light wood planks, a surround tub and shower, and a new pedestal sink, but it needed some color. They'd decided to paint the walls a deep blue.

"After we paint all the rooms, we can start working on the master bath next week," Jerod told them.

That was their biggest project besides the kitchen. Painting was messy work, though. Jazzi reached for the scarf she used to cover her hair. The guys donned their hats and they all headed upstairs.

Jazzi took the bedroom in the far-right corner. The walls were lime green, not very restful. The owner had liked their idea of painting it spice—a warm, golden brown. It took her until lunch to finish three walls and she still had one wall and all the trim to go.

While they ate, Jerod told them about an estate sale Franny and her mom had gone to. "Franny bought a dozen cherry chairs that I went to pick up for her. They had three coats of paint on them. She's refinished one of them and it's beautiful."

"Did she get them at a great price?" Ansel asked.

"They were a steal. She even told the owner they were worth more, but he just wanted to get rid of them, didn't want to bother with them. Wait 'til you see how beautiful they are."

"Does she have a table to go with the chairs?" Jazzi had bought her long farm table in Shipshewana while she still lived in her apartment in West Central. It was built by the Amish and came with a lot of leaves. Back then, she used folding chairs when her family came for Sunday meals. But after Ansel moved in with her, they'd ordered a dozen matching chairs to go with it. Of course, these days they still had to use the folding chairs to seat everyone who came.

Jerod reached for another sandwich. "A few months ago she refinished a cherry dining table with three leaves. It's for a formal dining room, really dressy."

Jazzi wasn't into formal. She liked casual entertaining better. When they finished eating they trudged back upstairs to paint again, and it was a race for each of them to get done before quitting time. When they inspected one another's work, though, they were happier with the results than they'd expected.

Ansel had painted his room the same deep blue they'd chosen for the second bathroom and it looked elegant. Jerod's room was now light gray. They'd thought about powder blue, but the new owner liked gray better.

Satisfied with the results, they locked up for the night and went home. Jazzi let Ansel shower and change first because he was going to meet the guys at Chevys southwest. She fed and played with the pets until he left, and then she ate the fish dinner they'd bought at their favorite takeout place on Hillegas.

The evening stretched before her. She turned on music before getting out the ingredients to make dozens of shortbread cookies. She used an egg-shaped cookie cutter for half the dough and a bunny-shaped cutter for the other half. After she put them in the ovens she made a huge batch of sugar cookies, using a heart-shaped cutter for those. She was still decorating them when Ansel came home.

He stepped in the house and took a deep breath. "I smell sugar and spice." He came to see what she'd made. "These are so cute." Reaching for one, he paused. "Can I have a few?"

Grinning, she handed him one. "I might have enough. I thought I'd pack some for lunch tomorrow, too."

Biting into one of the shortbread cookies, he groaned. "Have I told you that I love your baking?"

"A few times."

"I don't suppose you're making any of River's favorites, are you?"

"Chocolate chip?" She rolled her eyes. "That happens to be your favorite, too."

"Not exactly Easter staples, are they?"

"In our house they are. I'll make some for the baskets."

He gave a happy sigh. "My life is good."

Laughing, she finished up and started putting her dirty dishes in the dishwasher. "How was your night out?"

He went to get her a glass of wine, then sat on a stool and reached for another cookie. "Thane and Walker were happy to get out of their houses and away from their wives for a night. They're tired of playing gofer and nursemaid."

"Already? That's what it's all about. For better or worse." She took another sip of her wine.

"When you're down and out I'll be superkind to you."

"Even if I can't bake cookies?"

"I'll bake them for you."

She leaned to bump shoulders with him. "It *is* true love. I'll remember that."

They left the cookies on the kitchen counters for the frosting to dry and went into the living room, then visited a while before watching the news and relaxing. Before calling it a night they bagged the cookies she'd freeze in the morning, then climbed the steps to bed.

They were stretched next to each other when Ansel asked, "Did Gaff call today? I thought you guys were getting closer on Misty's murder."

"Nuts! I completely forgot to tell you." She'd immersed herself in music and baking, and it had been nice not to think about murders. "Gaff's coming for me tomorrow at ten thirty. He's narrowed his search down to three travel agencies. I called Jerod to let him know I had to leave early tomorrow."

"Good. It feels like you have a trail to follow. Hope you get even closer to solving this thing." Then he turned to give her a quick kiss before they drifted off to sleep.

Chapter 29

On Friday the guys started putting shiplap on the focus wall in the master bedroom while Jazzi painted the second bathroom. They'd gotten to work earlier than usual, so she might be able to get it done before Gaff arrived at ten thirty, and she came close. She only left one side wall that wouldn't take much time for the guys to finish.

This time, with the bathroom window cracked to air out some of the paint fumes, she heard Gaff pull into the drive and ran out to meet him. She grabbed her sweater on the way. No wonder people were catching colds and having sinus problems, the way the temperatures bounced up and down in spring. But they were close to the end of March, and the days should start getting warmer and staying that way.

As they drove toward town, Gaff asked, "Are you and Ansel ready for Easter? I know you have your whole family over for holidays."

She gave a brief nod. "All the decorations are up and I finally baked the cookies I send home with people last night."

"Last night? Isn't Thursday the night you go out?"

"Usually, but Olivia and Didi are sick. What about you? Are you and Ann ready?"

He smiled. "Both boys are coming with their wives and kids. We're going to have a houseful. Ann's bought enough groceries to feed an army."

That news made Jazzi happy. Gaff and his wife loved family get-togethers as much as she and Ansel did. As they approached town, Gaff turned onto Main and parked in a small lot by a travel agency. A clay pot full of daffodils and hyacinths sat by the front door.

"I called to let the owner know we were coming," Gaff told her.

When they walked inside an older man who looked to be in his midfifties greeted them. He motioned for them to take seats at the only desk in the small office. The desk was solid cherry, the guest chairs soft leather. The space was cramped but elegant. Walnut file cabinets lined the back wall. The owner wore a white shirt unbuttoned at the collar with its sleeves rolled up. His watch probably cost more than Jazzi's pickup. "How can I help you? Did I plan a trip for whoever you're interested in?"

"We're investigating the death of Misty Morrow. We've been told she was close to a man who ran a travel agency. Did you know her?"

The man shook his head. "Her name isn't familiar to me. I plan trips for people who are very wealthy. They want to explore exotic places or have a tour plan that includes restaurants and events that are hard to get into."

"Misty wouldn't fit any of that criteria." Gaff studied the watch. "She met the man at a bar on Brooklyn Avenue."

"I didn't know there was a bar on Brooklyn, but then, I rarely visit that area."

Why would he? Most of the businesses on the street catered to the lower middle class. But then, Jazzi doubted the guy who'd met Misty there was a regular client either.

Gaff asked, "Have you heard anything about your competitors? Other travel agents?"

"I don't bother with the trips they plan. Sorry."

Gaff looked at Jazzi and shook his head before pushing to his feet. "Thanks for making time for us. We'll keep looking."

The man rose, too. "Good luck, and if I can be of any further assistance, let me know."

Before stepping through the door, Jazzi asked, "Is that your Lexus in the parking lot?"

He smiled. "She's a beauty, isn't she? My wife has one, too. Hers is red instead of white."

"It's classy."

The smile grew. "Thank you."

Jazzi followed Gaff to his car. At the second agency they visited there was a husband-and-wife team. The husband deferred to his wife so often, Jazzi couldn't see him spending time with someone like Misty. They scratched him from their list for the moment and drove to the third agency, on the north side of town.

A black BMW was parked near the back door, and when they walked into the office a man in his early thirties rose to greet them. He wore a light blue suit, expensive shoes, and an expensive watch. His sandy-colored hair was swept back from his forehead. He was stylish but not good-looking. He extended a hand for them to shake. "Hello. I'm Bartholomew Bercot. It's nice to meet you."

When Gaff asked him if he'd ever met Misty Monroe his brow furrowed, as if he was trying to remember. "Was she a client?"

Gaff explained that he'd heard she was seeing a man who was a travel agent.

Bartholomew gave a playful grin. "I don't have the time to date right now. I'm trying to get this agency up and running." He glanced at Jazzi. "Might make an exception if I met someone like you."

Sure he would, if it would benefit him in some way. She bit her bottom lip. She wasn't being fair. She didn't know anything about this man, but her gut feeling wasn't complimentary. She tried for a neutral reply. "You must work a lot of hours, managing the agency alone."

"Running any business is a big commitment, but I manage."

She guessed the man would have a glib answer for anything. "Misty liked to hang out at a bar on Brooklyn Avenue. Maybe you met her there?"

He grimaced. "Doesn't sound like a good place to make connections, at least not the right ones. Doubt if I'd interest anyone there into booking a trip."

"Probably not." But you might find someone who'd steal credit card information for you. She didn't say it, but she thought it. As far she was concerned, Gaff had found his suspect.

Gaff must have thought so, too, because he rose and handed Bartholomew one of his cards. "Thanks for your time. We'll keep looking until we find the man who knew Misty. If you think of anything, I'd appreciate it if you'd give me a call."

"Will do, and good luck." He tilted his head to the side. "I don't suppose either of you are interested in a small trip sometime soon?" When they shook their heads he walked them to the door and stood to watch them pull away.

At the next light Gaff glanced at her. "It's time I dig more into Mr. Bercot's finances. I'd say he's a candidate."

"He looked like the type who'd appeal to Misty." She watched the houses and businesses they passed on State Street as they drove south to town. "Are you having any luck with Ginger's murder?"

He shook his head. "I drove to talk to the ex-boyfriend from Peru. He's living with his parents while he takes classes on the GI Bill."

"What's he studying?"

"Plumbing. Wants to go into business for himself. Says he never wants to be part of a team again. Got enough of that in the military."

"The world needs plumbers. Lots of kids go to college. Not as many go to trade schools. He should do okay on his own."

Gaff shrugged. "Sounds more like he gets in trouble if he's expected to work well with others. When I asked him if he'd seen Ginger since he came home his parents swore that he hadn't gotten back together with her and that he was home the day she disappeared."

"But they would, wouldn't they?"

He gave a quick nod. "Still, I can't prove he was anywhere else. I can't prove he'd even met Ginger. I'm at a dead end again."

Frustrating. It felt like they kept taking one step forward, then stalling. Gaff pulled into the fixer-upper's drive, and she started to get out of the car. "Let me know if you find anything on Bercot, will you?"

"Sure thing. Hope we have more leads soon."

She watched him pull away before going into the house. The guys had already eaten lunch and all of the cookies were gone. No surprise. But so were all the sandwiches. They hadn't saved her one, must have thought she and Gaff would stop somewhere to eat. She grabbed a few chips and carried them upstairs to munch on while she inspected what they were doing.

The master bedroom now had one shiplap wall and the entire room was painted white. A black, wrought-iron fixture hung from the ceiling. The large throw rug she'd ordered sprawled across most of the wood floor, and a black, wrought-iron bed was centered on the focus wall.

Jerod crossed his arms over his chest. "Well, what do you think?"

"I like it."

"Not bad, huh? I think we're nailing this guy's taste. All we have to do is finish installing the two reading lights over the bed, then we were talking about calling it quits early. We can all hit the master bath on Monday. What do you think?"

"I never turn down leaving early on Friday."

"Then it's decided. If you clean up some of the stuff we left in the kitchen, Ansel and I will finish up in here."

She headed downstairs and had the kitchen spotless by the time they came down. They were all tugging on sweaters or hoodies when Gaff called.

"It didn't take long to find stuff on Bercot. He has a lot of complaints filed against him at the Better Business Bureau. People find extra charges on their bills for side trips they didn't take, and a few of them have had trouble with their credit cards after traveling overseas. He tells them that these things can happen in other countries."

"But no one can prove anything?" she asked.

"Not yet, but it sure looks like the guy likes to dabble with other peoples' money."

"He's a contender."

"He's at the top of my list. Thought you'd like to know."

"Thanks, Gaff. Have a good weekend."

"You too."

When she ended her call she shared what Gaff had told her, and Jerod shook his head. "Now Gaff needs to find out what Bercot was doing on the day Misty was killed."

"Easier said than done." But on the drive home Jazzi couldn't stop thinking about how flashy Bercot was. She finally picked up her cell phone and called her sister. "Gaff and I have found a guy who looks really suspicious. He drives a black BMW. You haven't heard anyone say they saw one on the day Misty died, have you?"

She was answered with a sneeze. "Sorry. No one's said anything, but I'll ask around again. It's been a while, and people remember BMWs."

"Thanks, Sis, and I hope you're better soon."

"Me too. You know, there's a coffee shop across the street from the salon that opens early. Maybe I'll ask there. The cops questioned people, but the clerks work odd shifts. It wouldn't hurt to try again."

"Good idea. Hope you get lucky."

Another sneeze. "I gotta go. The more I talk, the more I sneeze."

Jazzi pressed her lips together as she closed the call. "I wouldn't count on Olivia on Sunday."

"She's even worse?"

"Sneezes every time she talks very much."

Ansel chuckled. "Bet that doesn't slow her down too much. Your sister isn't the quiet type."

He had a point. They were on Lima Road, coming up to lots of food places. "How do tacos sound for supper tonight? I didn't get any lunch today and I'm hungry."

"Gaff didn't stop anywhere?"

"He had to get back to the station. No time."

"Then tacos sound delicious. I love Mexican." He made his way into the right lane to pull into the drive-through for one of their favorite takeouts. George lifted his head when Ansel pulled the full bags into the van. He sniffed the air, his stub tail wagging. He knew there was a taco in there for him. Ansel always scooped the meat out of the shell to put on a paper plate for him.

She could hardly keep from diving into the bag on the short trip home. Fasting wouldn't work for her. Once Ansel had parked the van in the garage, she grabbed the food bag and hurried into the house. Ansel brought the cooler and George.

The cats wound around her ankles so she took enough time to feed them, then grabbed three paper plates, planted herself at the kitchen island, and was ready to dig in.

"You *are* starving." Ansel grabbed beer and wine for them and then sat down beside her. The eating began.

Chapter 30

It felt odd not to rush on Saturday morning. Jazzi and Ansel didn't need to help Radley and Elspeth; they were completely moved in. They could fall back into their usual Saturday routine . . . with one difference. Ansel shooed the pets out of their bedroom and said, "Later."

George gave him a sad look. Inky yowled, then slunk downstairs. As he shut the door, Marmalade stretched in the hallway. She knew no one was going to fill her cat bowl for a while and she was okay with that.

After they showered and dressed Jazzi went to feed the pets and Ansel started pumpernickel toast. She glanced at the bouquet by the sink and raised an eyebrow at Inky. Thank goodness, every Saturday she tossed the bouquet in the heavy ceramic crock to make way for a new one. Most of the flowers were scattered across the stainless-steel countertop.

She pointed a finger at him. "Really?"

The cat ate his last morsel of food and licked his paw, staring at her with no shame.

"There are things that have higher priority in my life than feeding you the second I wake up," she scolded.

He came to weave around her ankles, purring. Her black cat was not only naughty, he was manipulative. She laughed and bent to stroke his smooth fur.

They'd set the timer on the coffeepot so Ansel filled two mugs and carried them to the kitchen island. "The house is in good shape," he told her between sips. "Want to go to the grocery store early so we can cook whatever you have planned for tomorrow and rent a movie after supper?"

"Sounds good to me." She bit into her toast. Ansel had spread it with a thick layer of cherry preserves—her favorite.

"What do you have planned for the meal?"

"Two big pots of gumbo and corn bread. Didi's bringing a Greek salad, but I'll have to make a dessert because Elspeth won't be here."

"We haven't had a coconut cake for a long time, and it sort of goes with Easter."

She grinned. "The kids won't eat coconut, but I'll make them some cupcakes without any."

"Perfect. I'll help." He always did. They enjoyed cooking together. "We have the ham and prime rib ordered for Easter, right?"

"We can pick them up on Good Friday."

Satisfied, he brought her the grocery list she kept under a magnet on the fridge. "Do you have everything we need on it?"

"Everything but the ingredients for the coconut cake." She scribbled a few more items at the bottom of the list, then helped him clean the kitchen. When she grabbed her purse Inky ran to the door, meowing.

Ansel laughed. "He wants us to hurry and get home so he'll have grocery bags to play in."

George lifted his head but saw the list and lowered it again. These days, he liked his doggy bed better than sitting in the car.

The store was busier than usual, and Jazzi was glad they'd come early. People were beginning to stock up for things for Easter. While Ansel grabbed chicken breasts, sausage, and shrimp for the gumbo, he watched her throw in boneless, skinless chicken thighs, ground chuck, a pork tenderloin, a bag of tilapia, and a flat-iron steak. "For suppers this week?"

She nodded. She always planned a menu for every night of the week. That way she knew she had all the ingredients she needed for their meals. "Orange chicken with rice one night, hamburgers another, pork stir-fry, sautéed tilapia, and flat-iron steak fajitas. Sound okay?"

He grinned, happy with her choices, but then, she planned the menus around what he liked. What was the point of cooking something he didn't want to eat?

They had to stand in line to pay at the checkout, but the line moved fast. At home, they were putting groceries away, and the cats were running in and out of brown grocery bags, when Chad called.

"Can we meet somewhere to talk? My family's great, but I've seen enough of them for a while."

She glanced at Ansel, and when he gave a quick nod, said, "When and where?"

"I'm at the coffee shop now. I just had to get out of the house for a while."

Ansel gave another nod, and she said, "I'm on my way."

It was a short drive before she pulled in the lot, and when she walked in the shop and saw Chad she was glad she'd come. Dark circles rimmed his eyes, his shoulders slumped, and his misery permeated every pore of his body.

She slid into the booth across from him. "You're looking pretty bad."

"I've been better." He rubbed his eyes. "I moved back into our place, but it's too empty without Ginger. Everywhere I look, there's something that makes me think of her. I'm thinking of selling it and finding an apartment."

The waitress came for her order. After she left Jazzi said, "I've heard it's common for people to sell their homes when they lose a loved one, but experts say it's better to wait until your emotions are calmer and you can think more objectively."

"Easy for them to say. They don't almost lose it every time they glance at her chair or use one of her favorite dishes. They don't have to lie next to her empty half of the bed."

Jazzi couldn't imagine how that must feel. She hoped she'd never have to experience it.

"On top of it all, the cops are questioning everyone I've ever met, and it's making me feel like I'm under attack. I mean, losing her is bad enough. I'm having trouble dealing with that. But people who don't know me very well are looking at me like I'm a murderer. It feels creepy."

Her coffee came and she took a sip. "People who *do* know you know better."

"I hope so, but who could blame them if they had doubts? Look at how many husbands swear they loved their wives and want them back, and a month later they're under arrest for killing them."

That was true. It was on the news a lot. "Gaff's looking into it. It's taking time to sort through things, but he'll find out who killed her."

"Look, even good cops can't make miracles happen. No one could find any evidence. What if nothing ever shows up and I'm under suspicion forever?"

Jazzi thought of Damian, in their last case, who was suspected of killing Jessica. There wasn't enough evidence to prove him guilty, but the detective couldn't prove him innocent either. It was horrible. She let out a long sigh. "I feel really sorry for you, Chad."

He reached across the table and patted her hand. "I can't tell you how much it means to me that you believe in me. I don't deserve it, but it's nice to have you in my corner."

She took his hand and squeezed it. "It's nice to be friends again. We ended things pretty badly."

He finished his coffee and reached for his billfold. "I know it's cowardly, but I'm going to rent a cheap apartment for a couple of months. I need time to deal with everything. My family's great, but I've lived on my own too long to move back with them. And the house is too depressing."

"I get it. Are you going to be all right?"

"Yeah. You called it right when you said I'd feel like crap for a year and maybe start healing the year after that. But I'll get there. I don't think I'll ever be able to get married again, though. I never want to repeat this. It's too hard."

He paid both of their bills and they walked to their vehicles together. On the drive home Jazzi hoped moving into an apartment would help him. He thought he'd never marry again, but he was still young. If he met the right girl, in time he might feel differently. Then she thought about how lucky she and her family had been. The only person who'd lost a spouse was Gran, and she'd been lonely without Gramps underfoot. When Samantha's husband died she couldn't keep up the big property they'd had. When she moved into Gran's house it had been good for both of them.

Once Jazzi got home she saw that Ansel had been busy while she was gone. He'd started fitting the horizonal cross members into the vertical posts of the porch frame. Her Viking did beautiful work. That part of the frame was solid and secure. She walked in the house and went straight to hug him. Crushed against his strong chest, she said, "You aren't allowed to die."

He chuckled. "I'm not sure I can keep that promise, but I'll try to stick around as long as I can."

She pulled away to look up at him. "Chad's going to rent an apartment. He said it's too depressing staying in his house, where everything reminds him of Ginger."

Ansel bent to kiss the top of her head. "This house wouldn't be the same without you."

"Then I'll try to stick around, too."

"Good, because I'm getting hungry. What did you say was on the menu for tonight?"

The man was obsessed with food. "Delivery pizza, then we can start cooking the gumbo for tomorrow."

"Works for me. George wants pepperoni."

"I want a supreme. We can pick off pepperoni for him."

"I'll call it in." When he was done he carried a glass of wine to the island for her and a beer for him. "After tomorrow there's only one week until Easter. Are we ready?"

"I still have to make a lot of candy for the gift baskets. What about you? You put in some horizonal pieces for the porch. After those it's mostly assembly, isn't it?"

He nodded. "If I worked a little on it every night, I could get it done by Easter. We might have to do our separate things. You make candy while I put up screens and a canvas top."

"We can survive doing our own thing for a week."

"Yeah, but I don't want to make a habit of it. I like working with you."

Her cell phone buzzed and she reached for it. Olivia. She pressed Speaker. Her sister's voice was scratchy. "After the salon closed today I drove across the street to the coffee shop and talked to the people behind the counter. A young girl who works the early shift during the week said that a man who drove a black BMW stopped in with his girlfriend the morning Misty died. When I asked what the girl looked like she described Misty. She remembered because she watched them leave the coffee shop and drive right across the street to the salon. The man had taken the lid off his to-go cup to let his coffee cool and spilled it on himself when he was getting out of the car. He gestured like he was mad, trying to wipe off his cashmere coat."

Cashmere. Bartholomew only liked the best. "I'm going to call Gaff to let him know what you found out."

"Good. Hope it helps." Olivia started coughing. "Gotta go."

"Olivia found something?" When Jazzi explained Ansel nodded. "That's gotta help Gaff. Give him a call."

When she finished sharing the news Gaff said, "Good. Let's go talk to the girl."

"Now? It's Saturday, your day off."

"Is she still at the coffee shop?"

"Olivia thought she worked the evening shift tonight."

"Perfect. Want to meet there? It'll be easier."

She was about to argue when Ansel nodded his head. "Go. If this cracks the case, it's worth it."

Because he put it that way . . . "Sure. Give me half an hour. It's on the south side of town." When she hung up she pursed her lips in a pout. "When will the pizza get here?"

"Not soon enough. We'll order another one when you get back."

She looked at the movie they'd rented and sighed.

Smiling, Ansel hugged her. "We can stay up late tonight. Once we make the gumbo there's not a lot we have to do for tomorrow's meal."

"The coconut cake."

That hit home. He frowned. "We'll make that late, too. Then we'll watch the movie."

Not her idea of a relaxing Saturday night, but she'd rather cook late this evening than wake up early to hurry to get things done. She leaned to kiss Ansel before she grabbed her sweater and purse. "Enjoy the pizza."

"I'm eating it in the living room while I watch a game on TV."

She grimaced. He and the pets would enjoy themselves without her. But enough feeling sorry for herself. She started to her pickup.

Chapter 31

Only two customers sat at a table in the corner of the coffee shop. Assortments of donuts lined the back wall. Jazzi spotted a row of them filled with Bavarian cream. Her stomach rumbled. She meant to buy a few before she left for breakfast the next morning. She and Gaff sat on stools at the long counter. The young waitress came to take their orders, and Gaff showed her his badge.

"You came to ask me about the BMW guy," she said. "Olivia promised me a free haircut if I talked to you."

Nice. Her sister must really want to put Misty behind her. It wasn't like she was a prime suspect anymore.

Gaff took out his pen and notepad. "What can you tell me?"

The girl repeated what she'd told Olivia.

"Can you describe this guy?" Gaff asked.

"Sandy hair slicked back. Full of himself. Looked like he just walked out of *GQ*."

Gaff nodded. "Did you see him leave the salon and notice when?"

She shook her head. "We got busy. All I did was pour coffee and sell donuts." The girl glanced at Jazzi. "Looked like you might want a few. Am I right?"

"Two Bavarian creams and two bear claws." Ansel loved those.

The girl brought them and rang up her order, then returned her attention to Gaff. "Is there anything else you remember?" he asked.

"He wore a big, fancy watch and cuff links shaped like dollar signs."

"I noticed those, too, when we saw him," Jazzi said. "They made a statement."

"Anything else?" Gaff persisted.

"Nah, that's it. I hope it helps."

"It did. It was just what we needed," Jazzi told her.

"I would have helped even if your sister didn't offer me a free haircut. If that guy killed that woman, he should be locked away, off the streets."

Gaff handed her one of his cards. "We're working on that. Thank you. If you think of anything else, give me a call."

The girl stuffed his card in her uniform pocket. "Good luck," she called as they walked out the door.

Gaff wore a wolfish grin as he slid into his car. "It's time for me to bring Mr. Bercot in for questioning."

"Do you want me there?"

He shook his head. "No, this interview will be official. You might as well go home and enjoy what's left of your Saturday night."

He couldn't have said anything that made her happier. She jumped in her pickup and headed home. On her way she called and ordered another pizza to pick up, and even though Ansel and George had already eaten theirs, he sat with her at the kitchen island while she demolished her chicken club.

"I thought you wanted a supreme," he said, watching her.

She raised an eyebrow. "Would you have been happy with one of those?" When he grimaced she gave a knowing nod. "That's why. When we share a pizza I think of one with lots of meat."

"We could order a medium pizza for each of us."

"Won't work. I can't eat an entire medium and you'd still be hungry after you finished yours." She was right and he knew it.

"So, how did it go with the girl at the coffee shop?"

When she told him, he looked happy. "Sounds like maybe you can forget Misty's case. It's solved."

"Fingers crossed." She finished her pizza and threw the container in the trash. "Ready to start cooking for tomorrow?"

Working together, they made quick work of the gumbo. The coconut cake was another matter. There was no way to rush baking. After they sprinkled the last of the toasted coconut on top of the frosted cake, they cleaned the kitchen and turned out the lights.

They'd settled in the living room to watch their movie when Gaff called. "Bercot kept his cool until we brought out one piece of evidence after another. When the techs went through his car and found a bloody fingerprint that was probably his, he finally lost it. He yelled that he was teaching Misty the racket, then found out she was skimming from him. They fought, and he lost his temper and stabbed her with the first thing he could grab—your sister's scissors. He thought he'd wiped all the blood off his hands, but he was in a hurry and must have missed one of his fingers."

Jazzi let out a relieved sigh. "Can I call Olivia to let her know?"

"She should hear it from you before it hits the news. And thanks for your help again," Gaff told her.

"Ditto. Thanks for *your* help, too." Before she recounted the details for Ansel, she called Olivia. "Good news."

Her sister sounded as happy as she could between sneezes and coughs. "All I'm going to do tomorrow is sleep."

"A sound plan, and now you can rest easy."

When she finally finished her calls she told Ansel everything Gaff had said. "Now all we have to worry about is finding Ginger's killer."

He gave her a pained look. "Bercot killed Misty in a fit of temper. It happens, you know."

She shook her head. "That's not what happened with Chad and Ginger."

He didn't argue with her, just looked doubtful. "We'll leave it at that. For now, let's watch our movie and relax."

They'd rented a mystery that was clever and fun. Jazzi got so involved in it that her mind didn't drift once to thinking about Chad's case. When they went to bed she was in a good mood and fell asleep quickly.

She woke refreshed. They didn't have to rush on Sunday morning and had extra time to sip their coffee and read the papers. Ansel had ordered the Sunday *New York Times* and enjoyed reading through most of it before the family meal.

"Stay and enjoy yourself," Jazzi told him when she started to the kitchen. "It's easy this morning." She put the pots of gumbo on the stove to heat up and made three pans of corn bread. Jerod loved the stuff and could wipe out most of a pan himself.

When she told her family that Gaff had found Misty's killer it lifted everyone's spirits. Walker and River had come without Didi and the baby, and Thane had come by himself. Over their meal, Walker told them that his cement company had a big, new parking lot to pave, and that since he'd started running the business again, they had so much work, he was thinking about hiring another driver. He'd already replaced Colin. Thane said his company was swamped with work, too. All good news.

No one stayed as long as usual. "Next Sunday's Easter," Jazzi's mom said. "We always stay longer then. We'll give you a break today."

As everyone filed out the door to their cars, Gran lingered behind. When only she and Samantha remained, Gran laid a hand on Jazzi's arm. "Your ex is going to need you this week. It's not his shoe. He's telling the truth."

Jazzi blinked, trying to make sense of the vision.

Gran patted her reassuringly and turned to walk to the car with Samantha. "Don't fret about it. Just believe him."

And then she and Ansel were alone. Jazzi had to admit it was nice to have the house empty early. "What do you think Gran meant?" she asked as she followed Ansel to the kitchen to clean everything up.

He shrugged. "Your gran's messages are mysterious, but you'll know when it happens." They made quick work of filling the dishwasher and putting things away, then grabbed more to drink and settled in the living room to bum around for the rest of the day. George scooted closer to Ansel's leg as they stretched out on the couch.

Inky and Marmalade pressed against her as she propped a pillow behind her head to read. Grimacing, she shook her head. They'd rented a mystery to watch last night and she was reading a historical mystery today. But fictional murders were a lot more entertaining than real ones, so it was okay. She started a new chapter to enjoy.

Chapter 32

On Monday Jazzi, Ansel, and Jerod tackled the master bathroom upstairs. In its own way it was going to be as big a challenge as renovating the kitchen. The owner wanted the ceiling and walls to be white, with a built-in shower in the center of the room. The center. Not tucked into a corner or on a far wall. They'd surround it with three walls covered with beadboard on the outside and tiles inside, then they'd paint the beadboard black. A sink would be on the wall opposite a shower head on the inside. It had taken serious measuring to make everything fit. The toilet would be on the far wall, facing the sink.

"First we gut it, then we have to start with the floor, right?" Jazzi glanced at the charcoal, square ceramic tiles they'd chosen to lay.

Jerod nodded, starting toward the old vanity. "I've already turned off the water to everything in here. Now we just have to rip and pitch."

Jazzi yanked the Formica top from the sink and carried it downstairs to throw in the dumpster. The guys followed with the vanity. She and Ansel disconnected the toilet and carried it down, then the two guys took the heavy, soaker tub. They kept at it until the room was empty. Then they strapped on their knee pads and got started on the tiles.

As they all worked in a row, on hands and knees, Jerod said, "If we can get this done in three days, we can do the widow's walk on Thursday and the balcony railing on Good Friday, then give the owner his keys. If it takes longer, we'll have to come back to do the outside jobs."

"Then what?" Ansel asked. "Do you want to take a few days off before we start another job?"

"What other job?" Jazzi reached for another tile to lay in place. "We haven't bought the next fixer-upper yet."

Jerod sat up to straighten his back. "I've been looking. Haven't seen anything. In this market it's hard to find something at a good price."

Ansel sat up on his knees, too, to reach for a picture in his back pocket. "I have an idea, but neither of you might like it."

"Show us what you've got." Jerod scooted closer to see.

When Ansel opened the page Jazzi gasped. She'd never seen a more hideous house. It was painted a bright leaf green, and it had an ugly brown roof that sagged in places. The front window looked like she could kick in its frame. "Are you serious?"

"It's right on the front corner of a short street that leads to an expensive subdivision out north. Once you pass it you're surrounded by half-million-dollar homes."

Jerod grinned. "So everyone hates it because it's an eyesore and it's so small."

"That's the beauty of it. You can't tell by this picture, but it has bedrooms built on to the back in an L-shape. I say we lift the entire roofline and make it a two-story, and we'd have plenty of room."

Jazzi narrowed her eyes, trying to picture it. "That could work. Did you drive by the place?"

"A while ago when we had a guys' night out. I looked it up on the Internet."

Jerod pointed to the asking price. "If we did this right, we could make a lot of money."

Ansel leaned back, looking proud of himself.

Jerod reached for the paper. "Want me to call to set up a walk-through?" When Jazzi and Ansel both nodded he said, "Then it's done." He took out his cell and punched in the numbers. After a minute he turned his head to say, "We can look at it tonight when we leave here if we want to."

"Let's do it. We can stay over tomorrow if we need to make up the time." Ansel looked at Jazzi for her opinion.

"Works for me."

Jerod finished the call and said, "The Realtor will meet us there at four. We can see how bad this house really is."

Ansel hummed as they started work again. They had half the room tiled before it was time for lunch. Once downstairs, Jerod went to peek in the cooler. "What did you bring for sandwiches today?"

"Tuna salad. I made it this morning. Kept it separate so it wouldn't make the bread soggy."

Both men smiled, but George came to sniff the air when they took off the lid and returned to his dog bed to pout. He wasn't a tuna fan. She'd brought him a slice of deli meat.

Jerod put a pile of chips on his paper plate to have with his sandwich, then turned thoughtful. "I'm glad Gaff caught Misty's killer and that's done, but I keep thinking about Chad. Have you heard anything?"

Her cousin was the best. He'd despised Chad for a long time and now he felt sorry for him. He had a loud bark but a big heart. She told him about meeting Chad at the coffee shop.

"Man, I feel for him. If anything happened to Franny, I'd have to sell our place, too. I couldn't stand looking at things that reminded me of her."

"You don't think that in a couple of years, you could look at those same things and have them bring back good memories?" Jazzi went to the cooler and came back with a bag of cookies, and both men reached for them.

Jerod shook his head. "I know Gran stayed in her house when Gramps passed, but it would take me too long to move past being miserable if I stayed put."

Ansel nabbed another cookie. "We designed everything in our house together. In my mind, you're such a big part of our cottage, Jaz, it would feel like the heart of our home was torn out of it."

"That's what he says now," Jerod teased. "Just wait till a flock of babes offer to spend the night there to comfort him."

Jazzi laughed, but Ansel sent her cousin a glare. "Not funny."

Jerod finished the last cookie, and they trudged back upstairs. They'd finished the floor and marked measurements in red tape before four rolled around. Then they took separate vehicles to drive north.

The temperature had risen again, the snow melted, and everything was even greener than it was before. The house looked even worse than it did in the picture. The yard had more weeds than grass. The first thing they'd have to do was treat the grass and hope it would fill in where the weeds died. When the Realtor walked them through the inside it was a mess. The wiring was illegal. It was so bad, they'd have to hire an electrician to make it right. The plumbing needed work, but it was minimal. Jerod and Ansel could do it themselves. The foundation was solid, but someone had used as few two-by-fours as possible to hang drywall. It rippled in spots. They'd have to gut it and add new ones.

The bedrooms added to the back of the house had been done right. There was only one small bathroom, but that was all right. If they added a second story, they'd add two more up there.

"What do you think?" Jerod asked when they finished the tour.

"I'm in. What about you, babe?" Ansel asked.

"We've never done anything like this before. Let's see if we're up to it."

Jerod offered less money than the asking price. The Realtor didn't seem surprised. "I'll have to talk to the seller and get back to you."

The offer made, they left and started for their homes. Gaff called on the way.

"The autopsy on Ginger came back and she *was* pregnant, not that I doubted Gran. I just needed it confirmed. When I told Chad, he broke down, said he'd blamed Ginger for something that was his fault. The thought never occurred to him that *he* might be sterile. At least that's what he says. I'm not so sure. Everything's pointing toward the scenario that he noticed she was pregnant, knew the baby wasn't his, lost it, and strangled her. I know that's not what you want to hear, though, so I want to be thorough. My team already talked to Ginger's coworkers at the factory, but I'd like to see them again tomorrow morning. Want to go with me?"

"Yes." Chad didn't kill her. She was sure of that.

"See you at ten." And he closed the call. That used to feel abrupt to her, but she'd gotten used to it. Detectives led busy lives.

When she returned her phone to her pocket Ansel's good mood had vanished. So had hers. He ran a hand through his blond hair, clearly upset. "She was having an affair. That's adding insult to injury," he told her. "Why don't you give Chad a call and check on him?"

She tried, but he didn't pick up. He didn't pick up later when they pulled into their drive. Spending time in the kitchen didn't appeal to her. It usually lifted her mood, but she was so distracted, she'd probably burn whatever she made tonight. Instead they threw Italian sausages on the grill along with peppers and onions and made Italian sausage hoagies. Then she helped Ansel finish installing the horizonal cross members for the porch.

She tried to reach Chad a few more times, but he wasn't answering his phone. She couldn't blame him. He probably wasn't in the mood to talk. Finally Ansel was worried about him enough that they got in the pickup, put George in the back, and drove past Chad's house. He wasn't home.

"Good, maybe he's with his family," Jazzi said.

"I hope so. A guy shouldn't have to be alone when he hears something like that." Ansel turned the pickup toward home.

They went to bed earlier than usual, neither of them able to relax enough to enjoy TV or reading. It was two in the morning when Jazzi's cell phone buzzed.

Chapter 33

"Jashi?" The voice was blurred.

"Chad?" She instantly awoke.

"The bartender took my keys. He won't give them back."

"Where are you?"

A clunk came on the other end. Chad must have dropped his phone. Another voice said, "Your friend's plastered. He's at my bar on Clinton Street, close to Glenbrook." He told her its name.

"I know where that is. I'm getting dressed and I'll come for him."

"Bring a barf bag or your car will need to be cleaned."

Ansel dressed and drove with her. "You might need help getting him on his feet and in the back seat."

When they walked in the bar together the bartender pointed to Chad, passed out, sound asleep, slumped over a corner table. "He hasn't paid his tab. Twenty-five bucks."

Jazzi added ten more as a tip. The guy had gone to extra effort. "Thanks for calling us."

"Are you kidding? I want Mr. Doom and Gloom out of here."

Ansel took one side and Jazzi took the other, and they woke Chad enough to half drag him to their pickup to drive him home. He leaned on their shoulders, sobbing.

"My Ginger was going to have a baby. A baby. Did you hear?"

"Gaff told us." Jazzi reached to keep him from leaning too far forward. He was awkward enough to carry now.

Tears wet his cheeks. "Washn't mine. I got nothin.' Shootin' blanks. Blamed her." He raised his hands to wipe at his eyes, and Jazzi almost dropped her side of him.

"Hang on to me," she warned.

He wrapped his arm around her shoulder. "You're sho nice. Know what? I'm an idiot."

"You've had too much to drink." Ansel grabbed under his arm to keep him standing while he opened the pickup's door.

"Not shtaying in my houshe," he told them. He searched in his jeans pocket and pulled out a key. "Hotel down the road."

"What's the name of it?" Ansel jammed Chad into the back seat.

Chad reached up and wrapped his arms around his shoulders. "You're a good hushband, the best. Glad Jashi got you."

Ansel struggled to pull free. "It's mutual. She's the best, too." He slid behind the steering wheel and pulled onto Clinton, driving north. "Where to?"

Chad chuckled. "It hash a red roof. Alwaysh keeps the light on for me."

Ansel gave Jazzi a look and they headed there. Chad fell asleep again on the way. It took both of them to get him inside the building, on the elevator, and into his room. Jazzi turned down the blankets and Ansel lowered Chad onto the bed. They took off his shoes and belt, pulled a blanket over him, and left him to sleep it off.

"Do you think he'll be all right?" she asked on the drive home.

"He's going to miss work tomorrow," Ansel told her. "He's going to be out for a while, and his head's going to feel like an explosion went off inside it when he wakes up. Did you see the inch of whiskey left in his glass? At twenty-five bucks, he had a few of them."

"He didn't drink that much when we were together."

Ansel's lips pressed in a tight line. "He wasn't trying to drown his problems back then. Finding out Ginger was pregnant probably pushed him over the edge."

They crawled back in bed when they returned home, but Jazzi slept fitfully. Rescuing Chad combined with Gran's vision to make strange dreams. When the alarm clock went off she was happy to put the night behind her.

Chapter 34

Jazzi and Ansel were dragging before they even reached the fixer-upper, and there was plenty of work still to do. On top of that, Gaff was coming to pick her up at ten. They got busy right away and had the three walls framed for the shower before Gaff pulled in the driveway and honked the car's horn.

"We'll put up the blueboard for the shower while you're gone," Jerod said. "Might even get the drywall up for the beadboard if we're lucky." Blueboard was water resistant and perfect when installing tile.

Gaff honked again, and Jazzi ran down to join him. She finished tugging her lightweight sweater in place as he pulled out of the drive. "You must be in a hurry."

"I was called to another homicide this morning. Put me behind." The drive to the airport went quickly, and soon Gaff was pulling into the factory's parking lot. "Ginger's friend is going to meet us in the cafeteria. I talked to her foreman, so it's all okayed."

The cafeteria had durable but worn flooring. The tables and chairs had seen better days. Vending machines lined one wall. There was no kitchen, so workers either packed their own lunches or bought food from them.

She and Gaff settled at a table, and in a few minutes a medium-height woman with graying hair, generous hips and thighs, and black-rimmed glasses stepped into the room. Gaff smiled and motioned for her to have a seat. "I'm Detective Gaff and this is my consultant, Jazzi Herstad."

Her married name. At work everyone still called her Jazzi Zanders.

The woman gave a nervous smile. "I'm Marcia Anderson. I worked with Ginger." She studied Jazzi's jeans and denim shirt. "What kind of work do you do?"

"My husband, cousin, and I flip houses."

Marcia's eyebrows rose. "You don't just do the decorating and pretty stuff?"

"Nope, all three of us do it all. I swing a hammer more often than I shop."

"Good for you." She returned her attention to Gaff. "Have you found anything new? We all feel awful about what happened to Ginger. She was such a sweet girl."

Gaff hesitated, then decided to be forthcoming. "She was pregnant when she died."

Marcia's hand flew her to lips. "No, she and Chad had been trying for a long time. They couldn't have a child."

"Obviously Ginger could." Gaff concentrated on her reaction.

"I just don't believe it. Ginger loved Chad, not that he deserved it. She wouldn't cheat on him."

"Why do you say he didn't deserve it?" Jazzi asked.

"Why wouldn't I?" Marcia's brown eyes glittered with temper. "He was horrible to her. Made her feel like a cheap floozy. The girl didn't have much self-confidence to begin with, but once he heard about her abortion, he annihilated any self-esteem she had. Kept asking her how it felt to murder babies."

Jazzi's jaw dropped. "He said that to her?"

"Over and over again. Told her how selfish she was to only think about herself and not the fetus."

A cold knot formed in Jazzi's stomach. Chad had told her he hadn't been nice to Ginger when she couldn't have a baby, but "not being nice" was putting it mildly. No wonder he felt so guilty, so ashamed of himself. His comments had been downright cruel.

"No one liked him here," Marcia said. "He was good enough to Ginger at first but never did anything to support her or make her feel special, wouldn't even come to the company picnics. Then, when she couldn't have his baby, he turned into a complete jerk. It wouldn't surprise anyone here if he lost his temper and killed her."

A sobering thought. Jazzi was having trouble sorting through the new information. "I thought Chad and Ginger were doing better lately, that they'd worked things out."

Marcia snorted. "For the minute. As soon as he thought she might leave him, he changed his tune. Decided to forgive and forget. Not that she needed his forgiveness. He wasn't around when she was alone, broke, and pregnant. I'm glad they patched things up for a minute, though. She got really scared when someone told her Chad had driven to Peru to ask around about her."

Gaff scribbled in his notebook. "When did that happen?"

"About a week before she disappeared, but nothing seemed to come of it. Chad treated her real good that last week."

Was that a good thing? She couldn't decide. Maybe he was buying himself time to find out more. Jazzi shook her head. Now she was beginning to doubt him.

"And she never mentioned someone new?" Jazzi asked.

Marcia shook her head. "I can tell you this: She was acting nervous and not herself a few weeks before she disappeared, and I asked her if she was all right, but she wouldn't confide in me. I know something was wrong, though."

"Do you know if she had someone she *would* confide in?" Chad had told Jazzi the same thing, that Ginger was acting different the last few weeks before she was murdered.

"You might ask the girl who lived down the street from her when she was growing up. They were still close."

Gaff poised his pen. "Did Ginger happen to mention a name?"

Marcia shook her head again. "If she did, I don't remember it."

Gaff thanked her for her time, and as he and Jazzi walked to his car, he said, "I'd like to follow up on what Marcia told us. Do you have time to drive to Peru with me tomorrow to ask around town to see if anyone saw Chad's truck there before Ginger died? Maybe track down this old friend?"

"Sure, Jerod, Ansel, and I will make it work. Do you have a picture of Chad's truck?"

Gaff rolled his eyes. "I'm a detective. I'm prepared."

Jazzi grinned. "Just checking."

She was restless on the drive to Wildwood. Marcia's description of Chad had brought back old memories of how sarcastic he'd been when they broke off their engagement. He could say mean things when he wanted to.

When Gaff dropped her off he turned to study her a minute. "This case is getting pretty close. If it's bothering you too much, you can sit this one out, but people really do open up more when you're with me."

She shook her head. "I want to know what happened, one way or another."

"If you change your mind, I'll understand." He stayed to watch her until she went in the house before pulling away.

The guys came to meet her, took one look at her face, then Ansel opened his arms to hug her. She stepped into his embrace.

"How bad was it?" Jerod asked.

Jazzi told them everything, not sparing how Chad had treated Ginger. Jerod rubbed his forehead, frustrated. "Your ex hasn't changed that much. He can still be a royal dirtbag."

"I didn't know he could get so mean." Ansel pressed her closer. "And he treated you like that when you moved out? He goes for the jugular when he's mad."

Jazzi shook her head. "He wasn't as bad to me. First, he didn't have anything much to taunt me with. And second, I'm not Ginger. He'd have been sorry if he tried."

"A word of warning," Jerod told Ansel. "She means it. If you ever want to kick her to the curb, be nice about it, or you'll regret it."

"No worries. It'll never happen. But I feel sorry for Ginger."

"That doesn't mean he killed her." Jazzi let out a long sigh. "And somehow they worked out their differences. Ginger must have forgiven him and they moved on."

"She's more forgiving than my Franny. I'd have to grovel for months if I ticked her off enough."

"Ginger's coworker said that she didn't have much self-esteem. Chad swore he felt horrible for hurting her feelings, and that might have gone a long way with her."

"Hearing it all must have upset you. If you want to go home for the day, we'd understand." Jerod motioned toward the stairs. "We got the shower walls finished, inside and out, and the shower's installed. We made good progress."

Jazzi reached for her tool belt. "I'd rather work. I don't want to sit around, thinking about things."

"Have you eaten?" Ansel asked.

"I forgot." That never happened. She had a healthy appetite for a girl.

He took her shoulders and turned her toward the kitchen. "First food, then you can come up to help us. You can carry your sandwich up to munch on while we work."

She grabbed a ham and cheese out of the cooler, then followed them upstairs. She hurried through the food in a few minutes, then grabbed a roller and tugged her scarf over her hair. The guys painted the ceiling and walls white while she painted the beadboard black. They stayed half an hour later than usual to finish. When they stood back and looked at it they were amazed. They'd never done anything this dramatic before, and it was a showstopper.

Jerod was pleased. "We should be able to finish the room tomorrow, even if you miss most of the day going with Gaff. Ansel and I can install the tub, the toilet, and the sink ourselves. If you have time, two lights and a mirror need to be installed over the sink, and you bought a rug for in here."

"I'll try to get those done before I leave."

They locked up and walked to their vehicles together. So far, even with the interruptions of her leaving with Gaff, they were keeping on schedule.

"Take care of yourself tonight," Jerod called as he climbed in his pickup.

"What are you doing when you get home?" she asked.

"Gunther, Lizzie, and I are going to rototill the garden and get it ready to plant. They like helping me outside. I'm going to let them plant a row of spinach. It's early, but it might make it."

It might. Spinach liked cooler temperatures. So did some of the leaf lettuces.

"Have fun." Ansel slid behind the wheel of the van. "Maybe we should plant a garden."

She gave him a look. "Next year. This year we'll be lucky if we finish the screened-in porch, tear down our old garage, and build the new one with the breezeway to the kitchen."

He chuckled. "I guess you're right. We got a little ambitious again, didn't we?"

"But this should be the last time," she told him. "Any more projects and we're buying a new house."

He sobered at that thought. "I got the message loud and clear, but you're going to like these when they're done as much as I will."

He was right about that, or she'd have vetoed them. They each had equal votes.

Once home, they stayed outdoors for an hour, starting to install the screen panels for the porch. Jazzi was as excited about finishing the project as Ansel was. The cats would love being able to come outdoors. She just hoped she never looked out the kitchen window to see a coyote staring in at them.

After they showered and changed they started supper, and Ansel made a point of keeping up more small talk than usual. He wasn't fooling her. He didn't want her to fret about Chad. Pork stir-fry was on the menu tonight, so they cut a pork tenderloin into bite-sized pieces, sautéed them, then chopped onions to add to it. They cheated by tossing in a bag of frozen stir-fry vegetables and minced garlic, then splashing everything with soy sauce. While she made that, Ansel boiled Ramen noodles with no package seasoning to drain and add to the rest.

He took a huge helping and gave her a nod of approval. "Simple but delicious."

She liked it, too. Between them, they finished the entire pan.

"Ready to relax?" he asked after a quick cleanup.

She reached for her Dutch oven. "I'm going to make some soup for lunch tomorrow. Cooking distracts me more than watching TV. And Jerod loves my chicken tomato soup."

"The one with the penne pasta? So do I. I'll help you."

The recipe made a big pot of soup, enough to take half tomorrow and freeze half for another time. Working together, it didn't take that long to make either. But it helped her shift her mood. By the time they headed to the living room she was ready to watch the news and unwind.

Chapter 35

Jazzi had the two lights installed over the sink and the mirror hung before she had to leave with Gaff. The soup was in the kitchen for the guys to nuke when they wanted lunch. She and Gaff would stop somewhere to eat this time because it took an hour to drive to Peru.

She'd seen the scenery so many times, she only glanced at it, and was relieved when Gaff parked near the row of shops downtown. He handed her a picture of Chad's pickup, and they went from shop to shop, showing it to people and asking if they'd seen it. No one had until they reached the Butt Hut. Tanya Yorke was walking out of it. When she saw Jazzi she stopped and stared. "What are you doing here?"

Gaff held out the picture of Chad's pickup. "We're asking people if they saw this vehicle in Peru a while ago."

"Yeah, I'm the one who called it in. Why?"

Jazzi was pretty sure her face gave away what she thought of that. She wouldn't trust anything Tanya told her. "You said Chad came to Peru to question people about Ginger, but no one remembers that."

Tanya shrugged. "Why would they? It's not like it was earth-shattering. But you should ask Parker about it. He stayed out of sight for a while. Didn't want trouble if Chad heard he used to date Ginger."

Gaff frowned. "Did Parker talk to Chad?"

"Didn't I just say he hid and didn't want to see Chad?" Tanya opened her fresh pack of cigarettes and took one out. She put it between her lips and looked between Gaff and Ginger. "Got a light?"

They both shook their heads. "Neither of us smoke," Gaff told her.

She dug around for a lighter, lit the cigarette, and took a few long puffs. "You ask me, Chad came here because he suspected Ginger was seeing my man. If he'd talked to me, I'd have set him straight. Parker doesn't need nobody but me."

"But no one else saw Parker but you?" The accusation was clear in Jazzi's voice.

"Not my fault Chad's easy to forget, not like my Parker."

"Right. Well, thank you for your time." Gaff handed her one of his cards. "Would you mind telling us where we can find Parker?"

"Sure. He's at his parents' house, studying. He's gonna get him an important job and make good money soon."

"And where do his parents live?" Gaff wrote down the directions she gave him. With another thank you, he left Tanya and led Jazzi back to his car. Once inside he said, "You were right when you told me that girl is weird."

Jazzi laughed, his comment was so unexpected. "I'm wondering what this Parker is like."

"We'll soon find out." Gaff drove to a nearby small town and stopped at a house on the north edge of it. The two-story was well-kept, a brick façade on the bottom, white siding on top, and black shutters. A weeping cherry tree anchored a flower bed on one side of the cement walk leading to the front door.

Jazzi blinked. It wasn't what she'd expected. After meeting Tanya, she'd thought Parker's family must be on the seedy side, too. An RV was parked by the side of the garage.

"Well, a bit of a surprise," Gaff said. He must have made the same assumptions she had. They walked to the house and rang the bell.

A woman in tan slacks and a crisp blouse opened the door to greet them. She had dark hair cut in a bob and wore mascara and lipstick. She looked better than Jazzi usually did when she didn't have anywhere to go. "May I help you?"

Gaff displayed his badge. "I'm a detective and this is Jazzi, my consultant. We'd like to talk to your son, Parker. We're wondering if he saw this pickup in Peru or in the area a while ago." He showed her the picture.

She frowned and shook her head. "I haven't seen it, but I'll get Parker for you." She walked to the base of the stairs and called up. "Parker, there's a detective here to see you."

A tall man who looked to be in his early thirties came down and frowned at them. "Is this about Ginger?" He wasn't gorgeous like Ansel, but he was good-looking, with his mom's dark hair and deep blue eyes.

Gaff showed him the picture of Chad's truck and then a picture of Chad. "Tanya Yorke reported seeing Ginger's husband in Peru, asking about her, before Ginger's death. Did you see him?"

Parker motioned them into the living room and took a seat across from the couch. Gaff and Jazzi sat beside each other there. Once they were comfortable Parker grimaced. "Tanya called me about seeing Chad, too. She warned me to hide, that she thought he was coming to give me grief for dating Ginger in high school."

"Did you take her seriously?" Gaff asked.

"Not really, but why take a chance? I stayed home that day. I do most days anyway. I'm studying for a degree."

"But you never saw Chad?" Gaff persisted.

Parker shook his head. "If he came to Peru, he didn't try very hard to find me." He glanced at Jazzi. "Have you met Tanya?" When she nodded he said, "Then you know she's not all that stable. She came into the restaurant one night while I was eating and asked if she could sit at my table. I didn't want to be rude, so I told her she was welcome. Since then she's decided we're an item. It's a little scary."

"That would be." Jazzi frowned. "Would she have a vendetta against Ginger because you used to date her?"

"She has a problem with anyone I spend time with, even a few of my buddies. She's tried to warn them off, telling them they're interfering with our relationship." He spread his hands. "We don't *have* a relationship."

"No, what you have is a problem." Gaff wrote a quick note. "Have you seen Ginger since you came back home?"

"We haven't talked to each other in years. She's married now, isn't she? I've been curious about how she's doing, but she doesn't come to Peru often."

Gaff studied him. "So, you had no idea she was pregnant?"

Parker shut his eyes, as if trying to block out the news. He took a deep breath to steady himself before answering. "She was expecting when she died? I bet she was happy about that. I feel horrible I left when she was pregnant before, but I didn't know. She never told me. I could have married her and brought her with me."

Gaff waited before saying, "Someone killed her before she started showing very much. Her husband was sterile, though, and that's raised some questions."

Parker stared. "Chad was sterile?"

"You didn't know?"

"How could I? I didn't see Ginger, but something's not right. There was no girl anywhere who was more loyal than she was. She stayed with me through thick and thin when I was young and stupid. She'd never cheat on her husband."

"But she must have," Gaff said. "Do you have any idea if she was seeing someone?"

Parker pushed to his feet. "I'm telling you, Ginger wouldn't cheat. Maybe a miracle happened and Chad got lucky. Has he been checked again?"

"Not that I know of. I'll ask him about it." Gaff stood, too, and Jazzi joined him. "In the meantime, thanks for making time for us. If we have any more questions, I'll stop in again." He handed Parker his card and they left.

Jazzi was surprised when Gaff started back to Peru instead of home. "I thought we'd stop to see Ginger's friend next," he said, "but it's hard to believe, in a small town like Peru, that Parker hadn't heard Ginger had returned a few times."

Jazzi hadn't thought about that. "Elspeth's mom hadn't known until her dad mentioned seeing her here."

"Her mom wouldn't spend time with anyone Ginger's age, but I'm guessing someone would have told Parker they'd seen Ginger. Everyone knew they were an item before he joined the military."

Gaff was right. When she, Jerod, and Ansel worked in Merlot on a flipper, everyone knew everyone else's business. "Maybe he studies day and night?"

"Right." Gaff shot her a look. "I read Parker's files, and that boy can look and sound like an angel no matter what he's done. You notice his mother didn't stay in the room. She didn't want to react, to give away anything if her son told a whopper."

"His mother seemed nice, really together."

Gaff nodded. "A retired English teacher. Well-respected in town."

"I wondered. I mean, how many people really use 'may' instead of 'can'?"

"Yeah, I feel for her. From what I can tell, the mom and dad are top-notch, have two daughters who have great careers, but Parker always gave them trouble."

"So, is Parker a suspect?" Jazzi asked.

Gaff sighed. "Not yet. I don't have anything to tie him to the case."

Bummer. It would be nice to have someone look as suspicious as Chad. Jazzi watched as they drove through Peru to where Ginger's parents lived. Gaff passed their house to a home three doors down. Pulling into the drive, he said, "I got the feeling Ginger spent a lot of time here."

The house was modular, long and narrow. Cement blocks led to the front door. Pots of pansies sat on each side of it, cheering it up. When they knocked a woman in pajamas and a bathrobe answered. She blushed when she looked at Gaff's badge.

"Sorry. I work the night shift at the grocery store. Stayed up for a while when I got home and slept in this morning."

"Understandable." He followed her into a small kitchen. Dishes littered the countertop and filled the sink, but everything else was spotless. "I'm investigating Ginger Geary's murder. We're here to talk to your daughter about her. We've been told they still kept in touch."

The woman's eyes misted and she blinked rapidly. "That girl deserved better than what she got. She used to come here to see Jolene." She blushed again. "I named her after the Dolly Parton song. She never liked that, said it made her sound like a home wrecker." She was quiet for a minute, then said, "Jolene's at work right now. You can find her at the feedstore near the railroad tracks. She feels terrible about what's happened."

"Has Jolene talked to you about it?" Jazzi asked.

"Not much. When she's upset she gets real quiet, holds it in. I wait until she's ready to talk. That hasn't happened yet."

Gaff thanked her, and they drove back to town. He found the feedstore, and they went inside. Big bags of all kinds of animal food—for dogs, cats, chickens, goats, and rabbits—were piled in high stacks against one wall. A cat came to wind around their ankles. A thirtyish woman with long, brown, limp hair came to greet them. The kindest way to describe her was plain, but she had beautiful eyes. When Gaff introduced himself and Jazzi, Jolene's expression pinched with sadness.

"Ginger came to see me the weekend before she died. She was a mess. She and Chad had worked through the drama of no babies and were happy again, but she said she'd done a horrible thing, so bad she couldn't make herself tell me what it was, she was too ashamed."

Wow. Jazzi blinked in surprise. They usually had to pry information from people, but Jolene must have been wrestling with Ginger's confession ever since she died. "Could you guess what it might be?"

"No, but it was even worse than when she found out she was pregnant after Parker left town. That was a horrible time for her."

Gaff pulled his notepad and pen from his pocket. "And she told you she was ashamed a week before she was murdered?"

Jolene nodded. "It had to have something to do with the new baby."

Another surprise. "She told you she was expecting?" She hadn't told Chad. A horrible thought crossed Jazzi's mind. "Had she decided not to keep it?" She hadn't even considered that Ginger might not want this child.

Gaff poised his pen, ready to write. "When did she tell you she was pregnant? As far as we know, she didn't tell anyone else."

"She was worried when she missed her first period. She took a pregnancy test as soon as she could. I thought she'd be ecstatic because she and Chad wanted a baby so much, but she was pale, nervous. Her hands shook. When I asked her what was wrong, she wouldn't tell me."

"Was she afraid of Chad?" Jazzi thought the news would be cause for celebration, not panic, unless Ginger was worried Chad might suspect the baby wasn't his.

"No. He made her feel horrible for a while, but that was behind them. She'd grown a lot, being with him. She finally told him that if he didn't start treating her better, she'd leave him. That seemed to snap him to his senses."

"She gave him an ultimatum?" Ginger had more of a backbone than Jazzi thought.

Jolene smiled. "That surprised me, too, but Chad was good for her. It was wonderful to see her bloom."

Gaff clicked his pen and rested it on his notepad. "If she wasn't afraid of Chad, why hadn't she told him she was pregnant?"

Jolene smiled. "She didn't want him to get his hopes up only to be disappointed. She was waiting to make sure she could carry the baby."

"Do you think it was his?" Jazzi usually wasn't so blunt, but she needed to know the answer.

Jolene's smile faltered. "I don't know. She was so scared, it made me wonder."

Jazzi bit her bottom lip. She suspected Ginger meant to tell Chad he was going to be a father and let him assume the child was his. "Did Ginger mention anything about seeing Parker again?"

"Parker? He was in her past. Chad was her future."

Jazzi paused before saying, "She drove to Peru to meet someone, though, and she died here. Was there someone else she was seeing in town?"

"I wouldn't know who." Jolene's shoulders slumped; then her expression brightened. "Maybe it wasn't a man. She was getting tired of Tanya Yorke harassing her, I know that."

Would Tanya go so far as to kill Ginger to keep her from seeing Parker? Even if Tanya only imagined it?

Gaff reached in his pocket for one of his cards, then paused. "Can you think of anything else that might help us find Ginger's killer?"

Jolene shook her head. "I'm sorry. Whoever it is, I hope you find him and he's locked up forever. Ginger didn't deserve to die."

Jazzi asked one last question. "Did Ginger ever mention any other man to you, maybe someone she worked with or met occasionally?"

"No, but I know when she and Chad were having problems she was vulnerable." Jolene took a quick breath. "I've even wondered if she slept with someone just to get pregnant, to give Chad his baby. There was a man where she worked who kept coming on to her. I think he was her foreman."

Gaff put his notepad away and handed Jolene his card. "If you think of anything. . ."

She shook her head. "Believe me, I've gone over and over everything she told me before she died. It doesn't make any sense to me that someone killed her."

"Thanks for seeing us," Gaff told her. "You've been a big help." But she looked dubious.

On the drive home, Gaff said, "Let's grab some takeout, then I'd like to stop at the factory Ginger worked at one more time. Is that okay with you?"

"Yeah. I'd like to hear what this foreman has to say for himself."

Chapter 36

They ate a burger on the way to the factory. Jazzi glanced at the clock in the dashboard. Midafternoon. She wasn't going to get to help the guys much at the fixer-upper. The day was slipping away from her. But Gaff was making progress on the case. She wasn't sure where it was heading, but they were learning more today than they had before. That would make Jerod and Ansel as happy as it did her.

It was after two when they walked inside the old brick building again and Gaff asked to see Ginger's foreman. Someone went to find him and told them to wait in the cafeteria like before. In a few minutes a man in his early sixties stuck his head in the room and asked, "You wanna see me?"

"Were you Ginger's foreman?" Gaff asked.

The man laughed. "This ain't that big a company. I'm everyone's foreman here." He came to sit at the table with them. Above average height, with a scrawny build, he had as many wrinkles as he did gray hairs. "What can I do for you?"

Gaff glanced at Jazzi. She shook her head. This sure wasn't the kind of guy she'd pictured hitting on Ginger. She gave him a smile. "We just came from Peru, Indiana, where Ginger grew up. She told one of her old friends that her foreman was always hitting on her."

This time he slapped his knee and gave a belly laugh. "Bless that little gal, too uptight, always worried about saying and doing the right thing. I hit on every woman here. Most of 'em get a kick out of it. I mean, look at me." He motioned to his thin arms and frame. "Anyone who's worked here long enough knows I'm the most married man a woman can get. Worship the ground my Betty walks on. But every woman needs a little ego boost once in a while, so I flirt with 'em. Never touch. No touching allowed;

my Betty would hurt me. And nothing crude. Just some innocent flirting to brighten the day."

Jazzi grinned. She spent a lot of time around men in her line of work and she'd met a few like this guy. Harmless.

"Did you ever say anything that would make Ginger think you were serious?" Gaff asked.

"She took everything too seriously," he said. "If I said 'Lookin' good,' she'd blush bright red to her roots."

Poor Ginger. She might have gotten stronger when she was with Chad, but she still had a long way to go. "You liked her?" Jazzi asked.

"Felt for the gal. You ask me, she got picked on all the time growin' up. Only got bad attention, nothin' good. Never met a girl so self-conscious, but the sweetest thing you ever met."

This guy knew people, read them well. "Did you notice anything different about her the few weeks before she died?"

"She'd had a rough time of it," he said. "First her man got all crazy on her. Then they finally worked through that, and then somethin' even deeper started eatin' at her. She'd stare off in space, all moody and worried, when she had any slack time."

"But she didn't say anything to anybody?" Gaff asked.

He shook his head. "It was deeper than that, somethin' she was keeping buried. My oldest daughter had that look before she told us she had cancer. She had to deal with it first before she could share."

"Is she all right now?" Jazzi asked.

"She beat it. Thanks for askin'."

As usual, Gaff thanked him and handed him a card. Jazzi was pretty sure what that pensive look meant for Ginger. Chad wasn't the father of her baby and she was deciding to not tell him, to pretend that he was the dad. But she was a pretty honest person, and she was ashamed.

Chapter 37

Gaff dropped Jazzi at the fixer-upper at three thirty. The crab apple tree in the front yard had been growing greener every day since the start of April, and in the time she'd been gone, it had burst into bloom. She stopped for a minute to admire it. It was hard to resist the beauty of the pink flowers covering every branch. But she had work to do. She ran upstairs to see the guys and tell them what she'd learned.

Ansel and Jerod were installing the deep bathtub with jets. They looked up when she walked in the room. Ansel had carried George up to supervise their work, and the pug came to greet her. Bending, she scratched him behind his ears.

"Great timing," Jerod teased. "Almost everything's done."

"Hey, if I can get out of the heavy work, why not?" She straightened to look around the room. "This turned out beautiful."

"Yeah, makes me want to install a Jacuzzi in our house," Jerod said. "It would ease the aching muscles after a long day of work."

Ansel's gaze never left her face. "Was this a good day? Did you get some good answers?"

She recounted each conversation with the different people they'd questioned.

Ansel scowled. "I was hoping you'd learn who the father of her baby was."

"So were we, but no one seemed to know."

Jerod asked the same question she'd considered. "You don't think Ginger would sleep with someone just to get pregnant, do you? Especially if she thought Chad was the problem, not her."

"I wondered about that, too, but I don't think so." A strand of hair worked itself free from her ponytail and she pushed it back in place.

"Ginger felt too guilty, too ashamed of what she'd done. That makes me think it wasn't intentional."

"Maybe she was just worried Chad would find out." Ansel propped his hip against the wall. "Misty's murder was a lot more straightforward. She cheated the wrong person and he killed her."

Jerod leaned back, too, hooking a thumb in his tool belt. "I think Jazzi's right. If Ginger had worried Chad was sterile, she could have just gone to a fertility specialist, found a sperm donor."

"That's expensive. She couldn't pay for that herself without Chad knowing, and who knows how Chad would feel about it?" Jazzi shook her head, remembering. "He had a fit when I suggested he adopt."

"Yeah, who knows who the donor is," Ansel said. "Chad didn't think anyone was good enough to make his baby but him."

Jerod frowned at that. "There are lots of happy families out there who adopt or opt for donors."

"We're not arguing with you, but Chad might." Ansel turned his attention back to the bathtub. "But I'm ready to get back to work. We're just about done. I want to finish up, and then we can make sure we have everything we need to start work on the widow's walk tomorrow."

"Enough said." Jerod bent to install another fixture on the tub. While the men did that, Jazzi grabbed a broom to sweep up scraps of caulking and other odd bits on the floor. After that she wiped down the shower and sink. When they were done Ansel grabbed George to go downstairs. Jerod and Jazzi followed him through the kitchen and out the back door. George watched from the driveway as they entered the two-car, detached garage where they'd stored the new, wrought-iron railings that would take the place of the old ones. They counted to make sure they had enough.

"Looks like we're set," Jerod said. "If Jazzi decides to stick around to work with us, we should be able to get it done and even leave early. She'll have plenty of time to get extra pretty before she goes out."

"Like I've purposely skipped out on you guys!" She made a face. "Besides, we're not doing girls' night out this Thursday. It's too close to Easter, so there!"

"Even better," Jerod said. "You'll have extra time to make lots of candy for my Easter basket."

She had to laugh. "I'll probably make chocolate chip cookies tomorrow instead. Ansel thinks they're part of the holiday tradition."

Jerod patted him on the back. "Good man. You know what's important."

"Are you ready for Easter?" Ansel asked him.

"We've stocked up on jelly beans, marshmallow chicks, and malted milk eggs. We try to go light on the candy and buy fun spring stuff for the kids' baskets—jump ropes, sidewalk chalk, frisbees, and bubbles. Lots of balls. Stuff like that. And we bought them a kid's portable basketball hoop for the driveway, too."

That excited Ansel. "Nice. You can change the height on those, can't you?"

"There are different settings. We can make the pole longer the taller they get."

George trotted toward the van, tired of their talking. Ansel laughed. "I guess it's time to go. We're doing an Easter egg hunt on Sunday for the kids, remember?"

"They'll like that. The more kids, the more fun it is." Jerod started to his pickup. With a wave, he pulled away first. They followed him to Jefferson, then turned in the opposite direction toward home.

After they parked the van in the garage Jazzi went inside to feed the cats while Ansel carried out more screen panels to put in the porch frame. George stayed out with him to sprawl on the cement patio. Once the cats were happy Jazzi left the kitchen door open so they could look outside and she went to help with the panels. They slid into place fast. She and Ansel had all the sides installed before supper.

"Let's eat on the patio," Ansel said. "I can grill the hamburgers tonight."

It was so early in spring there were hardly any insects, so Jazzi propped the screen door open, too, so the cats could go out to explore if they wanted to. She started making caramelized onions and sautéed mushrooms for the burgers and watched Inky and Marmalade.

Marmalade stayed well back from the open door, but Inky walked to its threshold and peeked outside. George was lying on the cement, and that made him braver. He put a paw past the door frame and glanced around warily. When nothing happened he put his second paw outside, and finally his curiosity got the better of him. He walked out to explore the patio.

Marmalade hesitated, but Inky meowed for her to join him. Marmalade took two steps past the door, heard a car drive past the house, and jumped back inside. She walked to the porch again and looked at everything on the other side of the screen. A bird flew overhead and she leaped back again. It took a good fifteen minutes, but she finally went to join Inky. And soon they were perched on top of the patio table, studying their surroundings. The screens were high enough that Jazzi wasn't worried they could leap out of them. It was fun to watch their tails twitch back and forth as they took in the new smells and sights.

She'd just finished the toppings for the burgers when Ansel called, "I'm ready to bring in the burgers. Want to watch the cats so they don't dash out the door when I come in?"

They'd tried that before at the kitchen door, but once the cats saw a spray bottle, they stayed away from it. Jazzi carried the bottle out to the porch while Ansel slid inside. He'd toasted buns to go with the burgers. They went in the kitchen to put everything together, then carried their paper plates out to the patio table to eat, shooing the cats out of the way.

It was pleasant sitting outside. Once the sun sank lower it would grow cool, but for now, they were comfortable. The backyard was gorgeous. Every spring flower was blooming—the daffodils, early tulips, and hyacinths.

"I want to plant some flowering trees," Jazzi said. "I love the pink crab apple at the fixer-upper. We should probably be buying one soon."

Ansel nodded. "Make a list of what you want. I'll plant them. They won't bloom this year, but they'll be pretty when we finish all our projects."

Jazzi glanced at the top of the porch. Open sky. "What's next? We put in the screen roof, then drape canvas over it?"

"That's pretty much it," Ansel said. "I should have it done by Sunday. We're not doing guys' night out either. I can work on it tomorrow night."

It wasn't until they went inside to clean up that Jazzi realized how much she needed a nice, calm night like they'd just had. By the time they closed and locked the house to head upstairs, she was relaxed enough to drift into a dreamless sleep.

Chapter 38

Jazzi wasn't in the mood for another sandwich for lunch, so she browned ground chuck and seasoned it for nachos. She packed the meat, shredded cheese and lettuce, and a bottle of salsa in the cooler, along with tortilla chips and other toppings.

"It smells good," Ansel said, lifting George to carry to the van. "You've made me hungry."

Her Viking looked more scrumptious than usual today in worn jeans and a white T-shirt. White tees were her favorites. He looked good in or out of anything, but the white set off his golden tan and white-blond hair. "I'm taking a lot of food, but we probably won't have any leftovers."

He grinned. "Doubt it. We're not going out tonight, so what's for supper?"

"Something quick. I want to bake cookies. How does chicken marsala sound?"

"Only you would consider that quick. I never had it before I met you and now it's one of my favorites."

Hers too. She grabbed the cooler to leave. Inky meowed at the kitchen door, wanting outside on the porch. Jazzi petted him but shooed him away. "It's not quite warm enough for that yet. And we need to finish the roof before you can stay out there on your own."

He sauntered nonchalantly around the kitchen island, but she knew what he was up to. He'd wait for them to open the door, then make a fast dash to squeeze out ahead of them. She grabbed the spray bottle and he gave her a look, then stalked away.

They left the house and locked it behind them. On the drive to Wildwood Ansel said, "I have an idea to run by you. I'd rather stay longer at the fixer-upper today and finish the widow's walk *and* the balcony railing so we can have tomorrow free. We're down to crunch time on getting everything ready for Easter and there's still a lot to do."

"If Jerod's okay with taking Friday off, I could bake and make candy tomorrow." She started tapping things off on her fingers. "Then, on Saturday, I could make the scalloped potatoes so that all we have to do is pop them in the oven Sunday morning. The spoon bread, too. Since Elspeth's not coming, I need to make the lemon meringue pies and carrot cake."

"Are we in charge of deviled eggs?" Ansel asked.

She nodded. "But we can make them the day ahead, too. We'll wait for Sunday morning to roast the ham and prime rib, and it won't take long to roast the asparagus either."

He sighed. "That settles it. I'm asking Jerod about getting everything done today so we have all day Friday to work at home."

Not a bad idea. They had plenty to keep them busy. When they pulled into the drive Jerod was already leaning ladders against the house.

"I was just thinking that because there's no night out for either of you, could we stay a little later to get both jobs done? Then I could give the owner the keys and we'd have a three-day weekend."

Ansel chuckled. "We were just talking about that on the way here."

"Good, then let's hit it." He stopped to watch Jazzi carefully pick up the cooler. "And I bet you brought us a special lunch."

Her cousin noticed everything. "Nachos."

"Hot dang! You make them with everything—sour cream, black olives, the works. See? This is going to be a great day. Let's do this!"

George stretched in the driveway to watch them work. It was cool enough in the mornings that they wore long-sleeved shirts over their T-shirts. She and Ansel wore denim, but Jerod preferred flannel. They didn't waste time. They got busy taking down the old widow's walk. They had to be a little careful. It was so rusted, pieces were cracked and broken in places. By lunch, they'd removed the shirts, warm enough in short sleeves.

It was a good thing Jazzi had made a lot of food because Jerod ate more than usual. She stared at her cousin. "Did you eat supper last night?"

He grimaced. "Franny decided to surprise me and made a pork loin with vegetables."

"That's a good thing, isn't it?" Ansel raised his eyebrows. "It's almost impossible to ruin a pork loin."

"You'd think, wouldn't you? But she hardly added any liquid to it, and the pork chewed like leather. The vegetables were shriveled, charred bits. There's a reason we only bring a vegetable tray every Sunday. It's better for everyone involved."

"But at least she tried." Jazzi reached across the table to pat his hand.

Jerod gave a quick nod. "That's why me and the kids did our best to eat the thing, but finally we gave up. I made everyone hot dogs for supper. I love my wife, but we're all happier if I bring in fast food or do the cooking."

"She'll get better someday," Jazzi said.

Jerod raised an eyebrow. "I hope not. That means she'd practice on us. I need to lose weight, but not like that."

Ansel laughed and waved at the nachos. "Finish them off. Jaz is making chicken marsala tonight."

"You're just trying to make me jealous. I'm grabbing pizzas on the way home."

When they finished lunch there were no leftovers. Jazzi tossed the empty containers in the cooler and carried it to their van. Then the guys climbed the ladders to the roof, and Jazzi tied rope to one section of wrought-iron railing at a time for the guys to pull up. When they had all they needed she climbed to join them, and they installed the widow's walk. Working together, it didn't take long. By three they were tearing off the balcony railing.

The wood railing was in worse shape than the widow's walk. They tossed the rotted wood in the dumpster, then Jazzi fed wood railings up to them.

The balcony rails took longer because they not only had to install them but paint them. Jerod called the owner when they had three sides done, and by the time he stopped on his way home from work to pick up the keys, every project was finished. By then it was six.

While Jerod led the man through the house, Jazzi and Ansel cleaned the job site. When they finished the owner came to talk to them. He told them how much he liked what they'd done. He was so enthusiastic, they knew he wasn't just being polite. His eyes gleamed with pleasure.

"I can't tell you how nice it's going to be to invite my friends here for Easter. The house is everything I wanted. Thank you."

When they left everyone was happy. The house was a job well done.

It was seven before she and Ansel reached the north side of town. They decided to stop for a bucket of fried chicken and sides on the way home. Not a healthy choice, but they didn't have it often and Ansel loved it. So did George.

They ate on the back patio, and the cats came to beg for scraps, too. Did anyone not love fried chicken? It was too late to bother with cookies, so they showered and changed and decided to make it an early night. She could spend all day tomorrow baking and making candy while Ansel worked on finishing the porch.

He was watching a basketball game and she was reading when Gaff called. She had looked at the ID and frowned. She didn't have a good feeling about this.

"Jazzi?" Gaff hesitated a moment. "I wanted to call to let you hear this from me. We got an anonymous tip today that someone had seen Chad's pickup parked on the road where we found Ginger's car. The caller had seen Chad walking back from the woods with a shovel. We used that to get a warrant to search Chad's house. When we got to his bedroom we found Ginger's missing shoe on his night table. He's at the station now and we're questioning him. I don't think he's going to leave. We plan on arresting him for Ginger's murder."

She didn't know what to say. She still didn't think he killed her. "Why would he leave Ginger's shoe on his nightstand? That's just plain stupid."

"He had her picture and a few other things there with it. We think he killed her in an angry fit, then regretted it so much, he couldn't throw her stuff away."

"But her shoe? That would incriminate him."

"People aren't always rational when they commit murder."

"I still don't believe it." She gripped the phone until her fingers ached. "Everything's just a little too convenient, isn't it? Someone who won't give a name calls out of the blue and then you find Ginger's shoe in Chad's house? He hasn't even been staying there lately."

"Detectives call that a lucky break, but I didn't expect you to feel that way about it. You've been a trooper in helping me investigate Ginger's death, though, so I wanted you to know before it hit the TV news and the papers."

"Thank you." Her words were clipped, but he didn't have to call her. He knew she wouldn't agree with him on this.

"Take care, Jazzi. Just so you know, though, as far as we're concerned, this investigation is over."

She clicked off the phone and pressed her lips together, fuming.

"They arrested him?" Ansel asked.

She explained what had happened. "I can't blame Gaff. All the evidence points to Chad, but only an idiot would keep that shoe. Someone's setting him up."

"You and Gaff have been stirring the pot," Ansel said. "You've made someone nervous."

"Nervous enough to break into Chad's house and plant fake evidence. It would be easy because he's not staying there." She clenched her hands into fists, she was so frustrated. "I wonder if anyone even checked for prints or signs of a break-in."

"There won't be any fingerprints. Whoever did it would make sure of that."

"I should go see him." She started to get up, but Ansel shook his head.

"Gaff said they were questioning him now. Then he'll probably call a lawyer. You won't be able to visit him tonight."

"Then tomorrow."

Ansel gave her a pitying look. "I doubt if he'll know anything that will help you, but he'll like seeing you."

She sagged back on the sofa. Ansel was right. All she could do was comfort Chad right now. She had no idea how to prove he was innocent, and neither would he. She straightened her shoulders. "I'm going to question everyone again. Somewhere there's something we're missing. I'm going to find it."

"Not by yourself you're not. I'm going with you. If the killer's already nervous, you might push him over the edge."

If hearts could swell, hers just did. She loved this man. "Thanks, hon. Do you think Chad's innocent, too?"

He dodged the question. "It doesn't matter. You think he is, and you won't be happy until you know for sure."

She sat up straighter, suddenly excited. "But I *do* know for sure. I just remembered. Gran told us. 'It's not his shoe. He's telling the truth.' Remember?"

Ansel's blue eyes widened. "I'd forgotten, but she did mention a shoe. Your gran's never wrong."

Jazzi gave a satisfied nod. "Chad's innocent. Gaff won't believe me, though, without evidence."

"You've convinced me. I'll do what I can to help you, but can we get a few things done around here before we drive to Peru tomorrow?"

"That would probably be better. Chad's family will be there in the morning to visit him. I'd rather miss them. His dad won't bother being polite to me."

"Even after you've worked so hard trying to help Chad?"

"Chad got his ideas about marriage from his father. It didn't seem like it when we first met, but the minute we moved in together, he dropped right into his dad's pattern. The man rules the house. The wife keeps everyone in that house happy."

Ansel nodded. "Just like my parents."

"Only you're smarter than your dad. You don't want to be like him. It took Chad a lot longer to figure out his dad's a jerk."

"And he still loves him."

Jazzi shook her head. "It was different for Chad. His dad's devoted to his kids. Your dad was a jerk to your mom *and* to you and your sister. All he cares about is the dairy farm."

Ansel grimaced. "Yeah, my dad wins in the jerk category."

She smiled. At least he could joke about it now. When they'd first met he didn't want anything to do with anyone in his family but Radley, Adda, and her husband, Henry. After meeting all of them, she couldn't blame him.

He shrugged. "You going to be able to relax a little before bed?"

"I'm going to try." But she was frustrated. There wasn't anything she could do right now. She settled back on the couch and picked up her book, but she couldn't concentrate. She tried to watch TV, but her mind kept drifting. She was still upset when they went up to bed. She doubted she'd be able to sleep. It had been a long enough day, though, that just when her brain started to whir, it shut down. She was surprised when she woke later than usual the next morning.

Chapter 39

Inky glared at her as she got out of bed. The cat knew their schedule and knew they were starting later this Friday than usual.

"Get over yourself," she told him. He stalked to the door to the hallway and wouldn't budge. He usually followed her into the bathroom and jumped on the counter to bat at the running water while she washed her face and brushed her teeth. Not this morning. He wanted her to hurry and go downstairs to feed him. She took longer than usual just to annoy him.

When Ansel grabbed George to carry him down the steps Inky raced ahead of them. Marmalade, being the sweet cat she was, padded alongside Jazzi. But Jazzi adored both of them. She filled all three pet bowls while Ansel poured coffee and brought it to the kitchen island. When they'd stopped for fried chicken the night before they'd bought donuts at the shop two doors down. More decadence, but it felt special eating them this morning.

Ansel glanced outside at the blue skies and puffy white clouds. "Looks like a beautiful day. We can leave the doors open so the pets can go in and out whenever they want to."

As she'd expected, they followed Ansel to the porch. He brought the ladder from the garage and got busy installing the screens that formed the roof. While he did that, she got everything ready to make the candy and chocolate chip cookies. She started with the cookies, doubling her recipe to make ten dozen. With four ovens, by the time she scooped out dough to fill eight cookie sheets, the first batch was baked and ready to take out of the oven. One more batch and she was done.

She started on three different fudges next. The mocha-caramel fudge used chocolate chips, espresso powder, and dulce de leche. Fruit and nut white chocolate fudge needed a pound of white chocolate chips, nuts, and dried fruit. And her super fudge used marshmallow crème. While the fudges cooled she started making homemade marshmallows, some of her favorites. And she ended by making lots of soft caramels.

When Ansel came back in the kitchen he stared in surprise. "You got a lot done."

"That's it for the day. What about the porch?"

He looked pleased with himself. "All I have to do tomorrow is cover the screen roof with canvas, but I need you to help me with that." He reached for a cookie. When she raised an eyebrow, he said, "Just one. You ready to visit Chad at the police station, then head to Peru?"

"Let me throw on a little makeup first." She didn't bother with much but always wore mascara before she left the house.

"I'm going to wash up." He had to shoo Inky and Marmalade back into the kitchen before they left. "The cats like it outside so much, I'm thinking of buying a doorbell security system for the porch and installing a pet door so they can go in and out, even when we lock up and leave."

"Not a bad idea." She ran upstairs, and when she returned she had on mascara and blush. She'd let her hair down to fall around her shoulders.

Ansel grinned. "That was worth the wait."

She rolled her eyes. It was nice to have a husband who always thought she looked better than she did. He drove her pickup to the station. They had to wait in the lobby until another visitor left. Only one person could see Chad at a time. *Please let it be his mother.* But when the door opened Jazzi braced herself. His father looked at her and scowled.

His lips curled in a sneer. "If you'd have stayed with my son like you should have, none of this would have happened."

Ansel stood to look down at him. "If your son had treated her better, there wouldn't have been a problem."

Chad's father looked him up and down. "You might be big, but I can see why she chose you. She probably has you eating out of her hand."

Ansel shook his head and returned to sit next to Jazzi. "You were right. He's as big of a jerk as my dad."

Mr. Geary sent him a withering look and stomped out of the room.

Ansel snorted. "I can see why there's no love lost between you two."

"I try to avoid him." Jazzi looked up when the door to the back opened again and an officer motioned for her to follow him. Ansel reached for a magazine to pass the time.

When she came out he raised his eyebrows in question, and she shook her head. She didn't want to talk about it in there.

On the drive out of town Ansel asked, "Is he pretty depressed?"

"He figures he's doomed. He swore he'd never seen Ginger's shoe, but he didn't think anyone would believe him, and the cops didn't. He said he locked his door when he left to move into a hotel but forgot to turn on the security. He'd started drinking before he walked out the door. Then he drank so much at the bar, we had to go get him. He woke up with such a hangover, he didn't even think about his house."

"That made it that much easier for someone to break in."

Jazzi nodded. Chad had been so down, seeing him had depressed her. She'd expected that, but it bothered her more than she'd thought. The hour drive felt tedious. They'd passed the turn toward Salamonie Dam when her phone buzzed. She glanced at Ansel. "It's Gaff. Maybe he has good news for us."

She hit Speaker, and Gaff's voice filled the cab. "You're never going to believe this, but you helped me solve another murder."

She frowned. "How did I do that?"

"Remember the young waitress who was stabbed at a truck stop where our trucker had been? When I talked to the local authorities about it and asked them about our guy, they started digging more. And guess what? They searched his truck when he came to town this time."

"It was him?"

"Yup, it seems he stopped her on her way to her car to proposition her. She wasn't interested, and when he grabbed her, she put up a fight and threatened to report him. He got mad and stabbed her with a screwdriver he had on the back seat. He used it to fix a messed-up windshield wiper and instead of throwing it away, he wiped it off and left it there."

"That's pretty arrogant."

"Or stupid." Gaff's voice grew serious. "It was a fluke that we helped catch him, but I'm glad we did. Now he can't harass or hurt anyone else. You should feel good about that."

"I do."

"You're still thinking about Chad. You gave him your best shot, too."

"I'm not done yet. I'm on my way to Peru to talk to people again."

"By yourself?" He didn't sound happy.

"No, Ansel's with me. I forgot to tell you about Gran's vision. She told us it wasn't Chad's shoe. Gran's always right. Chad didn't take it."

Gaff didn't answer for a moment. He finally said, "Your gran's never let us down. I wish you would have talked to me. I'd have gone with you today."

"And what would you tell your team at work? An old woman told you Chad was innocent? How would that go over?"

He huffed out a frustrated sigh. "I could have come up with something better than that, but you and Ansel be careful. Don't take any chances."

"We won't. We're almost there. Gotta go."

"I don't like this. You should have . . ."

She cut him off. "Ansel's parking now. 'Bye, Gaff." And she ended the call.

Ansel shook his head. "You're going to hear about this."

"So are you. We're in this together." She motioned to the feedstore. "I thought we'd start by talking to Jolene again. She was Ginger's best friend."

Jolene was trying to lift a heavy bag of chicken feed off a high stack when they walked through the door. Ansel rushed to help her. Biceps bulged as he lowered it to the floor, and Jolene stared. She tilted her head to gaze up at him. She opened her lips to thank him, but no words came out.

He smiled at her. "I drove my wife here to talk to you. You've met Jazzi."

Jolene turned her head, saw Jazzi, and turned beet red all the way to the hairline of her lank, brown hair. "He's yours?"

Jazzi waved her embarrassment away. "Don't worry. He gets that all the time. I'm used to it."

"He's gorgeous, but so are you. I've never seen a better-looking couple."

"Thanks." Jazzi gave her a brief smile, then grew serious. "Gaff arrested Chad last night for Ginger's death, but I'm convinced he didn't kill her. If you don't mind, I'd like to ask you a few more questions."

Jolene propped her hip against the cashier counter. "What makes you think he's innocent?"

Jazzi made a face, then said, "No one else would understand, but my gran has the sight, and she told me that Chad didn't take Ginger's shoe, but Gaff's team found it at Chad's house." She went on to explain about the anonymous call and why they'd searched Chad's home.

Jolene pursed her lips, thinking. "Is your gran from Appalachia? My great-gran came from there, and she had the sight, too. Before she died she told me not to worry about finding a man because when I turned thirty-one, a wonderful guy would find me. I have two more years, and that's fine. I don't mind waiting for him."

"Then you believe me?"

"My great-gran was never wrong either."

"And you don't mind if I ask you more questions?"

"If Chad didn't take that shoe, someone else did—the person who buried her. I want the right person found."

Jazzi gulped a grateful breath. She'd worried people would tell her to go away and not talk to her. "Way back, when Ginger and Parker were seeing each other, did they have any special place they liked to go?"

Jolene frowned, trying to remember. "They usually met at after-school events—basketball games and stuff like that. But when they wanted to be alone . . ." She stopped, eyes wide. "Parker would pick Ginger up and drive to a road between his town and Peru. They'd park there to make out."

"Do you remember the name of the road?"

"They didn't say, didn't want anyone to know, but I remember they used to walk across a farmer's field to a wood close by." She shivered and rubbed her arms. "Ginger was buried in a wood, wasn't she?" When Jazzi nodded she hugged herself. "Do you think Parker got her pregnant both times?"

"I don't know, but I sure want to find out." Jazzi thought for a minute. "When Parker got in trouble for small stuff do you remember what it was?"

"Stupid, teenage crap. Mostly breaking and entering. He used to brag that no house locks could keep him out."

Jazzi glanced at Ansel. He gave a small nod, and she knew he was thinking the same thing she was. Chad's security had been turned off, and Parker had let himself into his house. She smiled at Jolene. "You've been a big help. Thanks for talking to me. You didn't have to."

"If it was Parker, I hope you can prove it. Will you let me know what you find out?"

Jazzi took her number and promised to give her a call.

When they left the feedstore Ansel asked, "Where to next?"

"There's only one hardware store in the entire area. I want to see what kind of brands they stock."

He frowned as he drove the few blocks there. "What are we looking for?"

"The kinds of shovels they sell. When Chad and I worked on landscapes for fixer-uppers, he only used Leonard forged shovels, swore they were stronger and better than anything else."

"What do we use?" Ansel asked.

"Tabor. Jerod's favorite brand."

When they reached the hardware store and walked inside they went straight to the garden section. No forged shovels or Tabor. Craftsman, the ones her father carried in his hardware store at home. He was a big fan of them. The clerk who helped them was so nice, Ansel bought one from him.

"We can always use another shovel for yard work," he told her.

Right. He didn't want to waste the guy's time and wanted to support him. They climbed into the pickup, and she patted his leg. "You're a softie and I love you for that." Before they started to Parker's house she called Gaff.

"I'm just checking on something. You took the shovel at Chad's house as evidence, didn't you? So you've recorded what brand it is."

"Yeah, let me look it up." She heard him flipping through papers, then he said, "Craftsman."

"Chad wouldn't own one of those. It wouldn't be at his house, but we're in Peru, and guess which brand the local hardware store sells?"

"Did you learn anything else?"

She told him about the road where Parker and Ginger used to park to make out and the petty crimes of burglary Parker had gotten in trouble for. "We're going to talk to Parker next."

"Where did you learn all this?"

"Jolene remembered when I asked her more questions. I think we'll learn more from Parker."

"Not until I get there. If you're right, he's the one who killed Ginger. You're not seeing him without me. Stay put and find something to keep you busy until I get there."

"In this small town?"

"Go order something at the restaurant, drink some coffee. I'll meet you there. But don't do *anything* until I get there. I'll use flashing lights. Just hold tight for a while."

She put her phone back in her pocket and looked at Ansel. "Did you hear that?"

He grinned. "We did forget to eat lunch, you know."

How had that happened? Usually Ansel and Jerod suffered loudly if they went too long without food. Gaff found them, sitting in a booth, staring at empty dishes and sipping coffee, when he got there. Ansel glanced at his watch. "You must have been flying. You got here in forty minutes."

"Time flies when you have flashing lights."

Ansel tossed a generous tip on the table and they followed Gaff to his car. Jazzi sat in back because Ansel's legs were so long. He'd have more room if he rode shotgun. Gaff drove to Parker's house, and the three of them walked to the door together.

This time when Parker's mother opened it she didn't look welcoming at all.

Chapter 40

"Parker's in the middle of taking an online exam," she explained. "You can't bother him right now."

Gaff held up his badge. "Fine. We can wait. I'd be happy to talk to you until he's done."

She stared at him, surprised. "I don't know how I could help you. I never met this Chad."

"Are you going to invite us in, or would you rather answer questions in my car?"

She blinked and held the door open wider, motioning for them to follow her into the living room. She perched on the edge of an armchair, her hands gripping its seat. She looked from one of them to another and waited for Gaff to start talking.

He took out his pen and notepad. "We could start by having you show us where you keep your yard tools—shovels and rakes."

She frowned but wordlessly rose and led them to an oversize, double garage. She pointed to the tools hung on hooks on the far wall. Gaff went to study them. "There's an empty hook. No shovel here. Do you know where it is?"

She shrugged. "I use a gardening shovel for my flower beds. I'm not sure who used that one last."

Gaff made a note, then studied the other tools. "Your husband must be a fan of Craftsman."

"He swears by them. Gets them at the store in Peru."

With a nod, Gaff said, "Thank you. We can return to the house now."

She fidgeted once they were all seated again, more uncomfortable than she'd been before. She glanced at the clock. "Parker should be finished soon. It was a timed test. He only has ten more minutes."

"Good. Can you tell us when and how often your son has left the house in the last two weeks?"

"He's a grown man. I don't keep track of him."

"But I'm sure you notice if he's here or not."

She frowned. "He can't stay underfoot twenty-four hours a day. He'd go stir-crazy. He goes out in the evenings to meet his old friends."

"He never goes out during the day?"

She blinked. "He might have. I don't pay close attention, and most of my meetings are scheduled during the day."

"Your husband still works?"

"Part-time. He doesn't have to, but he likes to stay busy. We both do." Footsteps sounded overhead, and she jumped to her feet to hurry to the bottom of the stairs. "Parker! That detective is back to talk to you."

He didn't come down immediately, and she stayed near the stairs to call again. "Parker! Either come down now or I'm sending him up."

They heard movement, and soon Parker came to join them in the living room, sitting across from them. He wore an annoyed frown. "What now?"

Gaff glanced at his notes. "We've taken Ginger's husband into custody and we're trying to build a case, but we've found some conflicting evidence."

Parker shrugged. "How am I supposed to help with that?"

"We found the shovel that was used to bury Ginger. It was a Craftsman, but Chad doesn't own any of those. Your father does, though."

Chad's mother stepped farther into the room, a worried look on her face.

Parker looked bored. "Maybe Chad bought it in Peru after he killed her. That's where Dad got his."

"It wasn't new. It had been used a lot from the looks of it."

Parker turned his attention to Ansel. He and Jazzi were sitting close together, a little distance from Gaff on the couch. He studied his work boots. "I heard somewhere that Chad was a landscaper. Did you work with him?" When Ansel shook his head he said, "Maybe he borrowed it from a friend or employee. A lot of people buy Craftsman. It's a good brand."

"Maybe that's what happened." Gaff studied his notes again. "Chad wasn't living in his house when we got the anonymous tip that made us search it. He swore he didn't know anything about Ginger's missing shoe."

Parker glanced at his mother when she gave a small gasp. He raised an eyebrow and she quickly recovered. "What did you expect him to do? Confess?"

Gaff glanced at the mother, too. "Do you know anything about the shoe, ma'am?"

She gave a quick shake of her head and looked away.

Gaff went on. "We've looked at your records, and you were brought in for questioning a few times for breaking and entering."

This time, before he answered, Parker narrowed his eyes and leaned forward in his chair. "*Questioning*. That's it. The town blamed me for everything that happened here. I was never convicted."

"Only because the officers never found any fingerprints."

"I'm assuming whoever did it was smarter than that." Parker's gaze never left Gaff's face.

"There were no fingerprints at Chad's house either."

With a wry smile, Parker spread his hands. "Probably because no one broke in."

"No, I mean *no* fingerprints. Not even Chad's." When Jazzi frowned at that Gaff added, "I sent a tech to check after I talked to you."

Parker waved that away. "Most people watch *CSI*. Everyone knows better than to leave fingerprints these days, *if* anyone went to the bother of sneaking into Chad's house. Did they take anything?"

"No, but we don't think that was the purpose of the break-in." Gaff moved his pen farther down the page. "The autopsy confirmed that Ginger was pregnant. She was far enough along that the doctor is hoping to make a DNA match to the father of her baby."

Parker's mom teetered for a moment, then put out a hand to steady herself. She came to sink down onto a nearby chair. She'd gone so pale, Jazzi was worried she might faint.

Parker scowled at her. "Are you going to be all right? Should I take you up to bed?"

"I'm fine." She raised a limp hand.

She didn't look fine, and Jazzi felt sorry for her. Parker had sounded irritated.

Gaff turned to study him. "Do you remember the last time you saw Ginger?"

"Sure, before I left to join the military."

Gaff shook his head. "I don't think so. I think it's when she asked you to meet her at your old spot on County Road 8, the day you killed her."

Parker rolled his eyes. "I hear a lot of guesswork. *I think*. Who cares what you think? I don't see any proof."

"We have pictures and measurements of the tire marks in the mud at the side of the road. I'm guessing they'll match your vehicle's."

The mother reached out to grip both arms of her chair.

Parker's eyes flashed temper. His face contorted. "And why would I meet her?"

"Because you'd been seeing her and got her pregnant. Again. Chad was sterile. It couldn't have been him. When we found Ginger's car there'd been a struggle in it. It looked like she'd opened the door to talk to someone, and that someone had yanked her out of it. You lost it when she told you she was going to have your baby but return to Chad, didn't you?"

Parker sprang to his feet, furious. "How would you have felt? All she did was come to Peru to whine to Jolene about how bad Chad was treating her. That's how we bumped into each other. She needed a shoulder to cry on. And then she needed someone to make her feel better, but the minute he stopped insulting her, she forgave him. Just like that. And then she told me she was going to have a baby. My baby. And she was going to raise it with Chad, that I didn't know how happy I'd made them. When I told her I was going to fight for custody, she swore she'd tell Chad I forced her. Can you believe that? I got mad, and she kept trying to explain how sorry she was for hurting me, but I didn't want to hear it. The more she talked, the more it hurt. I just wanted her to shut up!"

"So you strangled her."

"I didn't mean to kill her. I loved her, at least I did once. But this is the second time she was going to take a baby of mine, then leave me."

"You're the one who left Peru," Gaff reminded him.

"I had to, but I would have taken Ginger with me. We didn't have to break up."

Jazzi glanced at Parker's mother. She looked numb. Somewhere during the questioning she'd shut down. Jazzi reached out to touch her hand. "Should we call your husband to come to you?"

She nodded silently, then hung her head.

Gaff made a call, too, for the nearest authority to come to arrest Parker.

Parker sat, staring out the window, upset and angry. The waiting was horrible. Ansel put his hand over hers and gently squeezed it. Boy, she was glad he was with her.

When Parker's father finally came home and a sheriff came to take Parker away, Gaff drove them back to their pickup. "I've called the station and explained what's happened. Chad will be free soon."

"Thank you." Jazzi felt shaky. She couldn't imagine how a day could be worse than this one. All she wanted was to go home, have a glass of wine, and curl up on her couch, safe and secure. She didn't want to think about anything. She especially didn't want to go over the events of the day.

"Take care, Jazzi, and thanks for the help. Have a nice Easter." Gaff left her for Ansel to comfort.

Ansel helped her into the pickup. She usually fussed about not needing help, but not this time. He climbed behind the steering wheel and let out a long sigh. "Easter. Maybe we can recuperate tomorrow and enjoy ourselves on Sunday."

Jazzi doubted it. She thought it would take a while to work past the way she felt now.

On the drive home she turned on music but didn't really hear it. She stared out the window without seeing. Like Parker's mom, she felt numb. And maybe that was a blessing.

Chapter 41

Friday night was a wash. For once, she and Ansel skipped supper. Neither of them had an appetite. They didn't think about food until Ansel made popcorn to eat while they watched TV. The nice thing about being married to Ansel was that he didn't mind comfortable silences any more than she did. She couldn't have begun to put her feelings into words right then.

They called it an early night, and Jazzi slept fitfully. She was emotionally exhausted, but her brain still wanted to sort through the day's events. They both woke later than usual, tired even after a night's sleep. But they had things to do.

To start, Ansel hauled the Easter baskets they'd bought for each family out of the spare bedroom closet. They filled them with plastic grass and then divided up the bagged cookies and candies Jazzi had made for them, keeping a basket for themselves. Ansel stored them in the pantry while Jazzi started work on tomorrow's desserts. Once the cakes and pies were cooling, they went outside to attach the canvas roof over the porch's screen ceiling. They finished that and were carrying their ladders to the garage when Chad's pickup pulled into the drive.

He came to greet them, wrapping Jazzi in a tight hug. "Thanks for believing in me." He looked at Ansel, including him, too. "Both of you. Gaff told me what you did, going to Peru to question everyone again."

"Gran told us you didn't do it," Jazzi said.

Chad gave a tentative smile. "I'd forgotten about Gran and the sight. She told you that we wouldn't work out. We should have listened to her. How's she doing?"

Jazzi smiled, too, thinking of her. "She's Gran, hasn't changed much."

"That's a good thing. She's a neat old lady."

"Don't tell her that. She says you're not old until you hit one hundred."

"I feel old now." Chad looked down, breaking eye contact for a moment. When he looked up again he grimaced. "I heard Dad gave you both a hard time in the lobby before he left the station."

Jazzi shrugged that off. "I didn't expect him to be happy to see me."

"But he knew you were there to help me. He could have at least been civil." He glanced at Ansel. "You must have wanted to pound him."

"Your dad and mine aren't all that different. When mine came for our wedding he insulted everybody he saw."

Chad gave a somber nod. "If I don't go to my parents' house for Easter, it will hurt their feelings, especially my mom's. But then I'm moving back home on Monday. I thought being at a hotel would help, but I just sat around feeling sorry for myself and thinking about Ginger there, too. I'm going to go to work, come home every night and clean out everything we owned—and I mean everything—to start over. It's going to take some time to get myself together."

"Good luck." Jazzi knew it was going to be hard for him.

"Thanks again. I'm not going to see anyone for a while, but I appreciate what you did." He got back in his truck and pulled away.

Ansel wrapped an arm around her. "You'll probably never see him again. We'll bring back too many painful memories."

"That's all right. He needs to move on. I'm part of his past."

They walked into the house together, poured drinks, and carried them to the patio. They gave themselves a half-hour break, then Jazzi said, "We still have a lot to do for tomorrow."

Ansel helped her make the scalloped potatoes, deviled eggs, and spoon bread. Once everything that they could do ahead was prepped, Ansel threw hot dogs on the grill, and they carried them into the living room to eat while they watched TV.

Ansel clicked to *Queens of Mystery.*

Jazzi stared. "Are you all right?"

He laughed. "You love mysteries and I've heard this is a fun series."

"And you're going to watch it with me?"

He gave a crooked grin. "We'll see who solves it first. I have to start practicing to get ahead of you."

She finished her hot dog, then left her couch to snuggle next to him on his. Watching the show, they both laughed at the same places. Yup, she'd picked the right man to spend the rest of her life with.

By the time they went to bed they were both better than they'd been yesterday. They might even be able to enjoy themselves tomorrow. Ansel was already getting excited about the Easter egg hunt.

Chapter 42

They got up early to start the huge ham and prep the prime rib. The asparagus could wait 'til the last minute.

Once Jazzi had the ham in the oven Ansel carried bags of plastic Easter eggs from the laundry room. Jazzi stared at them all. "You have to be kidding."

"We want every kid to find a basketful." He dumped out the first batch. "We can fill each one of these with a quarter." He opened another bag and took out roll after roll of them.

"Are you trying to start the kids out with a college fund?" she asked.

He rolled his eyes. "Look at what else I bought and then you'll understand." He walked to the hall closet and returned with two bags, filled with boxes. He pushed one toward her. "Open it."

A pink ceramic piggy bank was inside. She turned it over, and it had a rubber stopper that could be removed.

Ansel grinned. "My grandma gave me one like that when I was a kid. When we went to her house to visit she'd pay me to do small jobs. Every week I'd open that bank to see how much I'd saved. I know Jerod and Walker give their kids allowances. They can start saving, too."

"I'm taking it your grandma's gone?" She picked up the next box. It held a blue pig.

Ansel nodded. "I really missed her when she passed. She was always fun to be with, and she made us feel special. We can be special to our friends' kids."

"We already have a strong start. They sure like coming to our house."

With a nod, he handed her a roll of quarters, and they got busy filling plastic eggs. When they ran out of money, they filled the rest with foil-wrapped chocolate eggs. When they finished they took the eggs outside to hide them all around their yard.

It was a beautiful day—warm, but not too warm. They had a big yard. They started hiding eggs in the flower beds near the house, tucking them under leaves near the edges and sliding them under bush branches near the garage. They dropped some in plain view on the small hill Ansel had made to give the pond a little privacy, dropped a few more on the downside of the hill before they reached the pond. They hid more around the gazebo and picnic table, then started around the edge of the pond to drop more in the grass and bushes surrounding it.

Once every egg was gone they headed back to the house. When they walked inside the aroma of ham and prime rib roasting in the ovens made Jazzi drool. While Ansel set up games in the basement, she made the glaze for the ham and filled rimmed cookie sheets with asparagus to roast. Together, they set silverware on the table, put the desserts on the kitchen island, and stacked the new matching plates they'd bought.

At eleven they went up to change into dress clothes for the holiday. Ansel wore deep-blue dress slacks and a light-blue shirt. Her Viking looked splendid in blue. It accented his eyes. She wore her favorite white spring dress with splashes of red flowers and stepped into low red heels. She let her hair fall in loose waves and took more time than usual with her makeup.

At noon everyone had arrived. Gran and Samantha and Jazzi's mom and dad wore their church finery. Olivia had on the new dress she'd bought in Chicago—a bright, sunshine yellow with a wide black belt and matching yellow heels. Even Thane wore a button-down shirt rather than a T-shirt. Jerod and his family wore the clothes they'd bought for Easter Sunday, too. Lizzie kept holding onto the hem of her dress and twirling. Gunther stood taller than usual to show off his new suit. River's was similar, but light gray. And baby Noreen looked adorable in the Easter dress Olivia had bought for her—girly pink with lots of frills. Walker and Didi wore light gray, too, to coordinate with River, and Jerod's parents—Eli and Eleanor—wore matching pale-yellow shirts with black dress slacks.

Jazzi felt her heart swell with pride. Their group cleaned up pretty good. Everyone was gathered around the appetizers, yakking and laughing, and Ansel had to raise his voice to get their attention. "Before we eat our meal we have a present for each kid here." He handed them each a box with their name on it, and they got excited when they saw their piggy banks. "We thought we'd give you a start on filling these, so some of the Easter eggs we hid have quarters in them and some have candy. We can take our food and drinks outside to watch you look for them."

That was all the invitation the kids needed. They raced out the kitchen door and spread out to start looking. Jazzi sipped her wine and touched Ansel's arm to get his attention. As Walker and Didi went with River, and he found eggs, she watched him put one in his basket, then one in Noreen's basket. Jerod and Franny were helping Gunther and Lizzie. They were doing the same. Many times one of them would point under a bush or flower to show Pete, hanging on to Jerod's hand to walk without falling, where an egg was hidden and then help him put it in his basket.

Eleanor smiled from ear to ear at them. "Jerod told me that every kid had agreed to put all of the eggs on the driveway and split them evenly between them so no one got more than someone else."

A lump formed in Jazzi's throat. "Our family's pretty special. We're so lucky."

Olivia came to stand near them and nodded. "If I didn't have a big sister who always came to my rescue, I might be spending Easter in jail."

Jazzi snorted. "Gaff never really believed you killed Misty."

Gran ate the last cracker with Boursin cheese on it and sipped some of her red wine to wash it down. "You came through for Chad, too. He doesn't think so now, but he's going to marry again, and the next girl will come with kids. He'll finally have the family he's always wanted."

"You saw that in a vision?"

Gran nodded.

"Hope you haven't seen Thane and me with kids." Olivia glanced across the patio at her husband. He and Eli were studying how Ansel had constructed the screened-in porch. "We've agreed we don't want any. Ever."

"He's all right with that?" Ansel asked.

"He's relieved. He said he'd rather invest in a lake cottage and a boat than a kid. We're trying to decide if we even want the bother of a puppy."

A worried frown furrowed Ansel's brow. Jazzi grinned at him. "I haven't changed my mind. I want kids, just not right now."

Nodding, he returned his attention to the egg hunt. When the kids started moving to look around the pond he went to help them. Jazzi had wondered how long he'd be able to resist. Eli and Thane went, too, to keep the kids safe around the water. Yup, all good men.

Half an hour later the kids all gathered in the driveway and spread out eggs with quarters in one spot and eggs with candy in another, then the men helped them divide them up. Before they finished, Jazzi slipped into the house to put the asparagus in the ovens and to load food onto the kitchen island.

When it came time to eat Jerod sliced the ham and Ansel sliced the prime rib. Then everyone settled at the long tables. No one hurried through the meal, not even the kids. They joined in the conversation, talking about what the Easter bunny had brought them this morning.

River said, "My friend from school got a new brother for Easter. He's five and he's brown."

Olivia looked confused. "How do you get a new five-year-old brother?"

"His mom and dad went someplace, and they gave them a new kid." River glanced at Walker. "Can we go someplace like that?"

"Two's enough for us," Walker said, ruffling a hand through his hair. "We couldn't be any happier with the ones we have."

That made River smile, but Gunther frowned. "How do you get a brown brother?"

Gran pushed away her empty plate. "He probably has a white mother and a black daddy, or he could be Chinese or Burmese. None of that matters. Kids are kids, no matter what color they are, and they all need love."

Gunther glanced at River. "We'll help love him, won't we? If he comes to your house and Lizzie and me are there, we'll be his friends, too."

"Giving love makes you happy," Gran said. "But so does dessert." She looked at Jazzi. "I love lemon meringue pie."

A not very subtle hint. Jazzi went to clear Gran's plate and brought her back a slice. Other people had finished, too, so she cleared the table while Ansel carried over the desserts and small plates. Everyone had finished their cake or pie before Jerod finished eating prime rib. Then everyone went outside to drink and watch the kids draw pictures on the driveway with their sidewalk chalk and blow bubbles with the different blowers Ansel had bought. A few of them made such huge bubbles, it was fun to watch them float away before they popped. Jerod ate carrot cake while the kids entertained themselves, and then the guys and kids headed to the basement for games—pin the tail on the rabbit, a big rabbit piñata, and balancing Easter eggs on spoons for races. At the end of the celebration, Jazzi and Ansel handed out a treat basket to each family as they left.

Ansel and Jazzi stood outside and watched people drive away. Then, hand in hand, with George trailing behind them, they walked to the pond and circled it before heading back inside to clean.

Jazzi rinsed dirty dishes and Ansel loaded them into the dishwasher. "I'd call today a success," he decided. "What do you think?"

"It was perfect. Just what I needed." Misty's death hadn't bothered her nearly as much as Ginger's. She'd never gotten to know either of them, but she doubted if many people would miss Misty. A sad thing to say, but true. It would take Chad a long time to get over Ginger. Gran had made her feel better, though, when she said, "A kid's a kid. They all need love." Maybe Chad had figured that out. Maybe that was why he'd be happy to love the kids that came with the next woman he'd love.

Ansel wiped down the farm table. "I was surprised when Olivia said that she and Thane don't want any children."

Jazzi shrugged. "Everyone has to do what's right for them. Different things make people happy. It's smarter to admit you don't want kids than to have kids you don't want."

He thought about that for a second, then nodded. "You're right."

She cut the leftover ham from the bone to put in a baggie for sandwiches. There was no leftover prime rib. As a matter of fact, there were only a few slices of carrot cake left, besides the ham. But then, there had been a lot of people at the table. She loaded the platter in the dishwasher, then dried her hands. Wrapping her arms around Ansel, she said, "You're going to make a great father."

He tugged her closer. "And you'll be a great mom."

"I hope so." She couldn't picture that in her mind, but she liked kids. Surely she'd love her own.

Smiling, Ansel stooped to kiss the top of her head. "I know so. Let's go upstairs and practice for when we're serious about making a couple of our own."

"Practice makes perfect."

They started for the stairs and George trotted after them. The cats rushed to the living room to snuggle on the couch, but when they kept going and Ansel looked at his pug and said, "Later," they all sprawled at the base of the steps to wait. Easter was a time to celebrate, and they might have to wait longer than usual this time.

Recipes from Jazzi's Kitchen!

Easy Salmon

I cut a large piece of salmon so there's one nice-size piece for each person.

Season the flesh side with salt and fennel seeds, pressing to make them stick. (Sometimes I season it with beau monde instead.)

In a hot skillet, coat the bottom with olive oil.

Add the salmon pieces, flesh side down. On medium high heat, cook for 5 minutes.

Turn the salmon so that it's skin side down and cook for another 4 or 5 minutes with a lid partially covering the pan.

You can see if the salmon is cooked through by looking at the color on the sides. It turns from a dark color to a lighter color when it's cooked. When it's cooked through it's ready to serve.

Chicken Seville

Heat 2 T. butter or olive oil in a large, deep skillet.

Sauté 8 skinless, boneless chicken breasts quickly and season with salt and pepper.

(If the chicken breasts are really big and thick, I cut them in half horizontally to make them thinner. Be careful with your fingers!)

Sprinkle with:

> 1 t. dried tarragon
> 1 t. dried thyme
> 1 t. dried savory
> Add thawed frozen pearl onions (small bag)
> 2 c. chicken stock
> 1/4 c Dijon mustard

Add:

> 1 15 oz. can artichoke heart halves and quarters, drained, marinated in oil
> 1 15 oz. can black olive slices, drained
> 1 15 oz. jar of roasted red peppers, drained and cut in chunks

When everything's heated through, thicken it with 1 T. cornstarch mixed in 3 T. water.

Sprinkle with parsley.

While the chicken cooks, I like to boil new potatoes to serve separately with the chicken Seville.

Chicken Marsala

Dredge 4 skinless, boneless chicken breasts in flour. (If the breasts are big and thick, I cut them in half horizontally to make them thinner. Be careful with your fingers!)

Sauté in:

    4 T. butter and 1 T. oil

When brown on both sides, add:

    1 chopped onion
    1 pint sliced mushrooms
    2 t. minced garlic in jar

When vegetables are soft, add:

    3 T. Marsala wine
    2/3 c. beef stock

Scrambled Eggs with Potato Hash

In a skillet, heat 2 T. olive oil
Add:

> 6 small Yukon gold potatoes, thinly sliced
> 1 t. minced garlic
> Salt and pepper

Cook till tender.

In a bowl, mix and set aside:

> A dozen eggs
> 3 T. water
> Splashes of Frank's Hot Sauce, to taste

In a second skillet heat 3 T. butter
Add:

> 1 diced onion
> 1/3 c. frozen diced green bell peppers from bag
> 3/4 lb. sliced cooked ham, chopped into chunks

When these are sautéed add the egg mixture. Cover the pan to help the eggs set.

Once the eggs are almost set add the cooked potatoes. Stir them in. Turn the heat to low and sprinkle shredded Swiss cheese over the top. Cover with lid until the cheese melts.

Printed in the United States
by Baker & Taylor Publisher Services